New King Palmers

New King Palmers

Peter Cowlam

_____cHp_____
CentreHouse Press

Copyright © 2016, Peter Cowlam
www.centrehousepress.co.uk | inquiries@centrehousepress.co.uk

British Library Cataloguing in Publication Data
A catalogue record for this book is available from the British
Library

ISBN 978-1-902086-13-2

...though truth and falsehood be
Near twins, yet truth a little elder is...
—*John Donne, Satire 3*

Thespian Hoe

1

There was one among many ancient family myths that the Maison d'Oc deemed worth its salt – a small point, but one that Eliot's newest appointee spent more time discussing than he thought wise. Then she questioned every condiment adorning his table, relishes whose classes he told her were four: *garum*, *liquamen*, *allec*, *muria*. A late dinner Eliot gave us, when all that Daphne sought was information.

She finds me 'evasive' (she says) about my filial loyalties. I tell her there are things – nuances, points of speculation – that even I don't understand. I do not know precisely what it is I owe the earl – the last Earl d'Oc. I do know his friendship with my parents was formed before I entered the world, in 1958, and I can easily recall my earliest contact with him, which was through my mother, Deidre. That was when I was still quite small. He was introduced as Eliot, and came to our house only when he knew my father planned to be at home, and not in France, or Italy, or more frequently America, that vastness of hope and enterprise. It was there that he (my father) went to live and work and end our family woes, in a fresh beginning and the second instalment of family Keyes, a name I was glad to drop.

There, alas, Bill Gates and my father never came together on the project closest to both men's hearts – the computer power delivered with so much aplomb to so many million desktops all round the world. That wasn't down solely to the abrupt difference in the way they set their goals. And I don't overlook that at twenty-five years his senior, my father belonged to a different generation.

My earliest recollection of his lifelong entanglement in the abstract world of electronic information exchange goes back to our London ménage of the early 1960s, where the desk in his study was littered with flow diagrams, scribbled calculations and handwritten Boolean operations I couldn't understand. Unlike his much younger rival, he could not rid himself of the corporate priesthood overseeing these endeavours. Where Gates and his Microsoft viewed the individualised computer universe as an interconnected stand-alone, a conflation of lists of things to do, and an overlay of windows into the processes that did them, all my father saw was a complex command line (which you the user were expected to type in), and humming away beneath it a clever systems subroutine, whose job was to parse that line grammatically, and on the basis of that send you spiralling into a cascade of options and sub-options.

That mentality my mother knew as wilfully cumbersome, and was probably the glaring light bearing down on *their* differences. Perhaps too it was one of the reasons they went their separate ways. She was, I think, remarkably prescient, for now we have the benefit of hindsight. We can see, obdurately attached to *his* architectures, the computer as a business and not a personal tool, a complicated machine requiring specialists, on a range of hourly rates only lawyers or accountants take for granted, in order to get the thing to do precisely what you wanted it to. That was always bound to be his undoing, and for me personally is a powerful reason why things to do with the family are filled with a sense of Martin Keyes's absence.

D'Oc was stately in his visits, always driven over by his flunkey in his limousine. He showed us the rigid exterior of someone whose political accommodations were already over-prolonged, and was a slight man lost in the gloss and leather of his rear seat, burdened with endless papers, and subject to the diktat of his document case. His beard, impeccably trimmed, he wore as a German goatee, a sunny straw colour in those days, but now faded to a lifeless grey. As a boy I was mildly repulsed by the florid texture of his flesh, his reddish face and the pinkness of his scalp – that part visible through his thinning hair, which when it receded was argent-coloured.

If d'Oc called it was my father, a big man in a grey cardigan, who emerged first, thundering from his study to answer the door – two chimes *affettuoso*, a mood not consonant with the prevailing gloom of our house. The two men shook hands affably, and only as d'Oc crossed the threshold did Deidre appear, her face already brightened by a smile (a rarity). That strange new aspect found itself fully lit when the hall was crossed in sunshine, if only for the instant the door remained open. She was never so pleased to see her husband. I looked down through the balusters in their abrupt, ninety-degree winding at the summit of the stairs, and was told to come down and say hello to the earl. This went on for years. His remoteness (from what I later learned was the third circle of power, to which I belonged, and which I'll tell you about) disqualified more than formal acquaintance with the Keyeses' little boy, an only child, though it didn't preclude gifts whenever he came. As I try to recall the order in which they arrived, I'm sure only of which came first, a golden-furred miniature teddy bear he'd bought in a Munich gift shop. It spent its days in the hollow of my pillow, or in a discussion circle on my bedroom floor, where it had for company a gigantic yellow chick, a glove puppet, a Mr Bendy, a small locomotive with a clownish, painted face, and a red hotel I'd acquired from our household Monopoly. Only odd pieces remained of the oval track the train had circuited on. The bear, or Heimlich, was followed by a pair of *Lederhosen*, a get-up setting me apart from other boys who lived in our neighbourhood, with an oak-leaf trim to the slits of the pockets, tight openings I couldn't get my hands in. There was a cuckoo clock he personally shipped from Zürich, which hung above my bed until I was twelve. Its hourly announcement was the cushioned strike on a bell followed by an airy, throaty double note as the cuckoo sprang from its open door. The metronomic clack of the pendulum either put me to sleep or kept me awake. When all it ever did was the latter, it was removed to Deidre's office. I ate a lot of Swiss chocolate. When I was six I was given a short-play vinyl the earl had found in a house clearance in northern Germany, its muddy purple label printed in Dutch. Both sides, A and B, featured the brothers Nathusius, recording-artist covers who had once shared a stage with Lennon and McCartney (that must have been their Hamburg days). 'Help', and 'Love Me Do' ('Luff, luff midoo'), were sung in breathy deviations from the originals.

With the clock gone the earl made gifts of educational value. Then, when my parents divorced, he treated mother and son to short holiday breaks at his place in Hoe. I still have the large-format book I was given at this time, its every other page a monochrome plate, and the whole a celebration of Stuttgart and its industries, where his family had interests – consumer electronics and photographic products. Dating to that period too is a leather-bound Grimms, which is still in my bookcase.

2

At some relevant point I might be willing to show how enlightened Deidre's attitudes were, though the monumental plans she dreamed for a boy's education were too rigidly ambitious, and were formed even before I was born. That, I would think, was the earl's influence. Our first visit to his corner of Paradise was by car. At that time Deidre drove a two-door convertible, a white, spotlessly clean Triumph Herald. That little run around was one in a distinguished line of service, whose fate, long before I learned to drive (or officially learned), was breakage in our local scrapyard, a rite performed without solemnity or ceremony. Our journey into the windswept hills of Hoe wasn't the shortest. The stops Deidre said we had to make inflated the whole thing over nearly eight hours – this for a destination just shy of the Tamar Bridge. There were points where I dozed. What began in a winding, tree-lined suburbia at the edge of southwest London zigzagged into a bewildering alternation of dual carriageways, trunk roads and narrow country lanes, and a gambol county to county. All detours were into dirt roads through a scarring of fields, the clay shovelled away by little yellow diggers, where square or rectangular building plots were laid out with brick and string. Piles of breeze blocks awaited the cement and outer skin to turn them into conurbations. Deidre had brought her camera and a notebook, and took what seemed to me far too many pictures.

With all those detours, that first visit to Hoe did not take place until under the sweep of headlights. There was a fleeting glimpse of its streets. A pair of iron gates followed, then the church, in shadow, and the cemetery overhung with yews. The car swung sharply at a fingerpost into the lane we were looking for, its entrance black, its depth a chasm, with a tottering hedgerow either side. The earl's retreat was at a turning once you had made the slow bobble over a stream and its bridge. The one important detail I had jotted down in our notes was shown as a hairpin left. Those same directions made salient two brick pillars, and from there a long carriageway in a gentle curve under a line of pines, whose tops were shrouded in mist the following morning, a sight I was woken to in a dawn raucous with rooks. The earl had had guests, but they'd all gone home, and only his kitchen girl remained. Her name, Annie. She was stooped, and lean, and friendly, and led me to the kitchen table, where in the waves of heat from the range she ladled a bowl of vegetable soup and quizzed me as I ate.

She was there for my breakfast too, and I met her again when I had set off to explore the extents of d'Oc's estate, a baronial house with medieval hall, where the land beyond his gardens was hilly pastures spread out and down as far as the River Yo. He'd got moorings there, and there was a boathouse, with stone steps in a plunge through a wildness of shrubbery, and a railing, and a barn door, which I found to be padlocked. I came back by a stony byway skirting his and a neighbour's meadows, and nosed my way into a dilapidated outhouse I had expected to be empty. That was not the case. In the cold shadows, at a workbench, under heavy beams and cobwebs, was Annie, alone, in a precise, frozen pose as she wielded a soldering iron, intent on a tin jug whose handle her reddened thumb pressed into place. She smiled. We talked. I told her how long I was here on holiday, and that got us onto school, and a lot I said about Deidre, and the home-education regimen she and a handpicked group of others had co-ordinated. There were five starlets I shared my class with, from the pigtailed youngest (a sly sickly girl) to the woolly-jumpered oldest, a boy with a button nose and freckles, as I, Humf, fell somewhere agewise in between. That grouping changed as our circumstances did.

I stepped out into the bright sunshine. Arrayed regimentally with pots and terracotta garden tubs were thirteen steps up a flagged terrace, a flight I began to climb. As I reached the count of twelve and sprang to the summit, I could see, through the tall rectangular panes of glass, the two friends Deidre and d'Oc drinking coffee under the vines of the conservatory. They had got, in the eddies of greenhouse heat, all the roof lights open to the sky, that arc above our heads an intense sapphire, with hardly a passing cloud. I held back and heard their conversation, an exchange eerily symmetrical with the one Annie and I had allowed to peter out, d'Oc asking how I was getting on – as a scholar, as an athlete, as a civilised social being. That Teutonic severity of tone (which I knew him for) had softened into godfatherly ministrations (tact I'd never known him for).

I had seen all along Deidre's secret desire to announce that her son was a child prodigy, but so far that had not entered her conversation. She replied to d'Oc much along these lines: that Humf was a strong swimmer, was agile in his gym shoes, showed stamina over distance, that he knew how to say in French he had found his pen, that he understood the rudiments of algebra, and that I'd shown my hand as a big-ender in the formal arena of debate. She steered these and other remarks onto safer ground and a discussion of infant genius generally, where d'Oc, who had seen *Idomeneo* in all of Europe's major houses, was known to have strong opinions. I think I can summarise his views, d'Oc a Mozart aficionado, and especially so with the operatic canon. As to the kind of facility sometimes seen in the very young – a child pianist able to infuse the tender passions of love, or conjure the mystical other world in a Chopin nocturne, or the control in Rachmaninovian pyrotechnics – that was the result of gifted mimicry. For genius to persist into adulthood those powers of imitation needed the furnace and fires and fusion of originality, a fact that explains why so much promise is extinguished in adolescence. In Deidre's mind, a full, rounded training – above all, the capacity to learn – I don't doubt should have led her lone offspring to the public career she envisaged, whether in politics, the arts, or media. One day I'd be let loose on the world as every inch the Renaissance man, or the man of mode wherever I turned to conquest. She couldn't know her ambitions for me would come undone with the diffidence of my youth, where group spectacle was something I abhorred, and competition for public recognition I dismissed as not for the fastidious, a world of mediocrities politely squabbling among themselves.

She left for London soon after lunch. She was unable to stay for more than a couple of days away from the architect's practice she and two other partners were raising to heady new heights. She came back for me the following weekend, by which time my rapport with Annie, and the freedom of d'Oc's estate, had made me sad and reluctant to leave.

3

While visits to Hoe were a regular mark on the calendar, I hardly ever saw d'Oc at his London address. By the time I was twelve, Deidre had got into the routine of putting me on the train at Paddington, with a packed lunch and a purse stuffed with spending money. I was met off the platform in Plymouth, in the hum and haze of evening, under a low sun and a sky wispy with clouds, once or twice by d'Oc himself, the earl having driven across in one of his vintage cars. More often it was Annie who did the picking up, sent over if d'Oc was away on Privy Council business, or for whatever other reason. For the route out to Hoe she liked to putter round Charles Church and its ruins, and point things out, those remains a favourite of hers, a city landmark burned out by incendiary bombs on two successive nights in 1941 (her awe was palpable at the national aspect of her personal history). We weren't exactly stand-offish on each of these reunions. As long-lost friends we were two animated faces under the flat windscreen of the VW she drove, her car modest, fatigued by its years of use, its livery a dull dove-grey, its outer shell mottled at the wheel arches, as still we chatted on. At that time the earl's country place, not then known as Thespian Hoe – the revised epithet was Deidre's, and a joke – was the pinnacle of Hoe's social life, with afternoon parties, fêtes and fundraising events. It attracted into its gardens hard-talking women in billowing *crêpe de chine* and fantastic coloured hats. There was a sprinkling of excitable-looking people from the Yo Valley Operatic Society, a group with close musical ties to the town's Anglican church, St John's. Its red sandstone I remember as dramatically lit in a slant of autumn sunshine. When I was older I was taken on visits to it, for education rather than prayer, with a notebook one of the adults always pressed on me. I can tell you, almost verbatim: the structure is known for its fifteenth-century screen, for its stained glass window (designed by 'eminent Victorian' Charles Eamer Kempe), for its Willis organ, and for its oak wagon roof, restored earlier in the century (by which I mean the twentieth). There were no surviving surface traces of the priory that stood to the plot's northeast, a cell of the Angers Benedictines, founded by a nobleman and supporter of William I, Henri de Mayenne, probably one of d'Oc's ancestors. D'Oc was always very meticulous about these details.

One other frequent guest at that time was Eliot's niece, Serenity Barr, who first appeared during her last year at Mount Christine de Pisan, a Catholic girls' school on the border of Dorset and Devon. She spent longer at Hoe than I did (usually), and dominated discussion at d'Oc's huge, highly polished dining table, and always sat where d'Oc could see her centrally lit, under the crossed angles of daylight streaming through the windows, all those panes leaded, the upper filters coloured. She held forth at her most combative in presence of Hoe's or Yo's operatic or dramatic troupes – their best acts reserved for the pause between courses, and the refilling of glasses. She was round-eyed with a large oval face, a symmetry her hair followed, with a centre parting, its strands right and left meeting, in her moments of stillness, at a point under her chin. All of it she tied to a bunch at the nape of her neck when it fell overdue for the scented shampoos she used. An apple fragrance, and in a later era aloe vera. She was freckled and robust, and was at her most relaxed in peasant smocks worn loosely over black or blue denims, the latter turned up a few inches off her ankle boots. I had my opinions too, but opted for Annie's company out in the kitchen, and escaped there whenever I could, where she'd always got a kettle on the range. One Easter afternoon there was no getting away. After a rehearsal of scenes – by the Yo Players, for an open-air *Twelfth Night* – I was pressed by d'Oc, then by a red-faced Andrew Aguecheek, to tell the story of Deidre's redesign of the small raised platform in Hoe's great hall, notionally a performance arena. She'd razed that and introduced removable plinths, a collapsible lectern, exits and entrances on every compass point, some ingenious stage machinery, and a lighting rig operated from a dedicated control box, whose sooty interior was itself lit up with points of light, when in use. After a first triumph, reported in the *Yo Valley Times* (a team of semi-pro musicians based in Exe, in a performance of Wolfgang's 'Dissonance' quartet), my mother used the prestige of Earl d'Oc's name, including it at the head of the client list she published, and always mentioned him in connection with professional awards she'd won.

The prime purpose of Eliot's performance space, here in this bucolic remoteness, had its first revelation with a fresh intake of MPs shortly after my twelfth birthday. Annie in her VW – who'd picked me up as usual – turned off the radio and nosed her way round a glitter of parked cars, pausing to say how busy she would be. We skirted the vast gravel arc round Hoe's great frontage, parking up in her reserved lot behind the kitchen garden. I asked her when she next went into town to buy me cigarettes, and not the mentholated ones. Deidre wouldn't be here for a few days, and there was a brand I'd seen advertised in a gold pack, with ornate *noir* lettering. She put it on her list. That same afternoon d'Oc supervised his newly baptised backbench debutants. They were men mostly, not yet out of diapers (their thirties), all of them a bludgeon of self-confidence, who as a collective, plus some yokels d'Oc had got in as extras, turned Deidre's timber frames and light effects into a cut-down House, with combatants in a face-off across the floor, in the simulated tilt yard you got at PMQs. I was encouraged to come and sling mud from an elevated place on the Opposition front bench, in hooting camaraderie with a handful of Yo players, here for the beer and sandwiches after. That I enjoyed. It got more serious over successive nights, with each freshman MP given a few hours and a subject on which to write a speech, and deliver from Deidre's dispatch box, with polite interruptions and the rehearsed etiquette in giving way. On the whole the speeches were dreary.

When Deidre got back down she was here for the climax, a debate on the vampire claws of inflation, Eliot's chosen speakers unable to conceal our national depth of ignorance in the misty cavern of economics. They sat together, d'Oc and my mother, Eliot I don't doubt making mental notes, and Deidre beginning to look at home in her theatre as the evening reached its rounding-off. That, again, was Yo-inspired, a Jacobean masque and a reading from Francis Bacon: 'Courts are but only superficiall scholes to dandle fooles.' The next day – Deidre's last, and the MPs gone – I rambled in the windswept grass, and found in the ruins of an old stone cottage the right place to hide my cigarettes, a niche in a weed-strewn gable, where what remained of the roof was a rusty sheet of corrugated iron. I wrapped the gold packet of twenty in a treasure map torn from a picture quiz book, whose compass needle pointed to a north where the illustration was an oak chest. The legend came from Robert Louis Stevenson: *Yo-ho-ho, and a bottle of rum!* I ambled back, contented, and found Annie listening to the radio and preparing fish sauce *à la* Maison d'Oc. Then in the evening there were just the four of us for dinner – d'Oc, Deidre, d'Oc's niece Serenity, and me. The conversation took its course from the spectacle all of us had witnessed. Serenity pressed her uncle as to his privileged insights into the state as a machined entity of capitalism, with Machiavelli's Renaissance shadow lapping round our ankles. She listed his qualifications, through his ancestry of d'Ocs, a family known for its pliability in the straits and ethos of twisted accommodations. She had traced, in consolidated steps, a line of d'Ocs, Dokkes and D'Arcs in its trade with the Habsburgs throughout the Austro-Hungarian Empire, which in its lesser incarnations had burrowed deep into the Viennese bureaucracy.

'Vienna, robust enough to repel repeated Ottoman onslaught, but not the d'Ocs.'

'Yes, that's fascinating,' Deidre said. 'Do tell us, Eliot.'

He was evasive, and offered us only his theory of the hierarchy and overlaps in a nation's circles of power. I can fit my own crude template to the model he described, if in retrospect I've understood it correctly. The uppermost sink is puffed with a gigantic question mark, a sign of bemusement, its job to represent the handful of unnamed persons – perhaps no more than a dozen – who between them own and control ninety per cent of the planet's surpluses. They're not accountable to parliaments or other instruments of the bourgeoisie – nor tenacious TV or radio interrogators, think tanks, committees, protest groups, persons of conscience wandering the streets, nor any others you can think of. The best you get is a dishing-out of entertaining anodynes, when in news lulls their identity is speculated on in newspapers. Below them, as the portal of messaging in a one-way direction – the direction is *down* – is the topmost echelon of industrial barons (d'Oc's romanticised term for the hated multinationals), twinned with its counter-parts drawn from the banks and other financial institutions. This is the second tier in God's distribution of mortal power (because yes, it's a religious setup). The important distinction in this and the tier below, the third or tertiary, that same one I found Earl d'Oc easing me into in my early adulthood, is the improbability of any of their members falling out or being ejected, and that's what ensures their structural cohesion, a class of unreflecting people whose duty is the protection of their own. In the glossary drawn up by newspaper hacks the purpose of circle three is jobs for life, and a safe haven for anyone in the ruling elite who can't meet expectations. That third tier, now that I'm committed to a fully labelled geometry – a geometry of angles, slopes and pyramids – is the pinnacle of private-sector management (or the boardroom), on a par with government, the monarchy, the security services, the media, the Church, and other sicknesses like that. The self-sustaining myth of social mobility, a fantasy that malleable populations are indulged in by presidents and prime ministers, operates only in the linear rig-up propping that bloated hierar-chy, unseen above us in the cloud. This is, in order of descent, bureaucrats, technicians, blue collars, the unemployed, thieves, rogues, petty villains. Here anyone is free to move up and down on the toss of a coin, or on the fall of heads or tails, subject to the fickleness and dictates of human ingenuity and the conspiracies of misfortune.

Without examples or specific mention of names, d'Oc offered his coldly logical conclusion as to the result of breaking that Faustian pact, that unspoken agreement implicit in the two overlapping circles cemented below the great question mark. The disgraced prince and the fallen politician are the stereotypes, or the double agent whose cover is blown, when materially all that's gambled is prestige, status, a stripping of medals, with the worst outcome internal banishment or exile, but outwardly a retention of social standing and a protective wadding of wealth. This toying with his guests was carried on as an after-dinner charades, with Deidre and Serenity insisting d'Oc reveal the true identity of the great question mark, a god-like monarchial instantiation some claimed to have intuited (it was a desert anchorite, or a zillionaire recluse) but never had dealings with. D'Oc denied all knowledge, suggesting his own limits lay in the topmost *visible* circle of power, whose purpose was threefold: to ensure the succession (of the instantiation, or the puffed-up question mark); to preserve and expand its empire; and to maintain the revered image people had of it. He would not depart from a conventional view of history, that living inscription written in the tome of human activity, where its conflation of events was defined by a tangible presence only of the great – men and occasionally women – in most cases warriors, statesmen and strategists. I think d'Oc even believed in the office of leadership – if not in the leaders themselves – as divine, and that explained why it had to be maintained so vigorously, with all that paraphernalia and circles of power. To that he added the refinement of secret codes, hilltop semaphore, with flames, flags or hand signals, and the later sophistications of Morse-like binary codes, private languages, tic-tac-toe clock-face grids, the Vigenère and other, much more complex ciphers, and an unassailability in the strategic use of prime numbers.

I listened in on Serenity's probing when d'Oc was forced to give out hints of his other role, outside his masonic circle (or Privy Council). That, in a flight of levity, and frustration at her uncle's taciturnity, she lampooned as priestly mysticism in the custodianship of ancient, jealously guarded secrets. By what means I don't know, but she'd heard of mysterious papers he'd got safely locked away, in an archive, the kind of written testaments conspiracy theorists fought among themselves for, often with bitter consequences, but seldom got a glimpse of. He agreed she might be onto something, and explained the importance of the work of his cabal, of its ownership of sensitive material – a buttress, he said, especially so in an era of diminishing deference to figures in authority. The means to reveal what 'really happened' in any given historical instant is a ploy, whose purpose is to demonstrate that the truth will eventually emerge under the pressure of democratic probes, but in reality this is yet another screen on the ancient way of doing things. The d'Ocs were a category of person invested with the power to write and maintain false histories over long periods of time, often decades, sometimes even centuries. Theirs was a bastion of awesome strength and penetration, spreading its sedition in every corner of domestic life. And to the contrary, it wasn't under pressure of the voted-in committee, with its instinct for sleuthing, by whose persistence the truth was forced from its stonework. It was never the case that what you saw, with each revelation, finally, was a reluctant easing of the portcullis. It was the diametric opposite, a demonstration of irresistible power, the raw implication that in capable hands a lie can be nurtured and maintained over extended tracts of human time. This isn't confused with the revelations of career historians, who – to make a professional name – propose that the world has got the saint or martyr wrong, in reality a weak craven in comparison with the powerful *Übermensch*, who is steeped in human practicalities and is not afflicted by conscience when mired in corruption. This is the hero. The saint is a moral bankrupt.

These are the things I took with me from Hoe.

4

I didn't consciously reflect on d'Oc or Serenity or any of their conversations once the return journey had reached the rail yards and warehouse frontages, and the train slowed, ominously, under the crowded house backs, in a looming of London's yellow brick. As such these holidays in Hoe dissolved into a working progress for the getting of qualifications, with university – a process I saw as self-abnegation – a step Deidre didn't think I showed enough ambition for. The lack of direction probably had its origin in our brief early days when the claim was still to be a family, and we remained, at least in theory, *en rapport*. As I said, I didn't go to school as such. On Mondays those who'd become my five fellow-pupils came to the house, where Deidre taught us geometry, German and drawing. The five began as snobby little six-year-olds in Sunday get-ups, flouncing in with expensive gifts, vying for teacher's attentions. I watched them into their teenage, when they were well informed, fashionable – and obnoxious. All of them read *The Daily Telegraph*.

Throughout, for the four other days of the week I travelled by tube, bus or both through the suburbs of west London, into the pillared little palaces – sash frontages, railings round the stair head, steps into the basement – where the pampered half-dozen converged for our assaults, under the varied expertise of what other parents Deidre had co-opted. There was a convalescing operatic soprano, whose geography class was pines, vines and a romanticised yearning for the south, always quoting Eliot's 'Burbank', and with a relish for Princess Volupine (but that's another Eliot, and another story). The only music I mastered under her was a few rudimentary piano scales. Of great outward severity was the guardian of our Wednesdays, who made us bat balls, swim butterfly and backstroke, hike up, down, and across the Heath, and who drilled us in the identification of town and parkland trees. In scope that was barks, summer leaves, and the tracery of branch and twig etched on the distemper of late November skies. Thursday was the Book of Numbers, in a large riverside property in Chelsea – statistics, and compound interest, and to complete the trinity stocks and shares. On Friday our teacher shared fraternity as a student herself (embroiled, I think, in a PhD, which went on endlessly), a conscientious writer type, who revelled in the love conceits of a donnish John Donne. I got all my literature from her, and a trip to the RSC. She said I had a beatific smile, a rare attribute in the triumph over my ambiguities.

All travel was out of rush hour, with class a ten o'clock start, when each of the five receiving neighbourhoods had relapsed into slumbers. On Wednesdays – with a baggage of books, a towel and swimwear – my walk from the station was a series of flagged avenues, which at a corner and crossroads met the perimeter fence of a primary school, to show me the fate I'd escaped. I remember only the name of its head, a Miss Sharkey, in large white serifs on a lime green sign. Her echo I still link with the eerie silence, and the blank chalked squares, circles and rectangles abandoned in the playground. Soon after that, we moved to a commune.

At fifteen or sixteen something changed, as I did begin to question d'Oc as to those circles of deceit, and without Serenity's intrusion, now that she'd got her social life at Cambridge. (She studied law. Today she's a Lib Dem peer.) D'Oc had got one of his stock candidates for an afternoon in Hoe, a damp-haired baggy-eyed GP standing in a by-election in the Cotswolds. I met that specimen briefly, after he'd been coached, the earl putting him to hard, unbroken hours on one of Deidre's plinths, rehearsing scripted platitudes suited to either of two instances, the doorstep or the soapbox. He drove off in a gust of encouraging words from the earl, who sat me down in the sunshine and had Annie bring us a pitcher of cider. I asked him for personal examples of anyone in a fallen state from the upper echelons. I was on the track of anyone publicly visible, who, having bent the remorseless codes of English classism, was permanently blackballed. I had reached that point of youthful scepticism in wanting to test his assertion that an angel in the dust, grounded by broken wing beats, nevertheless retained the trappings of power and the prestige of outward appearance. He looked at me rather joyfully, and spoke slowly, referring not to his archive in London, which I was later to plunder, but to his personal diary, recounting a final meeting with the Duke of Windsor, who as King Edward VIII had had the misfortune to count, among other forces ranged against him – up to and at the time of his abdication – Cosmo Lang, who was Archbishop of Canterbury from 1928 to 1942. The occasion (of that final meeting) involved the present Prince of Wales, our next king, who hadn't much opportunity to see his great uncle. It was January, in the Bois de Boulogne—

The prince drove up and stood outside the car. D'Oc could see his expectation pale at what he was walking into. Inside the duke's house he found its flunkeys garbed in the same scarlet and black as his own servants at home, which under the weight of family obligation struck him as pathetic. He glanced round the hall and lit on a small table with a red inlaid box, whose inscription proclaimed *The King* (and that was 'also pathetic'). Surprisingly, the indoor atmosphere was filled with the piquancy of incense. Just as disconcerting were the walls, almost visibly reverberant under the waves of plastic music. Then here was the duchess at last, who tore herself from the babble of conversation, a sudden departure that silenced her guests. One of them shook the prince's hand, then muttered something incomprehensible in Wall Street French, then, under the colossal strain the effort entailed, swooned in the arms of a footman.

Earl d'Oc escaped with the duke into a small sitting room, where they discussed the former monarch's memoirs. Incumbents in the upper echelons of English life had been interviewed when research for the book was underway. There was a Dictaphone recording detailing Privy Council insight into Wallis's liaisons. It was material the duke said he'd never wish to use, though he'd had the recording transferred onto old-fashioned reel-to-reel. Now that cassette tape had also been invented, he wanted it transcribed again. Their conversation ended when Charles entered the room, who found his uncle still in good form, though crumpled and dependent on a stick. Due to a cataract, and an operation he'd had, he kept that eye closed most of the time, yet was talkative and expansive in his gestures, most of which involved a huge, monstrous-looking cigar.

They talked about the duke's relationship with his father, which had been difficult, and remained problematic even when George V died. Then Gan-Gan too was a hard woman (the prince's own epithet for Mary, Charles's great-grandmother). All in all the one-time heir had had his bringing-up in the strictest code. That, he said, explained his antipathy towards older people generally, and tradition in particular.

While he mulled things over thus, the duchess flitted in and out, who even at close quarters was astounding for her age, though the mask she wore could not disguise a multitude of lifts. She found it hard to speak, and to do so clenched her teeth and froze the muscles round her jaw. To the young Charles she was hard-hearted, flighty, superficial. Her charm, if it dazzled, was structured by her role (at that moment that of hostess), and the glamour she seemed to exude was void of human warmth. Her main topic was whether to wear a hat at the Arc de Triomphe.

Touchingly, uncle and nephew talked about how difficult, for the last thirty years, Charles's family had made the duke's life. Charles asked him frankly would he like to see out his life in England. The duke hesitated – perhaps for fear of what pyrotechnics Wallis would greet that proposition with. In other circumstances he said he *would* return, but was sure no one would recognise him – and anyway, most of his contemporaries were dead. To Charles it was too tragic – his existence here, the people round him, the faded gentility, the dingy atmosphere. He was relieved when he left. Then d'Oc resumed his conversation with the duke, and agreed to take the tape and get it converted.

He took his commission back to London, and found a recording studio in Brondesbury, where the duke's tape was remade. The producer was a slight, brown-haired man (already thinning at the crown), who by the strain on his purse and the grain of his mind was at odds with his VAT accounts. Much hope he invested in those great many unwashed tramping through his engineering space, among whose trios, quartets, quintets – sometimes a lone *chanteuse* – he trained an eye for someone he could manage. This was the 1970s, when studio styling consisted of complicated hairdos, Byronic photocalls, a fantastic wardrobe, and reverse LP sleeves in a showcase of clever or witty lyrics. Years later the Duke of Windsor died. Not long after that the earl's man who sold him his studio time bawled aloud and thumped his VAT bins, on seeing his livelihood abruptly swept away. A rival impresario had found the shining way, and in the pubs of south London trailed a rougher beast to Bethlehem. In crashed the Punks, donning an aesthetic he – too old by now – wouldn't know how to tamper with.

Endless reruns of *Edward and Mrs Simpson* spluttered out into twilit living rooms all over the kingdom, and that offered pause for thought. In an inspired moment our man from Brondesbury tracked through his library of master tapes, and pulled out the late duke's research piece. This must have crossed an editor's desk, because hinted at in someone's god-forsaken *Mail* or *Express*, or something equally disreputable – via the pleached paragraphets of the gossip page – were hither-to undisclosed revelations surrounding the abdication – a story that never fully ran, being too complex for a tabloid readership, for whom any opening sentence must bear the reek of soiled underwear.

That, I said to d'Oc, was typical of him. He'd led me to the foothills, and with the summit or climax in view had turned my gaze in another direction.

'Is that the best we can do?' I asked.

'Try to think of what it would mean for me,' he said, 'if too much of this got out. I'm more than just the purveyor of propaganda. I too have a life. Finish your cider. It's you English who've put me where I am.' He felt safer with street entrepreneurs than he did with old Etonians. 'It's easy to sneer.'

'Who's sneering? Anyway what do you mean?'

'The fate of the duke's tape, and Wallis's liaisons—' They were important, apparently, because of implications for him.

It was too cryptic, and I didn't understand, but now I con-sciously aimed to remember the things d'Oc said.

5

I have just this one note about his solid line of predecessors, who'd controlled the central European salt trade since the seventeenth century. I offer it as another aside, another ob-liqueness, one that d'Oc gave me on a sultry afternoon, as we gazed out from our garden chairs over the River Yo. His story this time was of an innocent shoemaker who rode out of his way in delivering a pair of boots into a dukedom he had never traded with before, leagues distant from his workshop. There the terrain was rugged, of meagre cultivation, and a maze of dusty highways whose routes or destinations weren't easy to pick out. He got himself lost, and by nightfall his horse was lame. He stumbled on an entrance to a cave and went inside to look. Its interior – not a crypt, as he'd thought, but a disused salt mine – was filled with coffers, under the dead gaze of comrades now only skeletons, sitting in a circle. Myths ever since have filled those coffers with coins, a golden trove that the shoemaker emptied into his pockets. No one records the fate of his horse. We're left only with its master, in a heaven of mental arithmetic, counting out his newfound wealth till well after sunrise, when in the flush of morning he found his way home. His village elders wanted to know what it was he'd found, and quizzed him – in a cajoling, coaxing way. When he refused to reveal the vault's location, he was accused of theft and put on trial, news of which spread as far as the castle at Oc. There the count had his horse saddled and rode out and arranged for the shoemaker's release, and brought him back to his citadel, where he was asked for and gave information, and was rewarded.

The count had long maintained a secret map identifying other such mines, and now circled in blue pencil this latest addition to his collection. He arranged for a merchant fleet, under a flag of convenience, anchoring men and mules off the shoemaker's shoreline, and sought out, in its mountainous hinterland, the spot where he'd blundered on his treasure. There were delays – treacherous weather a blight on all shipping. Other events made it possible that the newly discovered cache – valuables, documents, official seals (or so the count anticipated) – had already been plundered. His expectations weren't unfounded. The geological constitution of rock-salt mines makes them ideal for the storage of papers, as I know from samples I've seen – outline contract agreement d'Oc's ancestors forged with the House of Habsburg, drawn up when the empire wanted cash for the wars it fought, and a tax on salt was a way of getting it.

There was other information I stole from Eliot's archive, when he'd become too ill to see to what extent I'd infiltrated. Instance the Roman sack of Jerusalem, celebrated in a carving on Titus's triumphal arch, which was erected by the senate after his death. It shows his army parading in the streets, with its trophies – a seven-branched candelabrum, a gold table, musical instruments – a print of which I took from a book Eliot showed me.

Then Rome itself was sacked, by the Visigoths, a wandering Germanic people with kingdoms in Gaul and Spain, the Gallic territory stretching from the Loire to the Pyrenees and the lower reaches of the Rhône. That raised questions as to where the treasures of Rome and Jerusalem had gone. In answer, Eliot held the key to an unopened room in his London house, where he kept his archive, and said he knew. He said also much Roman wealth was in the form of gold coins, struck in various mints, one such being at Arles, a point relevant to the lucky shoemaker whose mythology is added to above. Arles was the east point of a golden triangle Eliot liked to plot on modern maps of France, with Albi at the north and Montségur distant to the west, the latter one of the last strongholds of the Cathar Church, whose riches were held in a fortress. That institution briefly eclipsed the rule of Rome, but its doctrine entered the annals of Christian heresy, and under Pope Innocent III a crusade was launched (the Albigensian crusade). Miraculously, during the siege, a way out was found, and treasures were secretly removed, though the fortress was captured eventually, then destroyed. Many French Cathars fled to Italy, where persecution wasn't so systematic, though by the 1270s the Cathar hierarchy had disappeared, as had all its treasure. I'm supposed to believe that d'Oc was heir to that as well.

Entrances and Exits

1

When my home education was coming to its close, d'Oc wanted to know what direction I thought I'd take. Deidre hadn't a clue, but told him my operatic soprano – who also taught history – and later one of my teachers from the commune, thought I had shown interest in the fourteenth century. Richard II, Wat Tyler, John Ball, Wyclif, the Peasants' Revolt, Simon Sudbury – all that. There were also comedy shows I liked to watch on early-evening TV (with some, I later learned, not intended as comedy at all). I made the same mistake with serious radio discussions on books and poetry, which I misinterpreted as parody, Goonish in its hilarity, an error underlined when I searched the listings, surprised not to find Peter Sellers in the role of benighted man of letters. There were yet other ways I didn't know the world. Once, when Deidre was driving us across central Europe, I got the map-reading hideously wrong, and rather than the nice *pension* south of Salzburg, we arrived northeast of Innsbruck, at well after midnight, with no prospect of anywhere to sleep. She poured money into a payphone and got through to the earl, who gave us an address. Then there were times I was sent on errands and came back with the wrong thing – a gismo not the right size, or with too big a thread, or for Japanese speakers only…. I wouldn't ever willingly negotiate an exchange with the person who'd sold it, as that would entail too much conversation at a demotic human level. Instead I'd try again for the right gadget – and gadgets anyway tended to fall apart in my hands. It was only ever theory I felt comfortable with. Practice was always rebarbative.

Deidre didn't know what to do with me, and she didn't think her ex-husband would either – my father Martin Keyes, now living in California. That didn't stop her packing me off across the Atlantic, usually with the earl as escort. Her plan seemed to be that regular doses of paternal love, nurture and advice would help me to a useful occupation. I don't know what Martin was expected to do once he'd seen the truth, emergent only gradually, or what to make of it, given this new triadic relationship, with its complications, with its changed domestic life, here in the scorching heat of Palo Alto. He wasn't much good at informal coaching, reducing these cosy get-togethers to a lesson in learning, with tips on strategy and method – for look where that approach had taken him. I could only guess the tone and texture of reporting hearth to hearth, from his to Deidre's, when he too had no idea as to the right career for me. He could see my only onslaught on the world as a granite wall I'd built to keep it out. Perhaps I'd be a useful asset in a think tank. Or had I considered speechwriting?

No, I hadn't. Well in that case, if Deidre wanted his intervention, he said he'd do his best to get me trained in the witchcraft of computer source code, in a sepulchral backroom somewhere. I hadn't his mathematical flair for science, and felt only repulsion at the contradictions of commerce, technical expertise put to solutions for office and accountancy systems. I couldn't therefore become a computer programmer. A blank. For that reason, and not that I knew it then, the earl's help was also asked for. The result of the phone calls he made, just a few years later, once I'd lost my way ('I found me in a gloomy wood, astray / Gone from the path direct...'), is the ready-made career I did nothing to warrant. I'm one of those legions, those parasites, whose deserts aren't just. My life of easy money has been so effortlessly put in place through a stratum of powers active in the cloud above. I have found myself nearer than most to the footstool where rests that punctuating stop propping the great question mark up in the azure.

I did not emulate my parents' spectacular successes academically, getting only an upper second in anthropology, my *alma mater* and its alumni not an especially noted one, though Bamber Gascoigne did preside over its one semi-final showing, in an early *University Challenge* (1960s). That sense of not having connected with the world I carried into campus life, where my two friends, Ollie and Ellie, lived at the comic extremes of provincial public transport (I name it only as a distant northern town). The bar was a dive, and not helped by its cavern atmosphere, and all the staff in black. My life was a diet of canned soup and smothered crumpets – warm ooze for a man un-bearded in an almost permanent winter. What a song, those cold afternoons at parallel fifty-four (or thereabouts).

These straits were useful for getting through exams, as cramming was made easy under the soporific exhalations, the moist purr of the gas heater. My once-weekly recreation was a petite, curly-haired *fille de joie*, whose mechanical workday coitus suited me temperamentally. Eventually the compulsion of bodies in conjoint struck me as overwhelmingly bizarre, and I gave up shagging altogether. Nowadays I've found less irksome alternatives.

I blundered into a working life as a clerk in a series of shabby twilit offices. This was insurance, or import/export, or containerisation – or God knew what, till Deidre shook her head, I imagine deeply disappointed. I can't be sure exactly which of my two fathers put the money up – it must have been Martin solely, or Martin and the earl combined. It was certainly d'Oc who rang round his friends in the City, and on a series of handshakes eased me into partnership, the firm a management consultancy (more of which below). From the outset, I had my own office, a place of potted plants and minimal paperwork, *and* a secretary. For my colleagues, who betrayed not a hint of bemusement, the cachet they got was of Earl d'Oc heading their list of clients. By far, his was the most prestigious name printed on their résumé, which has since never been without him, or for that matter me.

That about wraps up the CV.

2

Until last year there were twelve partners in all, including me – then in the raking winds of early spring we suffered our first fatality. So now we're eleven. Our trading life began in the mid-'70s, under the corporate name Del Cad Telemat, a conflation clumsily got from the names of our founding fathers (no Freudian pun intended). These were two – a Marcus Deloney (technician), and his associate Andrew Cade (whose mantra was *money is merely a tool*). By the early 1980s Del Cad had truncated itself when Cade sold his shares. When I joined, our secretarial staff answered the phone with the same repetitive chant: DC for short, they'd say, or DC Telemat if asked to re-inflate. In the great push for communications the

Telemat transformed itself to Tel, then in that globalised fission exploding about us everywhere, the DC re-spelt itself to that theoretical duple, DotCom. One can't stand still of course, so the firm I work for now has rebranded itself again, and weaves its stylish logo round a very simple triform. I've a drawer full of newly printed business cards, with the emblazon DoCoTel.

My team is a gang of five, which given the right incentives continues to produce the designs and lines of code that clients such as Eliot endlessly require. I make a point of getting back to head office on the close of business at the end of every week, where our three floors over-stretch themselves in a glum rectangular tower – all cream and pale green cladding, and a blight of tinted windows. It's not that many strides from Finsbury Square.

Demands my clients made were not the most onerous my team had ever faced – at a technical level at least. What that quintet dreams up, in an afternoon gaze across the City Road, is suites of programs spawn of our standard database portfolio, with its data tags and search concatenations, and output smooth in its colour blends, void of jaggies and banding. There are jonquil and heliotrope flashings I had a hand in designing myself. It's all a scintillating prospect I do not go to bed too early for on nights before my days of labour. At inception I was given space and a secretary, Bonnie, whose adjoining office was almost as spacious as my own. Nowadays, the drive for profit and the squeal for human efficiency has meant her successor – Gillian, with a hard G – isn't exclusively mine, as I share her with two other partners. With that increase in her workload she lost her domain, which once it had been remodelled I spent five minutes looking round, soothing my temples in the subdued quiet of its lighting. In its pallor a brashly colour-branded symmetry of network servers was the new equipment DCT had shipped across the Atlantic. I closed the door on its hum of machine activity, the music of corporate onslaught, a scoring of PLCs whose trends and fluctuating fortunes we processed as numbers, to an end result of board-room fodder in pretty-looking statistics, and quarterly bills from us.

Between her letters and phone calls she – Gillian – managed my diary and organised my appointments. It's usual on a Friday to see her scoff a wedge of quiche for lunch, and leave – even at a quarter past five – an invasive miasma of egg and onion permeating her anteroom – a den no bigger than a broom cupboard – perfect foil, she says, for the blandness preserved in *my* office (good views I have, with windows that open). One point we do agree on most of the time is the order of eccentricity ranking my list of clients. At the top is a Swiss horologist, his High Street shop a mid-terrace in Kingston, which once you opened the door was filled with the twang of recorded music – guitar, lute and mandolin. His name was Bernauer. Bernauer had freed himself from the earthly con-straints those timepieces chiming in his shop measured out for other mortals. As testament to this, his back office off the shop was a kind of exhibition space, devoted to the little acts of deference he'd made to the march of science, which are some-times *too* remorseless.

I met him several years ago, when he wanted to know what kind of billing system DCT could offer, now that he'd bought himself a home computer. I wound my watch at a minute past midday, and under the tinkle of his shop bell wiped my feet on the mat. Bernauer was sitting at the counter, the frame of his specs the colour of gunmetal, with an eyepiece clipped to one of the lenses. His hair was cropped, and greying in the patches where it hadn't thinned, and had the sheen of silk under the bright white isosceles of light pouring from the lampshade suspended above his head. He put down a pair of tweezers, and could see my puzzlement. What I could hear, he said, was a Vivaldi mandolin concerto – its tempo unbelievably fast.

Cordial our meeting might have been, but on that day I did no business – not anyway with him. He got his billing system somewhere else (off the shelf, he said), though I left him my card. A few months later he sent a long agonised email, the gist of which I didn't understand until I returned to Kingston, where initially I didn't find him in his shop. A square of corrugated cardboard tacked to his window, with a message he'd scrawled in flame-coloured marker pen, told me how long he thought he was likely to be. Five minutes, putative – therefore I waited on the pavement, a biting wind rippling the pleats of my coat. I scanned his window, where a collection of Tissots in the velvet grooves of their display boxes he'd arranged in a horseshoe round a collection of ladies' wristwatches. A jewel-encrusted compass hung prosaically opposite a kitchen clock, and in the shadow of his door blind odd things I saw like a ship's chronometer, a sextant, a theodolite.

At last, Bernauer rounded a busy corner, just as I had started to tuck in my lapels and test the hollowness under those western paving slabs. He was tall, and slim, and now that I saw him not behind his counter, every inch a military man, wearing – wearing I don't know what – a Prussian cape (or something) someone had handed down. His lips were blue, his large ears pink and diaphanous, and his face ghostly. His five minutes (long up by now) were what it took to collect his lunch – a baguette over-filled and overdone with cress. And damn those queues. Nor for the moment could he put a finger to his keys.

'Here,' I said, 'I'll hold that.' The paper sleeve the shop girl had wrapped his banquet in retained a modicum of warmth, as did the tiny serviette he'd picked up on leaving. That I caught before it fluttered to the pavement, a crystallised surface a-glitter in the pale winter sun.

He snapped up the blind on stepping back inside, then strode across the two oblongs of sunlight with which that single action watermarked his floor. He began to discard his cape – a hand to the collar, his cold marble fingers working first one button, then another – and had not yet swept it off when he rattled the knob on the door past his counter. Over the pediment, in large red writ, was a keep-out sign.

'It's in here,' he said.

'Here' was the back room – the shrine to his obsessions – a litter of part-completed projects. I followed him in, and at an old-fashioned drawing board paused at the sharp precision of pencil strokes, ruled and squared on the shiny almond paper clipped into place along the top edge. This – a plan, and a front and end elevation – was the rural retreat Bernauer was busily designing for himself. I could make out certain details, such as a wind turbine, and solar panels, and an outer duct for services.

'Impressive,' I said.

He agreed – not immodestly, but in a hurry for his workbench, where his computer – now infamous for rival billing software – blew dissolving moon-coloured tulips into the sable void of a screen saver (not one I knew). One of many hard-pressed technical companions, its cover a glossy interlock of oak leaves, its open pages pressed facedown into the grain of the bench, was bookmarked in several places. It was called (and I've had to look it up, to remind myself) *The Solvay Formulation*, and its editor was AE MacEnnoy. I gave him his baguette, which he put to one side and ignored.

With a wave of Bernauer's hand, and a trailing thumb to the shift key, those tulips dispersed in a sprinkle of moon dust. Replacing them on-screen was a graphic Bernauer had been working on, concocted, he said, by a web technician, but derived from a drawing physicist Niels Bohr had made in the 1930s. He told me it was Einstein's light box. I asked what that meant. His pose thus, elbow cradled in the palm of his non-writing hand, index finger wrapped round the dimple of his chin, Bernauer beheld me partly in disbelief, but mostly with sadness, or perhaps it was pity. What it was, he said, was one of those famous thought experiments, where the variable was velocity – for nothing in our cosmos ever remained static (not even d'Oc's traditions). His box full of light – a device by which a single photon's energy, and the time of its emission, could both be measured precisely – Einstein had thought was the final demolition of Heisenberg's probability theory.

'So how was it supposed to work?'

Bernauer removed his cape. Inside the box was a shutter that opened and closed by clockwork, forming an aperture out of which the single photon was fired. You weighed the box before and after. With the difference in mass you were able to calculate the photon's energy ($E = MC^2$). You could therefore know at precisely what time this energy exchange took place – which of course was in violation of Heisenberg's uncertainty principle.

'Ingenious,' I said.

'Yes and no.' Bohr's response was a sleepless night, followed by work on the diagram Bernauer had adapted for his screen. The box was hung from a weighing spring attached to a bracket. Inside the box was a photon gun and shutter release, with a pre-set clock connected to both. Bohr's objection was this – that once the photon was fired the recoil resulted in the clock's uncertain position in Earth's gravitational field, and, correspondingly, its indefinite indication as to time – explicable, ironically, via Einstein's general theory of relativity.

In these and other things Bernauer saw himself as the facilitator. Egyptian pyramids he'd glued together out of balsa wood, on newly published theories as to alignment with the stars – that great heavenly clockwork. His *homage à Bohr* was less than satisfactory, since once the thing was set in motion the clock – not entirely inapt, I did dare to think – turned from its ticking argent to a blur of amaranth, its face and hands detaching themselves in a whirr of rotating gifs. The photon – no such thing, alas – faded badly from a needlepoint of chrome to an elastic streak of ellipses, and shaded to sienna. The shutter winked coquettishly.

Bernauer raised these points with his designer, who replied he had spent too long on the project already, and anyway, as virtual metaphor, he couldn't see anything wrong with what he'd done. He added – the words final, the tone non-negotiable – that quantum theory didn't encompass the kind of absolutes Bernauer seemed to have in mind. I took away his shipment disc, its origin a specialist working from a cobbled mews in Hanwell. Sounding more certain than I felt I said I would pass it to one of my boffins. The shop bell tinkled just as Bernauer began leafing through his bible of notes, pages sleeping in museum dust, observations that over the years he'd penned for the project, which I said I'd also pass on (so, till then, Bernauer...). His first customer for that sun-filled, cold, brittle afternoon was wrapped to her chin in the woolly stripes of her scarf, and had called for her Vienna regulator, which Bernauer was sure he'd repaired, and scratching his head now tried to remember where...ah yes, the storeroom here.

I had a call or two to make, and got back to the office late in the afternoon, well after Gillian (a hard G, remember) had gone, though she'd left me a note to call Earl d'Oc. I stood in the gloom of my window, for a moment caught dreaming under the pale inky blues banding the sky, where a first faint star, then another, then several more began to twinkle. Some way over the City Road a large yellow crane slowly swung a bucket of debris from where I had watched it being filled – a scarred pile of steel and broken concrete – but stopped in mid-stroke. I walked down the corridor into the technical area – a maze of cerise and maroon partitions – and found there only one in our research and development team, who by the furrows in his brow wrestled with something hugely intractable, and whose profile wriggled in the thinly fluid mask of green and yellow light emitted from his screen. I put a hand to Bernauer's disc, then thought better of it, and quietly closed the door. Instead I made that phone call.

So, now you have seen the sham and tokenism in the kind of

client account I bring to DCT, and the solitary bits of business I do. It's a deleterious effect on the company's balance sheet mostly. I got one of my web designers, eventually, onto Einstein's light box, and with the work done drove in a cab to Kingston and handed it over to Bernauer, insisting that was the best my technical team could offer. I loaded it from disc and ran it on screen. What would he think of a slate-coloured clock with its fire of luminous digits? Or the spring, in its purple shade of sloe? Or the gun, ejecting lemon-tinted photons? The shutter they passed through was round and black when closed, and a pinpoint of bright white light when open. The recoil was hydraulic.

I couldn't judge to what extent this was an improvement in Bernauer's mind – anyway, he didn't complain. He played with his toy for half an hour or so, then asked what staff I had for a second project, the man of clocks now having turned to the stellar sphere and ancient astronomy, and Christian metaphysics in the stamp of God and a bureaucracy of angels.

'That God who did not play dice.'

3

A grey sky. A cold morning, January. I stood at my office window, shoulders hunched, a confidential memo having landed on my desk (though now I think 'confidential' isn't the right word exactly). Its fleeting, impersonal babble, when I looked at it again, I read as a kind of decoy for the book of biblical spreadsheets ardently stapled to it. On delving into those depths, the crux of its holy writ was this – that confrère Bernie, our top man in accounts, had listed in column one my current client list, and in column two the year-to-date revenues those clients had returned. There are certain comic aspects in all such chiselled stone, where the secular hand won't always resist a paraphrase, the whole laborious process running A to Z (like this)—

Ableman, antiquarian bookseller, fourpence; Bernauer, horologist and amateur cosmologist, one and six; Campion, author and ornithologist, bad debt; d'Oc, collector, gratis; Effingham, after-dinner speaker, eleven guineas; Guthrie, scientologist, no accounts presented; Jeffers, guitar maker, no bill so far raised; Lemming, occupation unknown, an Austrian schilling; Orlando, student of press relations, gratis; Reuter, office management systems, goods in kind; Shearer, professional footballer, an under-twenty-one national team shirt; Smolin, physicist, campus tour, State College, New York City; Trethowan, film producer, £1,011 (eureka!); Vanderbliss, import-export, one crate KMW; Welbeck, web designer, calculation pending; Zukerman, violinist, framed, autographed portrait (photographic) [it hangs in one of the meeting rooms].

In column three were listed the DCT man-hours and resources I had called on in servicing these clients – often at short notice, and almost always to the detriment of more important projects. I had only to think back on the dreary histories and weary hours our talented programmers had spent in the tents of payroll, or the tabernacles dotting the deserts of corporate ledgerware, to understand what pressing work I had unthinkingly pulled them off. (Bernie, I am chastened.)

Column four was a pillar of salt, whose plinth bore the

inscription of what it cost to pay my fees and rent my office space. The balancing arithmetic was left for me to perform. The implication was of my presence here as very much in the minus, one of those acts of counterpoint that disregards the crank, oddball or celebrity, that child of our time who can, by the least promising process, turn up wonders for all humanity and even accountants to behold – flakes of gold leaf descending through a winter sky. Fortunately for me, at DCT wiser counsels than Bernie's prevail. My department running costs are low, so I am not yet considered for disbandment. What that department is is a kind of R and D of the humanities (every company should have one), and is tolerated because of d'Oc, because of his name, because, above all, his ancient title in connection with the firm is a legitimising asset.

His proximity to us, to DCT, is also a help. His pad in Kensington I had first visited at the age of twelve, and more frequently when fourteen. In my twenties, and as beneficiary of that legacy left by partners Deloney and Cade, I was asked if I knew his London address, and if so to look it up in the office street guide. It's a short walk from the Royal Albert Hall (in range, d'Oc said, of its hallelujah choruses). Back then I was treated as a kind of footman to his ancestry, those forerunners each with his hands to the levers of power. The engraved rules of empire are uttered *sotto voce*, testaments set in motion scion unto scion. I was asked to show interest in his predecessors, those who had overseen transmission of valuable objects and artefacts, hand to hand. What I was supposed to pay attention to was the plunder the earl had become custodian of, things he'd bothered to insure though had never, curator-like, spared the time to catalogue. On an A4 pad, it was my job to do that now (or rather then). He showed me round, after the *bonne* who ran his kitchen had brought me a cup of tea and a plate of biscuits. I paused to look at the hangings, a shadow world of portraits under a surface sheen from the chandeliers and wall lights. If I paused at a niche he told me to whom or what the blank gaze of its bust or protome belonged. He showed an expert touch to the fragile parchments he'd got in large flat drawers designed specifically for them. I asked, where had all of it come from? One of the many titled d'Ocs, he said, who in 1848, the year of revolutions, sought safe deposit of his treasures, with a shipment from southern France into England, by a route encompassing disused salt mines like the one discovered by our shoemaker (see above).

For a month or so I visited Eliot's once or twice a week, where the pattern of exchange was much as I've described – that human misery in the trail of his objects and artefacts. After each session I took my handwritten register back to the office, where it was typed, the top sheet entering a file that sat alone, and swelled very little, on the shelf above my filing cabinet. Eliot must have assumed the firm would find me a more genuine project. Nevertheless, he settled our invoices, all in the thirty-day threshold, even querying the size of some, but was soon less able to keep these appointments. I cast around for other options, and in a burst of innovatory goodwill introduced traffic-calming measures in the basement car park the firm shared with another. I'd noted how our senior partners were getting their Porsches badly bent through untidy parallel manoeuvres and an aggressive fleet of jalopies. The worst culprit was a rust-eaten station wagon, in transit at all hours, painted in the colours and pressed with the ensign of a company of chandlers, a brotherhood of salty dogs stoically holding out on the top floor of the new building we had moved to. Those crude beginnings of the earl's precious inventory were half-heartedly resurrected just a few years later, when raw computing power moved from large corporate mainframes into servers and PCs. I took to and left at his house, his museum, an IBM-compatible, pre-loaded with a database and a software suite to run it, and got further, quicker, into cataloguing the thefts and riches written in Eliot's family history. Soon it clashed with his timetable, and the reporting he did for the Privy Council, and the project was dropped a second time, though now for over decade, when I didn't see him much – vague social calls only. After that lapse of over ten years he got in touch again, the call coming through to my office. I thought he'd want to talk about his heirlooms, but that wasn't the case. His proposal was much more dubious than that.

That IBM-compatible had dutifully made its exit, and the room it once occupied was soberly liveried, and no longer an adjunct of his study – pale yellow walls, plain furnishings, and a lot less gilded clutter. I remembered a key he'd brandished, to a room he hadn't opened when last I had visited. I was ushered in. A new maid this time brought us coffee. I sat on a small square sofa, its dye a subdued olive green, and glanced up at a billow of bluish clouds in a mural on the ceiling, a high wind sweeping our interior. Quilted chairs were grouped in a semicircle round a low table where the coffee things, translucent cups and a jug, and a cafetière, had been placed. Under a framed mirror (shape a Gothic arch), and slightly off the wall, was a rosewood writing desk, with brass fittings, and a permanently open rolltop, that exposure made necessary by the presence of an up-to-date computer. Signs that someone regularly sat here and worked were phials of sickly bright nail varnish, in range a loud jaundice to musky bedtime violet, and also on the desk was a notebook, its cover a pattern of imitation marble. Arranged neatly on it were a red pencil and a silver sharpener.

He asked after my mother, knowing that Deidre now lived in semi-retirement in New Zealand. I usually visited under a blazing sun at Christmas, the bush where she lived dashed with the crimson of pohutukawa trees. She'd got a frame house in suburban Remuera (Auckland, a city I love), hand painted in subdued matt blues, in an acre plot with a large frontage and anchorage for the small power boat she kept. 'She's fit, and well, and happy,' I said.

He was genuinely glad to hear that. He gathered himself in small deliberate movements his shortness of stature dictated, and took his place in that half-circle of chairs, where he handed me my coffee.

'I've another commission I hope you'll accept.'

I assumed this was going to be a further catalogue of seals, documents, portraits.

'Oh no,' he said, 'that's all done. This is something different. And it's you I want. You, not the firm.'

As a nameless being in the third circle of power, I wasn't expected to understand the nuances of statecraft. He calmly assured me that everything he wanted me to do was bound to matters of the gravest national importance (this was the kind of thing he used to tell my mother, all those years ago). It was going to be of huge benefit to him – in the shuffle of crested documents he'd been working with, and now was forming replies to. My part in it was to descend to the grime of the London streets and bring him back a theatre professional, one whose career wasn't public property, with a name not known to the readers of tabloid newspapers or to TV audiences. I just about restrained a smile, but could not help internalise, on an ever-diminishing horizon, the ruin and detritus of the earl and all that nineteenth-century confection, with its etiquette, convention, with its crumbling code of honour, all a last shallow refuge and residue of empire. I imagined a remote, foggy, cobbled street, and the horse-drawn cab the earl would make available, as I trawled a stagy East End in search of the music-hall floozy, the powerless waif instructed to rendezvous at a secluded country lodge, and at the nod of his head to satisfy his needs. I blinked away those stereotypes and told him I had absolutely no knowledge of the theatre, and no connection with anyone in it. He went to the desk and rattled open one of its drawers, and drew out a sizeable paperback, a stage directory, its glossy paper cover centred by those two familiar Thespian masks, one with its smile of joy, the other despair.

'Have a look through this and make some calls.'

It didn't seem to be a question of how busy I might have been. To the query exactly what sort of person did he want, the reply was this: 'Someone able to cast a simply plotted play.'

'And what's the incentive? What am I to offer?'

'There will be, Humf, appropriate remuneration.'

I spent the hours before midday cocooned in my office, and kept to this charade for over a week. I could see by her puzzled frown how aghast my secretary, Gillian, was, and rumours must have spread I had found more to occupy my mornings than the crossword. Some in our team of technicians, young men, open-shirted, weary-looking, who till now got only pointless, token tasks from me, showed enough curiosity to look in with something pertinent to say, if they passed my office. Between calls I stood with my back to the desk and gazed thoughtfully through the window, at a blustery sky, or down at the life on the street, where the cars, buses and taxis crisscrossed lane to lane, and the pavements bustled with pedestrians – buttoned up and wind-blown. It was a joyous surprise when one of my partners ventured into my lair, where the distinct lack of industry, and at certain times a plate emptied of biscuits, were no longer expected signs. I'd often thought a good heraldic device would show 'reward' – the exclusive product of labour – as an oddly English legacy, unresolved by civil war, a beheaded king, and various factory Acts. I received memos, and found my name rising to the summit of the circulation list. I was even asked for the opening address at strategy sessions. No one quite grasped that after over a decade it was Earl Eliot d'Oc behind these machinations, or that my evasions were not the caution, the cleverness, of a man on the brink of a first commercial breakthrough.

Clouds covered the capital, and every day it rained. From that well-thumbed directory of theatre professionals I drew up a shortlist, which after a series of inconclusive phone calls was whittled down to just three names. The first was a man in his forties, whose CV had as its centrepiece sub-Saharan tours funded by the British Council. A close second was Ananke Klitt, thirty, whose tableau had gone into English schools. That had had public funding too, and listed as its aim the message to teenage girls, they *could* say no to sex. The third was Daphne

Hao, who was devising a one-woman show for the London fringe, and had taken a repertoire of well-known monologues into hotels at holiday resorts.

I passed this and other information on to the earl, whose reaction was a polite blank – no twitch to the corner of his mouth, not the slightest elevation of an eyebrow. I know, because he told me, that he interviewed each in turn at the Palace of Westminster, where only Ananke Klitt showed peasant awe at its statuary. He apportioned her a rushed ten minutes, and had erased her from his list even before he showed her out, with a gentle stroll through the news crews camped on College Green. Ananke, a little *too* earnest. It took days of cogitation for his only male candidate to make his presence felt. His moody, brooding eloquence betrayed his acute understanding of the ranking system as something the elect still view as a natural social order. Eliot cooled immediately. That introspection was too problematic, and was likely to disrupt his political purpose, eventually. Therefore our attention turned to Daphne, whose look was Scandinavian – a fair skin, hair an ash blonde in ringlets. He spent a good half-hour briefing her. He bought her tea in a polystyrene cup. Into this she stirred a sweetener. She seemed, he said, very probing in her curiosity, and asked if I minded that, and made much of the fact she'd called him Earl when he'd asked her to call him Eliot.

'Mind? Why should I mind?'

'I'm inviting you both to dinner.'

That pleasantly ironic occasion was served by an outside caterer, whom Eliot instructed as to the menu – salt sticks with a mango dip, followed by boiled fish, followed by a steamed pudding – all the kind of fare he thought she'd like. The main course came with those four condiments I regard as important enough referentially to have noted at the outset – *garum*, *liquamen*, *allec*, *muria* (or at least Eliot's version of them). Exact meanings are lost (I'm reliably told), but all these are mentioned in Roman writings on the subject of salt production.

'Salt,' I said, 'has been the earl's special privilege.'

She tested that green mush of mango on the tip of her little finger, poised at her lips as I told her how an ancestry of d'Ocs, Dokkes and D'Arcs had traded with the Habsburgs all over the Austro-Hungarian empire, and in lesser incarnations had infiltrated the Viennese bureaucracy.

'Vienna, robust enough to repel repeated Ottoman onslaught, but not the d'Ocs,' as I'm sure I must have said elsewhere.

Daphne Hao

1

Dessert all three of us declined. Coffee came in the fantasised rococo flush – lightness in the pinks, the velvets, the scrolls – of Eliot's drawing room. He placed his two foot soldiers – myself and Daphne – compass points apart on separate sofas, in a single line of vision from the winged chair, under the mantelpiece, where with a straight spine he took command. Daphne, not primed for business particularly, accepted an after-dinner mint and showed she'd got her notebook open at an empty page. I heard the click of a thermostat. In a lumber of aural coordinates the central heating purled and rumbled into life. At the sound of it she felt a chill, and automatically re-hooked the top two buttons of her blouse – all a fumble of finger and thumb. The commission, which Eliot didn't seem to think she'd have to consider or ponder much to make a decision, required familiarity with a name as new to me as to her. I shared her quizzical look when he referenced, in a Grove's he'd got in a glass-fronted bookcase, a short entry for the Bavarian composer-critic Gottlieb Nissel, an academy musician active in the nineteenth century. Nissel he said had lavished the best hours of his later life on an operatic magnum opus – ill-fated – in a collaboration with journeyman playwright Ludwig von Löchke, whose grounding was more textual than musical (he could not be called a poet). Löchke nevertheless produced a workable libretto, a concoction now consigned to the well-stocked graves of literature. It never outgrew its working title, *A Farewell to Salzburg*, in spirit a *Bildungsroman*, but reduced to a prison house of dialogue, whose subject was the life and artistic growth of Mozart. The project was abandoned on the emergence of Richard Wagner, whose operatic revolution placed the Nissel canon in a mire of music pedantry. Eliot pointed. Daphne, when she'd turned the key and opened the cabinet, stretched up and brought back to her seat not only the Grove's (or the section of laminated brick where Nissel's name appeared), but also a London street guide.

'Don't normally drive this far west,' she said. 'There's got to be a better way back than the jam I came through.'

She told us where she lived, somewhere off the Mile End Road, but the best I could show her, when I sat on her sofa and looked at the map, was how to escape the one-way web whose threads we were in, and head for the clear blue skies of the Bayswater Road. I followed a line with my index finger. Eliot smiled dejectedly.

She fetched her car shortly after that, from where it was parked several streets away, and left me in the hallway, in the soft glow and the crystal of its lighting. Eliot, in a search for paperwork he wanted her to have, did not follow us out. As I waited I cast eyes over his hangings, none of which I recalled from previous visits here, as a boy, or as a graduate, or in the early days of cataloguing. I got as far as the abbey church of Cluny, mildly repulsed by its gloomy-looking sky. That little flicker passed abruptly when Daphne reappeared. I watched her clamber to the pavement and trot lightly up the steps, where I opened the door fully, allowing her to straddle the threshold. Eliot joined us there, where he shook her hand stiffly and passed her a small brown envelope, into which he'd

slipped the libretto, expecting her to read it soon. I pointed to
the end of the street.

'Don't forget, left then right.'

Eliot retreated into the shadows, and for a moment stood
sideways to the huge gilded mirror angled above his writing
desk, where he adjusted his cravat. His eye caught not his own
reflection, which was frail and grey and unwilling to be old, but
the whimsical gaze that featured in all the family portraits.
Daphne, clutching her envelope, turned round sharply before
she reached the street. I had expected, on being introduced, the
kind of professional I never do well with, the girding a contented outer wrap in the triteness of career – but that was not the
case. I liked her. In time I'd come to admire her. Now, as the
distance gathered between us, she smiled.

'I'll be in touch,' she said.

That envelope she waved in valediction. She opened the door
of her little black car, then tossed it across to the passenger seat.

'Nice to have met,' I replied. I had my hand to the earl's
colossal front door, and began to push it to. She settled herself,
her engine in a purr, her two offside indicators a torch to the
whole street (such a noise it had, that flashing amber light).

She zoomed away, her blooms of exhaust blotting any last
trace of her perfume.

2

I had no better idea of d'Oc's commission for Daphne than she
had herself. I did know this. He'd sent her from his dinner
table, on a dry September night, intending no further personal
contact. For almost an hour after she'd left, he kept me
hanging on, producing a second copy of Löchke's libretto, *A*

Farewell to Salzburg, or rather its translation, by a certain John Ray, of Baltimore, and published by the Theodore Presser Company, in an edition not dated. It must have been the 1970s or earlier. Its cover was of flimsy stiffened paper, a faded lilac, with an old, eloquent, bookish-looking typeface. He told me to read it, and thoroughly get to know it. I took it into the office the following day, and opened it out on the oceanic waste of my desk, and gave it an hour of my time before coffee, baffled as to why Eliot was so interested in the sugared entertainments of imperial Vienna. I couldn't see how the thing could now be staged. I read it – probably wrongly – as a tragedy, with pivotal, comic moments tossed in haphazardly for audience relief. As I later learned (of course from d'Oc, that friend of the Enlightenment) the first of its climaxes owed itself to Mozart's letters written to his father, the year 1781, when Wolfgang was twenty-five. He'd been summoned to Vienna by Archbishop Colloredo, his employer, Vienna a place hard to get established, and so faced the possibility of an impromptu return to Salzburg, which was too provincial for a man of his enormous talent. Worse, he was prevented from staging concerts of his own, having to wait on Colloredo's say so, who as the whim took him may or may not include him in whatever was his timetable. Mozart in response began what Beethoven later plunged into more fully – a rebellion against the straitjackets of patronage – and looked for other backers, and in the process broadened his contact with musical theatrical life around him. That only infuriated the archbishop, whose bluster Mozart chose to interpret as dismissal from service (Wolfgang not then at the summit of European culture, but a servant to the vagaries of fortune). What Mozart says in reply to the archbishop (as I read it in Löchke) is more probably what he *wanted* to say, an outburst he reports in a letter to his father Leopold. As that little episode reaches its dramatised conclusion, the bewildered young musician is told that a verbal firing has no legal force – and anyway, he hasn't been sacked. Moreover, as a servant he does not have the power to resign. The situation is unresolved, so in the end it is Count Arco's task to boot the young composer out of court, which he does – literally – giving us the opera's only decent aria, and John Ray's comic translation of it, with its climax—

> Ejection so cruelly resolute
> On the toe of Arco's ignorant boot.

That alpine cadence was already a fading memory when Daphne phoned my office, her tone business-like, and limited in what it and she divulged.

'About this earl,' she said.

'Oh yes.'

'Well, really…!'

I agreed to meet, but not now. She was working on the southeast coast, so we'd have to wait for the weekend. I said I couldn't make it. When Eliot also phoned, with the same request, I had to disappoint him too. It was work-related, you see, and down to the circle I was in. Creative commercial thinking had written itself into a multitude of ring-bound tomes, which at DCT we'd filled to the limit with glossy methodologies. My ten other partners had given up their weekend leisure, yachting in the Channel, dawn-to-dusk hikes in the flatter bits of Kent, all togged up against a biting wind, and raking the scrub with field glasses – or all the other things they did (horses, glider planes, poolside aerobics, soccer for the over-forties, role play and bonding expeditions with teenage sons).... All because thrashing out our new management strategy was overdue. As our head of accounting systems had already pointed out, this promised to be so radical that only a redefinition of DCT itself, with its multiple substructures, was a proper target outcome. He resorted to terms like 'root and branch,' 'synergistic outputs', 'bell-curve quanta', 'streamlined operational matrices', syllables uttered with absurd self-parody. Perhaps he'd read one too many books from the blue-chip business school, with its swarm of gurus writing its Apocrypha. It was going to result in unlocking our office doors in the cold of a Saturday morning, when over sandwiches and jugs of filter coffee we'd absorb this new thinking into our practice. As things turned out I stubbed my cigar at four that afternoon, my thoughts having toyed with certain rival concepts (incendiary mostly), and walked to the window. I told the rest I was calling time – for still no coherent plan had been agreed.

I got across to Eliot's on Sunday night, and found him ashen and fatigued, and – unusually – lethargic. He took me into the study, with the rolltop, and on it that newish computer, where a girl from a temping agency, its nearest office a few streets away, had returned to that same project I'd started so many years ago, the house a museum, a hotchpotch of ancient books, faded brown parchments, gems, antique philately, busts, por-traits – works of art generally – old legal documents, all as I've listed above, under an icon of double-headed eagles. The dates have become important, so here they are as I am able to recall.

Cataloguing he resumed in 1992, the year of the monarch's *annus horribilis*. Its chapter of mishaps was a twelve-month span where the earl and his Privy Council cronies were called to emergency meetings, as someone got to grips with his numismatics list. Constitutional issues topped the agenda. Humble Humfrey Joel, scratching about in his lowly circle of power, shan't ever know exactly what the issues were – though not everything remains unclear. I was shown to, and read, one of Princess Diana's many chroniclers, his 'true' revelations a muddled exercise typographically, a world of orthographic gaffes, and so many missed opportunities punctuation-wise.

That tortured tabloid *Diana* saw Earl d'Oc and his friends close ranks around her, grey, learned men already planning the heir's public rehabilitation. Certain unfortunate incidents got in the way, though they seized on the Duchess of York, whose photographic revelations, from a sunlit South of France, were a useful distraction. The fire at Windsor Castle, and the Commons announcement applying the rubber stamp to the one thing everyone knew – that the prince and princess would separate – brought his project to a halt. In its current resurrection, just a few loose ends remained, and here he sat, imploring me, now that the management of outside staff was too exhausting. He turned the computer on, and in the glow of its screen weighed a copper-coloured phial, already part empty – drops for his ears, he said, his doctor had prescribed.

'"Loose ends",' I said. 'I thought you said the project was done.'

'I want you to gather it all together and produce it as a document.'

The earl and his documents.

'All right. But not here.' I copied his hard drive onto a CD and told him I would get someone back at the office to gather its word-processed outpourings into a single indexed file, with a contents list, an entirety I promised to reorganise as a coherent whole. It was then up to him to sign it off in draft before final printing, a scheme he agreed to.

3

I met Daphne on a rain-swept weekday afternoon in a café in Covent Garden, where she flapped her umbrella over the doorstep, and found a small square table near the till. I stood waiting at the counter, for an age before I was served. We had tea, only after she'd mopped up with tissues she took from her bag. Clumsily, I saucered a deluge of slops, my hands in a tremble, on setting down the tray. She was dressed more plainly than at dinner at the earl's, and wore her hair unpinned, with its loose curls touching her shoulders, and a shade blonder under the café's artificial light. Her social pleasantries were long and elaborate, and unmasked a motive I was slow to understand – or anyway that was her overture. The pronouncement following wasn't as harmonious, as she dealt with the earl and the terms of his commission. She said bluntly she didn't intend to take it up. I had no suspicions as to why, and asked her the reason. She produced Eliot's envelope, and from it tipped onto the table what would have been the first of her paycheques, which she told me to return. She'd too many other things to do. Having read through Eliot's schedule, a handwritten side of A4, prescriptive in its demands, and with no room for negotiation, she saw no possibility of fitting it into her timetable. I asked her what that timetable was, and got a long list of the kind of things she did.

She devised work. She'd got a one-woman show. She taught. She auditioned for parts. Her agent sent her everywhere. What she really wanted was the West End, film or TV. She'd got a contract with the Southeast tourist industry, which she couldn't just jack in. She garbed up, and visited couples, pyjamaed and nightcapped, just as they'd turned in. Seated at the foot of their beds, she sent them off to sleep with monologues chosen from a catalogue supplied by the concierge. Her most popular so far were: Titania (*Midsummer Night's Dream*); Clytemnestra (on Agamemnon's homecoming, Aeschylus); Antigone (as she laments her fate, Sophocles). Also in her repertoire were Wilde, his Mabel Chiltern (*Ideal Husband*); Saint Joan (GBS); Lady Macbeth; Salome (Oscar Wilde again); and two more Shakespeares, Portia (*Merchant of Venice*) and Isabella (*Measure for Measure*).

'Well, yes,' I said. 'That would keep anyone busy.'

More than this, what occupied her was a search for subject matter for a survey run by Channel 4, with calls for a synopsis and treatment for a fifty-minute documentary, as of course TV and filmmaking were a summit she'd like to conquer. I told her not to be put off by Eliot, whose list of written instructions slipped out of her libretto. I took it up, skimmed over. Her first task – her task specifically – was to draw up a shortlist of writers, for the job of reworking *A Farewell to Salzburg*, which as a play, under a new title, Eliot was adamant was 'scheduled' for the English stage. A rattle of change in the cash machine deadened the coy syllable forming and fading on her lips, which I didn't fully catch. I explained insofar as I could, though I'd have to admit, a play for the English stage – that really did surprise me. The earl, I said, was used to giving out orders and having them obeyed, a tendency that went with his circle of power and hadn't improved with age. I'd known him since childhood, and assured her I'd got a modicum of influence, and knew how to handle him.

'Leave it with me. I'll talk him round.'

I pushed the cheque back across the table, and with a smile told her to bank it. Shortly after that we struck out on our separate ways, in a silver mist. She phoned on a brighter day a week later, to tell me she had spent half an hour in the reference section of her local library, and had read Earl d'Oc's entry in *Who's Who*, and had found no mention of a Habsburg connection. I told her that shouldn't surprise her. She pressed the point.

'He's the kind of man,' I said finally, 'who in restaurants calculates the tip precisely, and that's the amount he leaves.'

'Well that tells me everything.'

'Have you got a shortlist?'

'Will you buy me lunch?'

'I'll buy you lunch when you've got a shortlist.'

It took her into October, when at last we sat in a quiet spaghetti house, hers a small bottle of Perrier and an egg and anchovy salad. I too wasn't hungry. I had toast, under a thin smear of pâté. She'd darkened her eyes, in a clever, theatrical way. There was a pinkish film applied to her lips. She wore a short skirt and a long, fur-collared coat. We chatted amiably, though I couldn't keep her off the Habsburgs, an elusive detail in the life of her new employer, in danger of being an obsession. I said there was no sleight of hand, and related some of the work I'd done on his inventory, his taxonomy of family relics. I even mentioned that document I'd been asked to assemble, which was now on my computer at the office. I made a point of stressing how extensively I'd worked on it, and could vouch for its moments of Habsburg history, things well aired publicly, but chronicled in a way the standard textbooks didn't. In a few days the whole thing would be ready for the printers, and once bound was probably due for shipment off to a secret library, overseen by d'Oc himself. She picked at a strand of grated carrot that had caught in the corner of her mouth. She didn't disbelieve me, but it didn't change her position. She said again she wouldn't go on with the project.

'How far have you got?'

She'd drawn up her shortlist – her specialist hacks – all capable of transforming Nissel's operatic flop from one dreary idiom into another. Her sparring candidates were a stock three, two of whom shared the same forename. I was given them collectively, the Neils Duff and Mee. Duff had won awards for demotic verse, and excelled in media ditties, which interviewing newscasters chortled over, the kind of thing that in lighter moments rounded off their summary of appalling world events—

> David Icke
> In a fit of spite
> Regularly abused
> The six o'clock news.

He had served time in youth theatre adapting the plays of Aidan Chambers. The other one, Mee, was active in semi-retirement, earning his fee with a tour of Home Counties sheltered housing, where he performed in hour-long shows, his audience a dayroom of dozing, dosed-up pensioners. One of his routines involved a trumpet, and a reveille. The third in her trio, the one I guessed d'Oc would choose, was a sour-sounding Leo Dicto (a chance, if well-chosen *nom de guerre*), whose résumé was the anatomy of creative-writer pugilism. He was a Yorkshireman. His outstanding achievement was a kitchen-sink screening, his only broadcast play, a distillation of lower-middle-class life, its comedy a painful collision of pathos, bathos and deep unthinking prejudice. It had found its way under the BBC portcullis, showing in the '70s, and was a career lift and a change in Dicto's fortunes, on the strength of which he ditched his day job, the teaching of English, drama and social integration, in a sixth-form college I know not where. I don't doubt a godforsaken wasteland. He was soon back teaching again, only this time the craft of screenwriting, and not to sixth-formers, but in country or seaside writers' retreats, his students not quite adult or skilled enough to satisfy Corporation diktat, with its tea-and-biscuit aesthetic, or clued up enough to learn its secrets. Daphne had spoken to him briefly, but only by phone. He was a virtual recluse, sur-viving in a remote moorland in a whitewashed cottage, where in the pantomime season he doctored a repertoire of Aladdins *et al*, served up for the village-hall life of the local community.

I showed her how pleased I was with this information, but it cut no ice. This time she really was about to resign.

'It's odd how this earl of yours won't communicate, except through you.'

'He's busy. And, is quite ill.'

'I can't work for him.'

'Don't be too hasty.'

'You've got what you want. Names. *You* can talk to them.'

'I can't.'

'Why?'

'I know nothing about the theatre.' I was an accident of fate, I said, the epitome of private life, a being a circle of higher powers had placed as one of twelve partners, now eleven, running a specialist IT and management firm.

'Humf, we are all accidents of fate.'

She was right about that.

4

I met her next on a frosty riverside, under a cold dusting of stars, when she was gloved, coated, and trussed in a scarf, and had got us tickets for a show. She assured I wasn't unsuited temperamentally to the concoctions she liked, or at all out of place in the compact little theatre she took us both to. It was intimate, cramped and draughty. All seats taken, all tickets sold. The piece – a spectacle of twisted classic poses, dry ice, a lot of writhing, and pools of violet light – seemed no more than a fusion, then a dissipation, of inner human energy, and so on in a tableau of tiny variations. I put my hands together politely. With lights up on the last handclap I thanked her very much, and retracted my hand from the small of her back as she led me to the greenroom, or no more than a bar, a shuttered zone with a hand pump, spirits, refrigerated wine, and not much seating. We were met by a stocky, youngish man, who acknowledged us as a pair, with a cheery, healthy hello, and for me additionally a hearty handshake, but soon after that the two were in conclave, discussing Daphne's one-woman show.

I sipped patiently at a lime-coloured cocktail as, in the part of a Polish medium, she explained her position centre-stage – a lined woman wearing a babushka. With that and other props for getup she communes with the dead, or rather the dead commune with her, or rather they commune with one another, camped in a circuitry of human flesh, or the conduit their hostess makes of herself. The deceased trio Daphne had been working on, in a staged descent into the footlights, consisted of Mary Wollstonecraft and Marilyn Monroe, and – because Daphne as a girl was conscientious at her Sunday school – Saint Ursula, whose martyrdom she said was symbolic. Her research there was through Jacobus de Voragine, Daphne claiming to have read exhaustively his *Golden Legend* (1265–66). I didn't mind hearing about her Ursula, a British princess who'd travelled to Rome with 11,000 virgins. There all 11,001 were killed by the Huns. Nevertheless, I couldn't quite imagine the kind of conversation Daphne had dreamed up, over a projected eighty minutes – all without a break – she taking on the tone and character of all three ghostly presences.

'Sounds incredible!'

'Yes, Roel.'

'And demanding,' I chipped in, though I wasn't able to participate any further in their conversation.

Her working title was *MMU*, or as she pronounced it 'em em mew', that last syllable struck with my defeated look for the wall clock.

'It's past ten, Humf. You rushing off?'

'I haven't eaten.'

'Oh, I know somewhere.'

That somewhere was the furnished lobby of a nearby Drop

In Asia, a cranberry plush with a golden thread of elephants, where we drank insipid fizzy beer and munched our way through a carapace of poppadoms, its platter twinned with a carousel of chopped onion relish, in a sprinkle of cumin and lemon juice (a recipe I urged myself I must write down.) I told her the earl had made his choice (as predicted, Leo Dicto), and also that Eliot wasn't prepared to relax his working method. The structure remained in place, with Eliot the project's apex. He would communicate with me, then me with Daphne, Daphne with Dicto, and in the other direction the reverse chain of command.

'That's ridiculous.'

'Here's your next payment. I hope, Daphne, you'll take it. How's the Channel 4 project?'

She underlined the point that Eliot's bank was Coutts, as she studied the cheque I gave her. 'I'm still thinking about it,' she said (the Channel 4 project). 'I'll get in touch with Dicto. The earl pays well. I'm calling a cab.'

5

Dicto took the job, and was quick to bank his first advance, another of Eliot's cheques from Coutts, and a sum that ran to thousands. The earl – ever strategic – in his next message along our staging posts 'advised' that all editorial decisions were his alone. On that he remained inflexible, to the point – and almost a breaking point – that I argued heatedly with Daphne, telling her no, d'Oc wouldn't change his mind. He never did. She phoned Dicto. Dicto she said sounded grumpy, but agreed (apparently). So now a basis for Eliot's master plan was put in place, which saw as first casualty the cast list Nissel and von

Löchke had arrived at, as fabric of their only operatic collaboration, their *Farewell to Salzburg*. Gone were Nannerl, Mozart's sister, Constanze (his wife), Leopold (father), gone were Archbishop Colloredo and the hard-booted, hard-hearted Count Arco. Gone Salieri, a musical rival (whether Mozart's poisoner or not). Wolfgang too disappeared, to cap it. That left us, in the final erasure, in Eliot's sweeping readjustment, a Germanic hatching of Italian opera turned into English slapstick, a sort of lark-ascending hobnail. I don't go delving into Grove's *or* groves, sylvan, sickly or otherwise, and I cannot say if that ill-fated opera was ever performed, its parturition belonging to an era and an idiom long over, and not ones I have studied. With d'Oc's jurisdiction, and its process of hagiographic cleansing, a sentimentalised Mozart, in his child conquest of the courts of Bavaria, Vienna, Prague *et al* (London, Mannheim, Paris *et al*), is replaced by the nebulous Simon Star, a boy who belongs to an England of deprived inner cities, in the here and now, and whose musical horizon extends over not much more than three or four chords strummed on a guitar. D'Oc's outline, as a synopsis I passed to Daphne, a page of A4 we drank latte over looking very puzzled, had dispensed with von Löchke's eighteenth-century Vienna, with a dramaturgy focused instead in a kind of temporal limbo. We see in the earl's instructions – which were very precise – an amalgam of the Tudor court and modern urban England. Dicto, unflinching if bowed under great duress, was expected to carry out this surgical adaptation, and with the dialogue he wrote must show a preparedness for any of d'Oc's incisions. D'Oc reserved the right to cut, amend, and introduce additional material.

You can see what a bizarre concoction all of it was just from the cast list, with the original touched on above swept away and replaced by the following—

New King Palmers
THE PLAYERS
King Chads, King of England
Sir Ossie, King's Chancellor
Lady Michael, King's Defence Secretary
Sir Nigel, King's Foreign Secretary
King's Musician
Palmers Ltd, an entrepreneur
Madame Zemlinsky, a fortune-teller
Star, an electric guitarist
King's courtiers, King's servants, King's vassal
Pincher, a merchant
Erato Electric, with Chorus (heard only)
A landlord
Two tabloid journalists
Revellers
A lutenist
Entertainers, and others

It's worth reiterating that d'Oc only ever had two meetings with Daphne, his coordinator of these pyrotechnics. He never at any time met or talked to Leo Dicto. Dicto – as the earl had stipulated – sent his works in progress to Daphne, Daphne passed them to me, and I passed them to d'Oc, who was specific as to each new round of changes, which he marked in red pen on laser-printed drafts. He was, too, and continued to be, generous with his cheques. Their loaded cargos I made a mental note of every time Daphne mused on the sums she was getting.

Run-throughs, rehearsed readings and even partial staging were a requisite before the work was complete, so long as I, a son of sorts, undertook to attend and agreed to report my findings to the earl. I don't know what special confidence he placed in me – my only skirmish with theatre had been as a boy, and at Thespian Hoe. He swore me to secrecy on one vital issue, which I was asked to withhold from Daphne until the play was ready for its opening tour. Its essence was this: that once the work was complete, and fitted to the formula as d'Oc had set out editorially, it encoded within it a message from the British Privy Council to its counterpart in the European Union. So now I begin to think not just about politics, but ciphers, acrostics, dialogue as crossword clues, repeated phrase patterns, the Vigenère and other tools of espionage – *le chiffre indéchiffrable.*

In those early days, before the first of our fatalities, I handled the paperwork only. That usually involved a padded envelope marked 'c/o Daphne Hao' (the name she traded under). Bundled inside was that ever mutating manuscript, in its litter of the earl's red pen strokes. The part I played in these multiple transits revealed nothing more to me than the play's changing title, with its final metamorphosis – *New King Palmers* – wriggling into being after two faltering sweeps of Eliot's pen, on the tail of its earlier incarnations. These were, *Star, Madame Zemlinsky's Dream, Leisure for Leisure, Rough Beast to Bethlehem.* Others I forget. But, finally, *New King Palmers* – that was the play. An impediment (and some argued there were many) to the testing of its scenes, with Star, or Zemlinsky, or the new king, was the arts community Daphne dealt with day to day, whose sensitive social vanes were regimented madly to the gales of political correctness. It was almost impossible to camp out in even a modest rehearsal space, with a willing troupe, *if* her aims were outside the community remit. She told me how absurd her profession was, at times, with its addiction to soft political funding. It had this tacit agreement to apply itself as the bandage on society's fractures, with what goes on as performance only an ersatz for the state's contract with its citizens. That was after decades of mass education and its carefully crafted failures. She lectured sternly. Where her creed ought to have been the driving vision of humanity's sceptics, instead she was urged to tell us safe sex was possible and that women were angry.

Not that, I think, she felt personally aggrieved about anything. A slight setback was that one-woman show she was planning, whose polyphonic monologues were intended to unmask the evil oppression the likes of Humfrey Joel, and his 'friend' the powerful Earl Eliot d'Oc, had subjected less privileged mortals to. That was all fine in principle, though from what I knew Eliot had spent a great part of his middle life arranging best care possible for the frailties of his ma, and apart from impeccable trysts with *my* ma, he exercised his evils largely over other men. Speaking for myself, I was jilted once, and decided that was enough, and ever since have viewed sexual politics at a remove, willing only to enter that debate via the chic, expensively garbed prostitutes I list in my address book, blondes and brunettes for hire, where the exploitation is mutual. That other kind of woman, the career gal, is as much a bore to me as the stock career male, and is likely to rise much higher in the world than I shall – and good luck. But now I had to admit: I liked the way she did things, the control she took, the goals she set and mostly achieved, her interest in her own destiny (as, well, yes, I'd fallen for Daphne).

According to Roel, and the committee he sat on, Daphne's three-pronged *MMU* wasn't a viable programme. Nothing could be said about Marilyn Monroe that hadn't been already. Other autopsy results (and do I detect masculine interdict?) had shown that feminist activism was so closely stitched into the fabric of Western civilisation that Mary Wollstonecraft need no longer be invoked, for hadn't her 'vindication' carried forward into a powerful sisterhood, transatlantic? And how about this, in summary: for a society faithless and afraid to express tender emotions, Saint Ursula was also dismissed. Daphne showed no hint of anger or disappointment on relating this, and said only I should now listen carefully for someone from the circus rampaging through the organ loft. I followed her into a cheap sushi bar, in an escape from the cold – a biting cold – and bought her lunch. I offered soothing words. I said perhaps with Channel 4 she'd have better luck.

'Not much chance of that, Humf. I don't have any material.'

I half had the solution, and thought instantly of d'Oc and his family history. The problem was, that wasn't a seam I could get to safely, with all it would take, metaphorically – ropes, pulleys, gangs of men and mules – in mining its ores. I knew how truculent Eliot could be. Lines on his aristocratic graph had plotted every mood from puce to blue. Much though I wanted to, I didn't promise anything, aware of how useful Daphne would find his archive. I hinted at it, in the reiteration of his name, found in all its variants as Dokke (with the Franks), as D'Arc at Albi with Simon de Montfort, or in its current form at Potsdam. I wouldn't give it up, asking myself what it was I could do for her, if in only vague portentous terms. I flattered myself I knew first-hand what kind of leech attaches itself to all kinds of empires everywhere.

'I'm sure something will turn up,' I said.

'Let's hope.'

I had now got the final version, tantalisingly, of Eliot's megatome, that private document my team at DCT, with Gillian's help, had got ready for printing, a thought that crossed and re-crossed my mind the next time I was parcelling up the Leo Dicto manuscript. Then, under d'Oc's fanlight, I met his family GP, a man in his sixties, thickly jowled, and looking unwell himself. His face was a purple patchwork where the razor had scraped at its lifetime's toil. He was leaving the house, and I was going in. He nodded gravely, but paradoxically sounded a bright hello. I stepped round and closed the door behind him. Eliot, when I found him, was putting his final touches to his Project Inventory, and had got rid of his temping girls. What was now required was scholarship, and academic expertise, and someone fulltime.

'Oh well then who?' I asked.

The answer was evasive, though that issue was eventually placed in *my* hands personally, with a choice I was asked to make. I was given, as the means of applying final authenticity to that whole bag of artefacts, one of the following: a granite-complexioned art historian, who lived in Woodstock, or a V&A curator, all of whose books her publisher had launched symbolically in Bath. Once I'd decided which, d'Oc's database would be open to her – a mere simulacrum now. I said I'd return to the office and come back to install software that made the help and search facilities easier to use, as one couldn't guarantee DCT's program suites were known to everyone – and besides, the one Eliot had got was old and outdated. Furthermore, there was sensitive matter he wanted sifting out, which I couldn't do unless under his direction, into a separate database I would also have to install, the earl and his privy ethos always applying a filter to the truth. And what was 'truth' anyway, if not the process of distillation, and wholly contingent. As Serenity had said to him all those years ago, during holidays in Hoe: 'We are all constructs of policy and schooling, or something running counter to them.'

D'Oc's niece had always made me think.

'Please do the interviews here,' said d'Oc.

'It's all such a shock,' I replied. I would have to get back to the office. I would have to check the diary.

'Yes. You do that.'

6

What reasons could I invent for phoning Daphne? I paced my office, but couldn't think beyond d'Oc's revisions to the Dicto script, a drama in itself, as that lumbered on, scene by scene, and always overdue. I received d'Oc's padded envelope and tore at it impatiently, then called her immediately on the only number she'd given me. It returned a recorded message, in an echo of stage Americanness – 'Hi! I'm not here right now…' – as then it reeled off a litany of workplace names and numbers, a laboriously lettered URL, and finally her email address. This I began to note on my pad (laurel dot hao at thespis dot…)

when her fatigued, live English voice cut in abruptly. Nothing seemed right. Her words were wadded in the echo of a public phone booth, or so it sounded. I strained to imagine what kind of hall or living room hung in private suspension around her – bits of graffiti, Cindy's or Sandy's telephone chat line, the numbers bold, bright, brassy, a battered directory, its pages stuck (just at the ones you want) with a chewed-out spear of Wrigley's, or someone's anxious semen.

'Ah, Humf,' she said. 'What news?'

'D'Oc's latest revisions.'

'He's kept himself busy, the seventy-eighth Earl of Gormenghast.'

'Very droll. We could meet, or I could drop it off.'

'Why not put it in the post….'

I said it was no trouble to deliver it personally, as I'd got business in Limehouse and could call in on my way. There was a palpable pause, but, with caution, she agreed.

The address she gave was a basement flat in a gridlock of tree-lined streets, in a tall terrace vanishing upwards into a cloudy, moody sky, its frontage dark green at its bargeboards, and a dirty white peeling from its windows. The brick was sooty brown. Her rooms spread out backwards from the pavement, kitchen first, then off the passage were doors to her lounge, bedroom, bathroom. I trotted down her cement steps and tapped gently on the single pane of frosted glass in the upper half of the door.

'It's open.'

Inside she was chopping vegetables, with a cleaver, its steel-bright blade about half the size of my document case. I was taken nevertheless by the delicacy her fist and flexible wrist effortlessly worked that deadly instrument with. She was talking on the phone, mouthpiece cradled under her chin, her head cocked inquiringly. Her hair was tied in a rose-coloured ribbon. I saw why it had sounded so cavern-like when I had called her earlier. An old service chute into the basement, now her kitchen alcove, was where she hung her phone and notepad – also a wok, a plastic colander, and a large red ladle. I waited. She and the other voice went through their catechism – a pause, a sentence, a pause – till finally she called a halt, and hung up.

She brushed aside a short lock of hair that had planted a lone curl on her brow, and put down the cleaver. There were golden cubes of parsnip heaped on the chopping board. I said how rarely I cooked myself, mostly ending up with pasta in a basket-hung bistro across the street from where I lived – all grapes and vines and a marine glaze to its tiling.

'That's too bad,' she said – and no good at all for my waistline.

I rummaged in my case and handed her the latest.

She led me to her living room, which was low-lit and dominated at its centre by a circular dining table, piled high with papers – scripts and correspondence – plus a dictionary (a *Chambers*). The paint on her walls, a seductive blue, had been reduced to strips and rectangles, under a patchwork of cuttings and photographs.

One I started looking at she said was a young Alan Epsy. 'You know him?'

'No.'

Ah, well this was Epsy in the part of Sir Fopling Flutter, looking *too* at ease in his Piccat shoes and a Chedreaux periwig (which all meant nothing to me). A series of black-and-white photos showed scenes from Brecht, Beckett, Pinter, and a string of more recent names I didn't recognise, in productions she admired for different reasons. There were too handwritten things, penned on gummed little notelets, their top-corner logo those two familiar Thespian masks – little trade secrets posted to herself. There were hand-drawn stage sets, designs she had kept of productions she'd acted in or directed. In one I identified Malvolio after his incarceration, *Twelfth Night* one of the plays my PhD home educator had taken us to see.

Now the awkward moment. She offered tea or coffee, but I sensed she didn't have time – so I left, having paused for one last look at her Malvolio. 'Reminds me of Bernie,' I said, 'our accountant.' She told me the production, and waved me on my way. That was not a great success, I told myself, repeatedly, even back at the office, a few hours later, the day turning to dusk, with a flicker of streetlights, and dusk to night when the lights glowed, and the moon was creeping over my windowsills.

Some days after that papers she sent to my office ascended, with great buoyancy, to the summit of my intray, in a handwritten envelope I intrigued over even as I tore it open. Its cargo was résumés, Alan Epsy's foremost. Clipped to all four was one of her compliment slips (its heading *Laurel Hao*, those two theatrical masks pinned to the top left corner). In neat, rounded, hasty ballpoint her note explained where and at what time they were having their first read through – not something she'd envisaged, she said, when Eliot served that dinner for three. (An odd number she'd thought at the time.) Would I like photocopies of the scenes to be read? I called her that instant and left a message saying that I would. Alas we didn't need to meet. There was time to post these other papers too.

7

I got over to the address in Hammersmith she'd written down, a basement, and above it a low-rise brick building. That you enter by a nondescript door before descent into a bituminous underworld, a yardage lit by naked bulbs and cluttered with props, costumes and electrical equipment. In atmosphere a damp subterranean calm was pointedly at odds with the rumble of traffic overhead. Those assembled ahead of me were about to read the play's first act. Already they had puzzled as to what it was about. Here's what *I* concluded—

The Palmers of Eliot's new title is an entrepreneur, who, ostensibly, is acting as artistic agent for a young, untalented musician, Simon Star (the antithesis of Earl d'Oc's Mozart). Action is located in and around King Chads's court, which has moved to its country retreat. Characters and events, though approximated to a UK in the late twentieth century, are shown as partially attuned to the Tudor era. This makes Chads and his court a fantasy of sorts, infused with symbolic meaning. But what does that mean?

King Chads's is a life circumscribed by tradition, precedent, above all ritual. The Tudor backdrop he is etched against illustrates the ancient system of power England is rooted in (an established order d'Oc upholds. His intention isn't satire). In different degrees the courtly characters reflect the two worlds – the mode of our contemporaries, and the ancient one of pageant. Two forces acting on the court are, on the one hand, a groundswell of opinion in favour of republicanism, and on the other suspicion at the aims and politics of the European Union.

Arriving at court is a ragbag of entertainers, including Palmers, a commercial adventurer who in the play's opening scenes is acting for singer/songwriter Star, but has other business interests too, apart from exploiting Star, something Star has only vague inklings of. Their position is understood completely by Madame Zemlinsky, a fortune-teller and Tarot adept, who in following agent and client to Chads's court is intending to outwit both of them and make off with their cash.

All three get embroiled in court politics, which at that time is dominated by the republican and EU questions, with personal complications brought by the King's Musician, an accomplished polyphonist, who must now act out new rivalries, in particular with Simon Star.

On the small deal table where Daphne was sitting was a jug of water, awash with ice cubes and a slice apiece of lemon and lime. She offered me a glass, and introduced her colleagues – three male, one female – whose résumés I had glanced over. She returned to their conversation, with a detour into the day-long workshop she'd overseen at an arts centre – 'some years ago' – way off in the skirt of Hardy's Wessex. Now, she'd revived it for a group of teenagers, a receptive troupe she'd worked with all that day, at a ramshackle venue a block from Loughborough Junction. With the young she always stressed importance on the malleability of myth, as a means of concealing incendiaries in that otherwise unassailable edifice, the monument to culture and tradition. She was adamant that not only theatre, but civilisation will not change without imagining forks not taken, *have* been taken. Every story, every myth, every salient fact of our history, we are duty bound to relive for the masks, mirrors and opposites each implies.

Those branches off in other directions are the accretion of small deviations able to bring us, whole, to the counterview of everything that is, and a revised value on the social forces making it so.

'That's fascinating, Daphne. Tell us more.'

Examples of 'branching off', ones she and her teenagers had been looking at today, she listed—

A Eurydice who survives Orpheus's fatal glancing back. A Narcissus who never at any moment gazes into any reflective surface. A Pandora's jar stuffed not with evils but with blessings (it is lost initially; it is recovered in November 1919, by Nancy Astor). Gawain as a lunar deity. A chosen people having not twelve, but eleven tribes. Likewise a spiritual leader able to muster only that number of disciples, eleven.

Inversions, reversals, masks added and removed, revealing not the masker but the masker's other mask, were the essentials of stage technique she urged her protégés to pay minute attention to, for how easy it was to show on stage who were the liars, who were the duped, how all of them form the vessel of humanity, a starred craft bearing as its load the narrative all are expected to carry to a scripted conclusion. It seemed to be a hobbyhorse of hers, and it got quite abrasive, until someone changed the subject, turning to me—

'So you're the Humfrey acting for the earl?'

I said yes, that was so.

'How *is* the earl?'

'Not well. The doctor's always there, but he doesn't improve.'

'Sorry to hear that.'

I was shown to a two-seater wicker settee, under the joint gaze of a stag's head and a bust of Agamemnon.

Daphne had not had time to change, coming here direct from Loughborough Junction, still in an earthy getup, a hooped top and garage dungarees. Her chair creaked. I watched as she unfolded her script and paused at the opening scene, which acts as a sort of triptych. Palmers centres, Madame Zemlinsky flanks. Daphne poured herself a glass of water. Epsy, assertive, said that he'd never read a play like it.

I put my fingertips together, and looked at him philosophically. He'd got his own ideas, brought forth as the trump card over those we'd already heard from Daphne, and grounded us back in the basics, with questions as to rationale, plot, character templates, the narrow gauge of motive. In the play's present instantiation, motive seemed merely incidental, grafted onto a milieu masquerading as more than the sum of its storylines.

'Are we talking, Humf, conspiracy theory?'

I said I didn't think so.

They argued it out, and having lit that touch paper I sat quietly, matching the wodge of CVs with the personnel grouped around me. Epsy took the part of Palmers (Daphne's other two males were Martin Held and Stewart Grange). Said Epsy had met the onset of baldness by closely shaving his head. These were his mid-forties, and what had been snowy tufts above his ears, and strands of silver topping his collar line, he'd cropped with puritanical severity. He was flabby but not unfit, had played Sunday sports, but now trod water at his local pool. He'd once had a promising career, performing on the steps of New York's Metropolitan Museum, which an impossible twist of fortune led to a part on Broadway. Other parts followed, at home, all of them in television. You'd see him in short sketches on satire shows – that faceless extra seated at the back of the studio bus, while to the fore someone better known succumbed to or dealt with the obstacles of everyday life, in the formulas of slapstick, the surreal, and everything in between. He'd had an agent once, and for the times the right figure too, and brooding Latin looks. He modelled shirts, then a stylish coat, then a particular way of eating cornflakes. His high point came with those popular juxtapositions invented by celebrity photographers, where with the remote fixed look of a man fit for the role of 007 he showed us how sharp an executive suit could be, pinned to a backdrop of everyday industry – scaffolds, men in hard hats, the churn of cement mixers. The debonair Epsy remained unaffected, as he gazed beyond these urban wastes. His climax was unattainably expensive sports cars, in a glitter of gold paint and gadgetry, which a now not so young Epsy earned company payrolls for, by driving through the terraced streets of Bermondsey. All ceased to be as kind when the hair at his crown thinned, then shrank through snowy shades of grey. A wonderfully resolute chin doubled itself overnight, then, after too many steak suppers, a once waspish waist ballooned through an abacus of new calibrations, all notched on the various belts he wore. A very good Palmers he'd make.

The r-less Stewart Grange had a museum interest in the cinema, and probably found that joke – that lost consonant dropped from his surname – wearying by now, or just a little tedious. For him Daphne had in mind the part of the King's Musician, whose first appearance is not until the close of Act

One, Scene Six, or I.6 as Dicto had notated it. Here was just
that kind of courtier the tabloids loved to villainise, a man
steeped in learning, rarefied beyond classification, scaling as
he did an impossibly elevated slope. Its opposing declivity
ended in those dens of mediocrity in the high versus lowbrow
debate – if debate you could call it. Political correctness cannot
wholly unstitch the proudest minds of what is essential in their
repertoire. No reason should exist as to why he must hide his
contempt for a multitude of artefacts beaten on the anvil of
popular taste. That position is openly declared when a wandering minstrel makes himself at home in the minstrels' gallery,
where much of the play's action is performed. This is the hub
of the King's country estate, where our interloper accompanies
a bawdy song with strumming on his lute. I know I rush on,
but this is its refrain—

> O down in the valley
> Along by the stream.

The King's Musician beats him with a whipstock and throws
him out. ('Whipstock' is one of few words Dicto retained from
the Shakespearean model Earl d'Oc gave him as part of his
research notes. Others dropped were 'leman', 'impeticos', 'gra-
tillity', 'testril'.)

So here we have one of the play's themes – the murk and the
dirty handshakes euphemistically termed artistic patronage.
There are internal complications too, which it took Epsy
(again) to point out, ones Daphne would need to address before
the first public light flooded onto the stage. The text Dicto had
so far delivered – under oppression of Eliot's scrutiny – opened

with a note on staging, which according to Epsy was aimed at a non-existent readership, and was a puzzle as to what it meant. King Chads's court is described, as I've set out above. We're in an England adumbrated as the one we know, with Tudor overtones. What were we supposed to make of this? Did, Epsy asked, the King and his fantasy environment have deep dramatic meaning? I replied I didn't know, foreseeing as imminent the moment I would have to tell Daphne of Eliot's hidden encumbrances. What would she say to the presence of d'Oc's diplomatic codes aimed at some counterpart, some impeccably dressed senior sitting in an ivory office somewhere at the heart of the new-Europe empire? What he had stipulated, and to this point only to me, bound us to the kind of secrecy where not a word of the final document he and Dicto eventually delivered was open to revision.

How did I read this, other than initially, in the way that d'Oc – in his bowdlerisation of Nissel, and against that play's un-likely reality – had re-accoutred its players? From the outset the King and others are partly got up for the Elizabethan stage: we have ermine, boots, rapiers, hose, codpieces, in implausible confluence with business suits and neckties, with props and articles made up of bill-folds and cigarette lighters, etc. By the final act (by the final act's scene five), much of this has changed, the King shedding most of his Tudor attire, while his Chancellor, Defence and Foreign Secretaries have regressed in the other direction. They have the look of a Cecil or a Walsing-ham (to quote the text's examples). Epsy continued to raise objections, with named authorities on semiotics and the stage, his sole purpose to cast slights on the author's lack of expertise, a writer who couldn't have known that dramaturgy is much better considered as a science. I scanned what text there was for acrostics, for complex polyalphabetic ciphers, then for simple allegories, or figures like litotes, or syllepses, or allusion or analogy, or meiosis, but in the short time we were there I could not penetrate to Eliot's secret, and therefore wasn't much wiser than Epsy.

Epsy could complain as much as he liked. Now that his best days lay in the ruins of his career, the one ghastly flaw I saw in him, and in people like him, was as advocate of a commercial worldview at its most reductive. I ask, was his bureaucratisation of all human activity, artistic or otherwise – was it not a mess of dead prescriptions and half-alive conformities? He'd press me for references justifying Eliot's text. Thereafter I'd find it an irrelevance having to thumb through non-standard tomes found round the walls of his study. Under a yellow lamplight, a figment of Epsy urged me to halt, an index finger poised over Walsingham's destruction of the Armada, in the banal hope of finding meaning. And so it turned out—

'So what is it with this Walsingham?' he asked. There was withering scepticism in that tone.

'Manoeuvrings,' I mused. 'If different in detail, aren't they the same in principle as those in Chads's court?'

'Why can't the play *show* that?'

'You'd have to ask the author, the premise being that for d'Oc what is at stake is what you'd call the soul of Europe.'

Epsy found that pretentious. 'Oh dear,' he said. He didn't show much thought for the slants on history Daphne's patron generously offered, but sided with her – or so he thought – when it came to the note on staging. Why would you have one? And was it an adequate guide through the superficial layers of

Chads's court, and beyond into the undergrowth of European history? That gradual costume change the text insisted on, amusing as it was as visual metaphor, he was sure would fail in its purpose. No audience he'd known would not wonder if the whole spectacle wasn't a science fantasy, whose underlying timepiece didn't run identically for each of its characters (a point that made me think of Bernauer).

All I could say was Dicto was a willing scribe.

'Naturally. He's no less acid in his opinion of *the people* than this earl of yours.' We were in an Eliot-Dicto duopoly.

I wondered if Daphne might dampen his outpourings, and regain control. Or instead continue to debate his points. She agreed that the tools the text made available were not sufficient to communicate something as nebulous as the remorseless tide of history – if that was Eliot's plan. For the sake of peace and progress, I also agreed. King Chads – not wholly the portrait of a man we knew, or knew of – was a lonely, heirless monarch in an England rife with republican talk, with a plummeting popularity since the divorce of his wife, a vapid Princess Moon. That much we can see. We read in Palmers the focus of lesser power, one rash enough to think of itself as a challenge to monarchy – Palmers a man street-wise and shop-soiled, and a recent beneficiary of Chads's patronage. I think I know that rashness for what it is, even when Chads, the butt of prodigious tabloid satire, is routinely depicted as the signatory of half-baked environmental schemes aimed at the long-term preservation of his planet.

Nor did Daphne see as authentic Chads's position *vis-à-vis* the people. It was an imperious act, when in order to win back some of the popularity ceded to his former wife, Chads had devised a rehabilitation scheme aimed at the nation's youth. His wife don't forget was a simple country girl turned fantasy princess, and beloved of the people. By Chads's grace and generosity anyone eligible for the scheme is issued with a guitar and chord book and encouraged to master them. For the successful, the reward is work in the entertainments biz. Palmers, *carpe diem*, has seized the opportunity, with a young Simon Star under his protection. Courtesy the King's largesse he is touring the pubs and clubs. With the three chords Star has learned he bumps along and scrapes a living (this the pecuniary state Star is led to believe).

So to Palmers, I.1, on his journey from Harlesden to the King's country estate. It's the start of the hunting season, and this is the remote rural setting where Palmers will present his protégé. The plot begins to scatter. One of its threads is the artistic rivalry between Star – or the Star Palmers has puffed up on the world stage – and Chads's official musician, now apparently jilted, if previously undisputed. Not so clear-cut are the latter's retaliatory instincts, which emerge and flourish once he feels threatened. Other than that he's a man who shares the play's general delusion, who by II.3 actually believes – as others do – that a sensitive, cultured English monarch can, in all honesty, prefer Star's rudiments of music over his own. He is after all responsible for masses and masques, whose madrigals, 'sung in a quincunx of trees...from the King's high windows...over the King's marble floors...have bewitched the world's ambassadors!' One suspects that Dicto knew that in Highgrove House the CD library featured the music of William Byrd.

Also *en route* from Harlesden is Madame Zemlinsky, who as

professional astrologer keeps to the same costume throughout – a dotted bandeau, hooped earrings, floral skirts. Whether rooted or in transit, her Tarot cards or crystal ball are near to hand. To Daphne, who took her part (and took it well), Madame Z was too transparently a fake, the last flaw that over my half a glass of water I was patient not to dispute. In one important sense Zemlinsky did live up to her claims, conceiving the world's past in a floating dream, a cloud or cumulus fringed with orange fire. It took effort or dexterity, engulfed in the murk of human destiny, in plotting a path through the world's perennial wars. War is a muddy conflict a certain kind of historian views as the abrasions of everyday life. Above this Zemlinsky knew that a man's bond was like a Japanese plum tree – a thing of Keatsian beauty, but fruitless nevertheless. With what ease she told her clients how fit the world was with its adman's rills and streams – yet all was sham in the glow of copper-coloured clouds. Presto! Ague in the end spites the flesh. A man doused in the daytime potions of money or love was as likely to wake in a staining of fire and ice, with dampness to his brow. His couch of rosy quilted dreams was a bed of lamentation, and *that* was the triumph of every working life. For a woman solo, astute and fending for herself, such practical wisdom was always her cachet.

In Palmers her calculations show no lack of insight. She'd got a better idea than his partner Star of their joint financial state. We're shown how – perhaps even before Harlesden – she'd discovered that the heavy coat he wore was lined with purses, and the purses were filled with euros. The world's fools and dreamers always flocked to a mercantile shrine. It was a matter of time before some sleight of hand was feasible, the means by which she'd relieve the travelling Palmers of all that heavy outer wear (much as Palmers had fleeced his songbird). All would eventually turn out well for Z. The runes she read were a pattern of universal destiny, for didn't she float above life's norms, having got at and understood its mechanisms – for so she summoned her genie.

There were other intrigues Zemlinsky found herself immersed in. As she had struck out on her own, there were, also out of Harlesden – carefully behind her – two black-blooded employees of the *Daily Screech*. Misfortune had seen them jettisoned from the perimeter scaffold on the edge of the King's estate, where they had gone to work each day. All fine until Chads's hapless young princess – then only trembling on the brink of divorce – had shed her midsummer negligee, and gone with her morning pineapple juice topless on the terrace. Immediately, adorning the *Screech*'s midweek centrefold, and a scoop, a raffish look on her photogenic face had with it a hint of musk from the bedchamber. Sensational! Especially so in light of those perfectly rounded breasts, their two pink erectile teats pleading the case of an heir (though only Chads had nestled his cheek and sucked).

Journalists Two and One – or Melissa and a man unnamed – had been mulling over, ever since Harlesden, possibilities apropos of Zemlinsky. Perhaps Zemlinsky didn't know. Once the divorce had been settled, Princess Moon had retired to the South of France with her entourage. That included the Astrologer Royal, one of those sphinx-like mystics whose fastidious gaze swept our desert of human affairs. Chads was a man whose sense of the ineffable embraced fortune in quite another guise, encompassing Jungian archetypes, nights breast-to-breast with the cosmos, days in search of a guru, and attunement to the vast chorus of life, from an encampment on the Serengeti.

Nor would Chads overlook the wisdom of world religions. That position had led him to value English society as the only true repository of human flourishing, broad in its ethnicity. You might therefore have expected that with his wife and her puerile entertainments gone, the post of Astrologer Royal was one he'd instantly dissolve. Whether by some bureaucratic oversight, or the simple fact that weighty sovereign matters preoccupied his mind, the post remained, and of course was now vacant.

Our two bastions of democracy urged Zemlinsky to apply for the post on moral grounds. The moral grounds were these – that the dismantling of their platform perched above the King's outer wall had annulled their rights to the kind of freedoms all truth-seeking persons of the press properly de-manded. What a dictator King Chads really was at heart. If that's the way he wanted it, well…. He'd been the butt of their jokes *before*. That was nothing to the plot they'd hatched since – a campaign fluffed up and assembled from information no monarch could imagine anyone acquiring. The plan hadn't worked out, for all it amounted to was further jeers at the King with his ecological escapades. Chads might well have the wherewithal to grow and rear organic produce, and connect it to a methane farm, but how could he expect us ordinary blokes to dig allotments after long hours at work, or rig up rain encatchments into our WCs, and did he seriously believe modern motors *could* be made to run on compressed air, or on cell systems independent of fossil fuels? Crazy guy, huh!

What was in it for Zemlinsky? Well, once she'd got herself into the royal household, any scrap of information she laid her hands on, they'd pay for.

Okay, she said – she'd think about it.

8

It proved almost impossible discouraging Epsy from a line-by-line critique of the text as we'd got it so far. It astonished him that the earl's I.1, set as it is in a pub interior, strategically close to King Chads's estate, with its blue-collar props – foaming quarts of beer, a dry-ice machine (to simulate a fug of tobacco smoke), and a bell (hurry up please it's time) – was anything an English aristocrat would know about. He mused openly that an organising intelligence other than my friend's must have been behind these scenes (literally behind these scenes). Ironically a King Chads as no more than a fantasised English monarch didn't trouble him at all, a persona sharing particular characteristics – as many are obvious, though some inscrutably are not – with Eliot's friend the Prince of Wales. Further, it was natural for Epsy, with his weight of bourgeois prejudice, to discount Chads as the drama's central character, ascribing that position to Palmers instead – about whom all introductory action might be said to revolve (a point I disputed). I told Daphne, addressing Epsy via that triangle – Chads-Palmers-Star – that in my opinion the play's foremost debating point was its incompetent musician, a fully formed representative of the debased culture mass entertainment has given us. From that simple premise multiple issues follow – powerful rumours ground in the mills of media cartels, the politics of states and superstates, the ambitions of individuals in a commerce-led society, the pros and cons of a constitutional monarch *vis-à-vis* the republic.

Republicanism was not a subject I had ever heard Earl d'Oc pronounce on, his monocle on or off, though he did once look at me obliquely when one of those sunny morning headlines blared a simple message to its millions – its one small deception the diffusion of floating quotation points – to the effect that Charles would never be King. That at least was according to the mother of his heirs. Palmers, phantasm born of an operatic pen, has good reason to thank the fictive Chads or the real Prince of Wales (whose trusts, projects and organisations are numerous), since Palmers the entrepreneur is a direct beneficiary, and has taken his share – and keeps on taking – from whatever royally blest coffers he can, all ostensibly to hoist his protégé Star high up on a pedestal, one marked socks and droogs and rock 'n' roll (a point at which the whole set-up goes over my head). It's an image intended to carry meaning, when Star is seen in a corner sitting sullenly on his amplifier, nursing his guitar, brooding but not Byronic (mooding and half moronic). Epsy thought it an insult, as a lumping of popular culture – all of it – with the worst of civilisation's outpourings.

I said I didn't think the earl had any quarrel with popular culture, nor did I see his indictment of it in I.1's saloon depiction, with its high ceiling, Victorian mouldings, its thickly raised wallpaper, surfaces a thin muddy colour, stained through the years of nicotine infusion. You'd argue his two tabloid journalists were nothing of that gene pool, seen as they are in quiet conversation together, cooking up stories on Chads's eccentric English ways, a king with principled views on art and architecture, a lust for blood sports, and in 'stark' contrast to that (a word over-used by reviewers and hack politicians) a penchant for organically grown farm produce.

My only concession to Epsy was in his emphasis on an ancient, and now calcified class system, acting as the prism of different kinds of culture in collision. Typifying that, Eliot grants his lonely paparazzi – a pair can never be a horde – an over-eagerness to meet the gifted Madame Zemlinsky, who can read palms, interpret the spread of Tarot cards, and divine kaleidoscopic intent in slops and floating tea leaves. Why is *she* here too – all the way from Harlesden, plying her trade? It's simple. Our two pillars of the press cannot penetrate the mystical aura that the universe and its monarchies are shrouded in. For that you need a mystic – outside of science, and outside the methodical arrangement of type on the page. This is an age-old axiom. For Epsy, the condemnation of all forms of populism is for d'Oc a moral imperative, where two scheming interlocutors, shifty with makeup and shadowy under lighting, nevertheless unveil themselves as fundamentally decent, upright citizens, but led astray. It seemed for Epsy I needed to reiterate: their interest in Madame Z is for her practical as opposed to cosmic insights, especially into the commercially minded Palmers (whose full dramatic epithet is Palmers Ltd). It can't be symbolic of anything other than gain or greed that Palmers is dressed in a coat reaching to his ankles, mostly. It conceals an obese being, bibulous and stereotypical of the business world. Epsy wanted that as a slight on his working origins. In reality, as a garment lined with purses, and the money Palmers has earned exploiting Star, it's a device, architecturally the first foundation stone in an intricate plot that opens with Zemlinsky in need of two strong men to help relieve the fat man of his cash.

There were just the five readers for that opening scene – Epsy, Grange, Martin Held, Daphne herself, and her one other female, Fiona Ibert. Parts they had to read added up to more than that quintet: Revellers (four of them), the Landlord, Palmers, Madame Zemlinsky, Star, and Journalists One and Two. Daphne cajoled. The other four aided and abetted. So – reluctant, diffident, uncomfortable with any public spectacle involving me – I was recruited into the read-through with a handful of simpler lines.

'You have such a perfect, gravelly tone.'

'Thank you, Fiona. Nevertheless, it's not theatrically trained.'

'You'll manage, I'm sure.'

9

Our meeting broke up, with Epsy, Held and Grange departing together, and Fiona Ibert – outstanding as a cartoonish, giggly Melissa – following shortly. All had doubled where necessary, while I, Humfrey (a partner at DCT), had my brief sunlit outing maundering through Star's light sprinkling of lines. All I required was an occasional, monosyllabic grunt.

I reported back to d'Oc, telling him how well the reading went, making no mention of Epsy, whose fastidious gaze into the play's entrails might have made for difficult conversation. D'Oc carried on, blissfully unperturbed – when anyway I was just the messenger.

On then to our next exchange, and the short life of that long padded envelope, its transit him to me, me to Daphne, this time with a note for her with a note for Dicto. Dicto it seemed had to be reminded of the importance of Eliot's pen – red and editorial – and that was no different now in the markings he'd made to Acts Two and Three. I don't know how you detect a withering look over the phone, but am told that was how you'd sum up Dicto's appearance when Daphne called him next. He exploded with expletives. The one question in Dicto's mind that really needed an answer was: are we to suppose Chads of this *New King Palmers* is a resurrected Edward VIII fused with a putative Charles III? Daphne asked what I thought. I responded evasively, but must have smiled knowingly (it must have been a crumpled smile). She tried another tack, but that didn't work. She invited me out, asking was I free next Wednesday. I thought I probably was.

When, finally, I delivered the revised Acts Two and Three, I saw to what extent Eliot was drawn, pale and gaunt, and how for the first time a darkish, purple malaise discoloured his eye sockets. I glanced, and it was only half past nine, and already he was climbing the stairs for bed. This was a bad moment, Humf. Could I call tomorrow afternoon instead?

'No,' I said. 'Fridays I'm booked with Louise for hand relief,' after which I always drove home with the radio tuned, then – a big blubbery satisfied walrus – sank in a tub of warm suds, with a sherry at my elbow. I left the script on his rolltop, and told him I would call in on my way to work in the morning. I got there at eight, and now saw something new – an effort, and a weariness – in the way he wound his scarf, as he stood, or rather stooped, under the sunny burnish of his fanlight. I knew how tenaciously he and his counterparts cocooned themselves in the cold shadows of a lodge whose whereabouts was secret, grappling with issues I easily guessed at, often through the night, and so on till the leaden strips of morning showed through the windows. I compared that with the tedium of *my* working day, hardly a parallel, but to me no less a burden, with its sackfuls of frozen nuggets, a load I hauled Sisyphus-like up a paper mountain. My fretful, ambitious partnership, citizens circumscribed by the barbs of our lower circle, smartly dressed professionals careering up and down in lifts, or striding the twilit corridors of DCT. All still nursed this fear that on the stroke of the millennium – its chronometers gone haywire – civilisation was doomed, its IT a compass needle shattered on a broken lodestone. That anticipated crash exacerbated what worries were already felt at the vulnerability of our management structure, when a new, cleverer generation of computer technicians, well primed by the manifestos of guerrilla warfare, stalked the jungles of electro-commerce, and any day now were set to seize the initiative. It meant more of those bleak Saturday mornings over endless coffee slops, trying to forge a strategy for combat.

I left work early on Wednesday, and met Daphne in the tiled concourse of the overground stop opposite the small theatre – a fifty-seater with bar and lounge facilities – where the pantomime she'd devised – *Jack and the Hee-Haw Tree* – had reached its last night but one. A coup of sorts, she'd booked for the title role a minor celebrity from afternoon TV. Naturally, I suspected a motive.

We took our seats at the back. The plot rested on a simple premise, that Jack – much like the boy that I had been – found it impossible to raise himself from the bend of his mattress any time before midday. This was greatly to his ma's chagrin, who now thought of evicting her son just as she had her husband –

a foul-mouthed swain she'd married by mistake. Jack can save himself, in one last commission to the pawn shop, where her only trinket, a ring of soft metal inscribed with looping initials, and set with an onyx, ought to fetch enough to keep the rent book closed, for the next thirty days at least. He gets a decent price, but like his father can't resist the dazzle of the arena. Fatally, he stops at the Ass's Bray and slakes his thirst. The sun is hot. He sits at a bench outside, in the shade of a hee-haw tree. The barmaid brings the ploughman's lunch he's ordered. This he demolishes, leaving only a ring of sun-bright cucumber and a string of tomato pips. He rolls and smokes a herbal cigarette, at which point all dissolves in dream – though here clever staging leaves it unclear as to what his dream is. Is it his mother and older sister berating him for wasting away the rent money, or is it a rope ladder unwinding from the hee-haw tree?

It's the ladder. Jack ascends, and is pursued by the barmaid, not much concerned that a good-looking boy has left his jacket and tobacco tin, but thankful for the pretext. Result: those last two daintily booted feet disappear above the fringe of light dusting the proscenium, cue for a first hint of thunderous footsteps, followed by the curtain coming down. In the rush for the bar I, as usual, Humf, was left behind. I studied the programme, still unable to recognise that famous TV name.

Curtain up, Act Two. We know this is giant country – its access ladder makes it also *upper* country – because thanks to a local joiner there is, stage left, an enormous throne. It remains unoccupied (even to the final curtain), but its presence has menace and meaning. A tiny mouse, painted on a painted dresser, is overwhelmed in the pinprick of its dimensions, a mite made minuscule by the hypertrophied mugs, plates, jugs and saucers it permanently grooms its whiskers among. In due course the sound system joins in too, reinforcing all these overstretched statistics with a shudder of nuclear footsteps, and a *Fe, fi, fo* in thunderous basso. Undeterred, Jack and his new companion explore this strange new universe they're in, and now understand the spirit of conquest. They start to gather trophies. From the props department come rubies the size of fruit, pearl earrings suited to the golfing green, banknotes bigger than portraits, and many things they can't collect – platters for coins, coins for studs, a hat you might camp out in. As you expect, this is an enterprise filled with peril, whose climaxes include a monumental boot, connected to a shin in a tartan sock, all neatly stitched to a voluminous trouser leg, the whole thing lowered on ropes and pulleys from a dark upper atmosphere crossed by lights and catwalks, and accompanied by thunderclaps.

Best bauble of all is a golden harp (or perhaps lyre for the giant's knee), angel-winged and animated, its vertical pillar none other than Fiona Ibert, daubed in gold-plate grease paint, and not a player I identified until I heard her voice (Melissa of the *Daily Screech*). The giant's pluck, slave to the dictates of all narrow aesthetics everywhere, has grated and fatigued his one and only instrument for too many years, with his dreary sentimental songs, too reminiscent of stormy landscapes, and rooted in a national life stunted by political misfortune. Pal Fiona confides in Daphne's urban Jack how ripe she is for a change of scene, and promises to do all she can to help when he and the barmaid plan to escape, laden with the best of the giant's treasures. But that's under threat of one other danger they need to be aware of. This upper country is a maze of earthy craters that scar and pockmark the valleys and fields and meadows beyond the giant's castle. Since no tradition ever renews itself without some mad departure, we learn that the giant's ancestors were an even more prolific race, prone to fall through the world's crust, and find themselves no match for the flesh-eating dinosaurs below. Doubtless that rope ladder hangs from the site of one such mishap.

Whole generations of cloudy-haired giants grappled with the problem unsuccessfully. Even the development of an advanced construction industry never overcame this persistent threat to civic life. Some things like this go on for thousands of years, until someone dabbling with alternatives finds a solution. A straw-sucking bucolic advised a carefully balanced diet, which by extension led to the search for the perfect slimmer's pill, an age-old quest that unearthed the naturally occurring hee-haw nut, which when harvested and crushed to a tonic gave up all its secrets as the best non-toxic curb on the appetite pharmaceuticals could devise.

Therein lay the key to Jack's fortune. When I later summed up our evening I described it as 'quaint' and 'bizarre'.

'All pantomime *is*,' was how Daphne replied. She was wearing a grey cashmere overcoat and a maroon neckpiece laced with silver fabric, tall, calf-coloured boots, soft gloves – and carried a leather bag. I'd hoped she was going to suggest a bistro or restaurant she knew, but she kept me on the street, talking, intent on what had to be said, and *only* that. Her news wasn't surprising. Epsy was difficult to manage. Dicto was bluff, a phlegmatic Yorkshireman, unsubtle, direct, even rude on the phone. The d'Oc project had given her sleepless nights. Her other work suffered. She had made no progress with

Channel 4. These and other exhalations – a cold agitation into the night air – fell short of a resignation speech, but I knew I'd been warned. I was flattered, I said, that she'd mentioned it at all, and to me, but now I was losing her and didn't know how to prevent it. I tried to show something other than superficial interest in her *MMU*, implying there might be useful material in that large family history overseen by d'Oc – the one I'd asked Gillian to send to the printers. Briefly she was interested, but the conversation ended when I made her no definite offer. How could I, given the wrath I knew it would stir Eliot to? Vagueness cost me, even when I motioned cryptically to a Michelin-starred steakhouse a few doors down the street. She took no notice and said goodbye.

10

Yet back at the office I did consider calling up that document onto my screen, and got as far as printing an extract on sheets of inkjet paper, if only a few flimsy pages. I read through several times, and almost picked up the phone, then with a diagonal streak of yellow marker pen I erased that whole proposition from my agenda, before folding it carefully and dropping it in the bin. I drummed the desktop with my finger-tips, then, because Gillian was out, I had to make my own coffee.

11

It ran its course and closed, *Jack and the Hee-Haw Tree*. There were plaudits. And a write-up in the local press. Then Grange, I heard, had received a better offer, and would play no further part in *New King Palmers*. Its second act Daphne had entered for a festival, now in its fourth year. Its planning committee she told me she was part of, though mostly it worked as a quorum of three, from a backroom with a laptop and landline. The theatre d'Oc was asked to hire was small, intimate, recently refurbished, and a winding walk up a solid wooden stairway. It was tucked away above a Sichuan restaurant. The small grouping forming the audience was other actors, writers, directors, well-chosen members of the press, and a mature woman with lots of forms and tick boxes, who worked for the Arts Council.

I admit to that tingle – that pre-performance chemistry, in a charged atmosphere, and the melting inner warmth of antici-pation – that broken magic spell when Daphne appeared on stage, garbed up as Zemlinsky, who before the performance got started – before she plunged into role – announced several important provisos. She explained, under a greenish-looking light, that this was a work in progress, and what 'progress' she wanted to show centred on Act Two – an ocean she didn't launch into without a summary of Act One. I think I might have judged from the jab of lead into the reviewer's notepad behind me how hazardous this, as a strategy, was, and could hear with what ferocity that broken pencil point was hastily re-sharpened.

Anyway, the performance began, with an irritable King Chads pacing about with his household accounts, impatient for his hunting boots. Chads has the bluest of blood, and to the blue collars in the audience was a man borne on ancestral wings, artificially. His triumph is his family crest, a symbol that had fluttered over the world's outraged battlefields. I am not surprised that for Chads the outdoor life had never lost its attraction. For now though the call of field and forest would have to wait. In came one of his advisers – his Chancellor – stepping onto that little lit stage of world affairs, flourishing his copy of the King's accounts. High office his might be, yet that too was anchored in the lower denominations of Eliot's circles. The present incumbent is douched in superficial airs, a slave to the structured sophistication of his profession. He had that contagion worldly ambition mires the human psyche in (I think of my partners at DoCoTel). He is ceaselessly gnawed at via his internal organs, ill with anxiety over his wealth and personal status. The world asks, does he do his job right? If not, the loss of it, or demotion through the euphemism of a cabinet reshuffle, is a serious blow to prestige. The man harbours great fears in the spreadsheet he is brandishing on stage (or ought we to call it a vellum?), troubled at how the King's lifestyle appears to the commoner, or *will* appear in the *Screech*, with its jokes and jibes at royal excess. Unswervingly, that's the course it's on.

To Chads this is all idiotic, when the greater part of his expenditure serves the office, not the man (i.e. the Crown and not the King). The problem is this: much of that largesse in recent months has gone on entertaining delegations from the EC, a sore point for the Chancellor, a man not known for his sympathy for the European project. One might speculate as to the tenor of conversation between the English monarch and this bourgeois *gentilhomme*. Does he plump for safe, overarching things, such as how the UK can lead the world in religious tolerance? Or what is the value of research into nanotechnology? Or has marriage as an institution finally collapsed? Chads was characterised as not afraid to cast himself forward into the decades, and so had just the right optics when his fawning interlocutors conceived of a new Europe in terms of how it proclaimed itself architecturally. Other topics he would certainly avoid. For example the CAP, and fishing – even despite his commitment to good environmental management and the virtues of natural farming. Nor would he touch on the current plight in the Republic of Letters, a precious jewel the Muses had given us, its lustre irremediably dulled now that it had fallen into the hands of professional academics and other intolerant people.

In due course we learn that the Foreign Secretary, Sir Nigel, has been sent on a delicate mission to Gaul, ostensibly to woo our old-fangled enemy. More importantly it's a first step towards the UK exerting its influence on the running of the new superstate, that amorphous entity increasingly a looming probability. This detour did not surprise me at all, even when, in a life under Eliot's aegis, I had never discussed with him, except in gnomic terms, contemporary politics. We sometimes talked about his friend Diana. In light of the latter I'm surprised at Princess Moon (divorced), the cost of whose wardrobe the Chancellor bemoans, as he does also her current relationship with the tabloids. These worthy institutions have made her, almost on the instant of the marriage's dissolution, a fairy heroine, while Chads is an evil spectre of medieval myth. All *is* sometimes black and white. It meant that for the King and his roving household the problem was this: what could be done to restore the monarch's popularity? The answer lay with the estranged Princess herself, who'd got the common touch. Chads should now seize the initiative, taking his lesson from her, with his grants, guitars and chord books. These we see issued *en bloc* to applicants just like Simon Star (or in his case Palmers, his agent). Though in fact the scheme isn't the King's at all – it's the Chancellor's. To the King it represents just another laborious duty – as yes, he did have to hear Star play, if playing you could call it.

The Chancellor also tells us he has just appointed a new Astrologer Royal, one of those household posts that Chads assumed had disappeared with the divorce of his wife. He is urged to look in on the minstrels' gallery, and sees for himself. There is indeed an astrologer, for there is Daphne, or rather Zemlinsky, easing her way into courtly life. Palmers is also there, showing off his prodigy Star, which not surprisingly is galling to the King's official musician, who as a man trained to meet the needs of Chads's sybaritic ear, is at a loss to understand the success his new rival is having. For dramatic purposes there has to be more to it than this – something beyond the aesthete-versus-populist dilemma. So now there's a hint that Palmers has some function other than Star's acting agent. This however is an episode drowned in the hullabaloo caused by the King's Vassal's failure to fetch King Chads's hunting boots, and is just the diversion Madame Z needs to steal the Chancellor's copy of Chads's household accounts, which carelessly he has left poking out of a pocket.

When Zemlinsky next meets up with the two journalists, they explain, proudly, what perversions of social behaviour have seen them barred from the King's estate and its environs. To compound what low opinion we've got of them by now, they try to acquire the document Madame Z has got for sale, without meeting her fee. Luckily Madame Z belongs to the same school of commerce as they do, and won't be duped. They haggle. This can hardly go unnoticed by the chance passer-by, and that, fortuitously, is Palmers.

This takes us to the fifth of Act Two's eight scenes, where the lights, dimmed on the empty street that Madame Z and her two tabloid hacks have just vacated, now flame up over Chads's cabinet room. The King has fallen off his horse, and hobbles in, tottering onto stage – in and out through the mental pools of light – all with the aid of a stick. As the King goes out, the Chancellor comes in. Then at last Sir Nigel appears, hot foot from Gaul, under a brassy blast of trumpets. Sir Nigel has failed to forge that closer alliance with our EU counterparts, and not only that – he has driven himself wedge-like between its two most powerful groupings, the Teutons and the Gauls. Now there is one of many comic-strip caesuras. This round, pompous Englishman, his brief the stewardship of UK international affairs, sounds off schoolboyish against all things continental. His worst, most magnified fear of the coming republic is the abrupt backing it has won from the banished Princess Moon. She many would like to see as its figurehead.

Enter Lady Michael, Secretary of State for Defence, reading from this morning's tabloid leader – a catalogue of Chads's household accounts. It's a crisis, and Defence thinks the only answer is war. The English must march on Gaul. On the face of it the Chancellor's approach is measured in comparison, but that is just a patina, and eventually he shares the same conclusion. He summons the King's jester – one of those all-wise Shakespearean Fools – who is instructed to bring Palmers into the cabinet room, a first concrete admission that the wandering entrepreneur is also a spy. Palmers is primed with a diplomatic commission, whereupon, swollen with pride, he reports that Madame Zemlinsky has almost certainly betrayed the

King's trust and generosity by leaking sensitive information to the press, resulting in this morning's headlines. That sets the Chancellor thinking, who nevertheless is not deflected from present concerns and Palmers's assignment. So, what is it? Well, what Palmers has to do is enlist the help of the UK's foremost metric martyr. A secret document to him will signal tacit government support for his cause, so giving him the strength to spread his views. That will have a decisive effect on public opinion.

Another slight pause in the pace of events sees the King's Musician more than ever miffed that Star, with his rudimentary grasp of music, is, incomprehensibly, that much more favoured than he. Fuelled by rumours of impending war, he seems the right man for Madame Zemlinsky's long-held plan – not only to relieve Palmers of his money bags, but under cover of the coming conflict to dispose of him altogether. From there we return to the cabinet room, where high-level talk is of Mack the Metric Martyr, and the plan the Chancellor has to deploy his band in the dispute with France. This is all summarised in the document Palmers has been charged to deliver, which offers specific detail as to how Mack and his men can arm themselves from army dumps and ammunition caches. Having thus equipped themselves, what more do they need in taking their fight to the mainland, to the heart of Europe? A brilliant strategy perhaps, except that Palmers disobeys instructions, and in unsealing the document immediately sees scope for himself as an arms dealer – as we know, a lucrative line of business – and seemingly the answer to his dreams and ambitions.

That's not the only scheme that Sir Ossie, the Chancellor –

hapless in his wizardry, at least when it comes to statecraft – has devised at short notice. With Palmers preparing for his mission, Ossie sets about deceiving Zemlinsky into reading a forged memo from the King, which with its royal crest and the beautifully duplicated flourish of Chads's signature, expresses the monarch's concern at the mounting powers of Strasbourg and Brussels – just the kind of gossip those of the cabinet's inner circle are happy to see batted about in the tabloids. Zemlinsky duly obliges and is duped into reading the memo. What information she passes on to her friends of the press, however, isn't gestated in a way the Chancellor envisaged – for such is that ceaseless organ of public conscience.

End of Act Two.

12

First sign of the misapprehensions the Nissel-Eliot axis was to saddle me with came in the foyer outside that little theatre, once Daphne and her cast had done their work. I stood for some time thumbing through the leaflets racked up a wall and spread across a tabletop. Others in that makeshift audience followed me out, drifting from the arena's two swing doors, and gathered into groups, in a buzz at what they'd witnessed. Soon a bluish haze of tobacco smoke crowned their exchanges, in a bewilderment of wonder at its paste-up, and what its costumes meant. Epsy was among them, having changed quickly, but partly still a stage phantasm, having not had time to remove his makeup. I recognised his voice, a glitter of self-accord as it rose above the hum enveloping all – to tell us what demands, and what physicality, given the script's rambling incoherence. A rotund, bustling little woman, with freckles, a fixed smile and doubloons for spectacles asked me if I'd like to be a friend of the theatre, and with one of those leaflets pointed out its subscription rates.

'I'll give that some thought,' I said.

Daphne, now in jodhpurs, a tee shirt and cardigan, with her ringlets of hair bunched at the crown of her head – all so eloquent – emerged from the dressing room. She smiled a great deal and starrily, finding herself engulfed.

'*Great* performance, Laurie.' There were fewer kind words for the play.

She drew me into her circle, where a hawkish, middle-aged, yet youthful-looking man made brave conciliatory attempts, offering his hand for a handshake, and beginning like this: 'Mr d'Oc, may I just say….'

'Ah,' I said, 'there I must correct you. Joel. The name is Humfrey Joel. Very pleased to meet. Regrettably the author – Leo Dicto actually – couldn't be with us tonight.'

A nervous pause exploded under the relief of collective laughter. A man with a ponytail and a pattern of pied checks woven into his shirt – a spectre piping minors out of Ham – slipped away quietly into the Sichuan restaurant. He returned with a small bottle of American beer, which he drank from the neck, just as I'd explained why Eliot also couldn't be here (emergency meetings with the Privy Council).

'What *is* the Privy Council?' Daphne asked.

I didn't really know, I said, which betrayed lifelong acceptance of Eliot's Masonic nature, though I thought that ought to make him appealing to theatregoers everywhere. Of course Epsy knew everything, and butted in—

'It's the sovereign's private chamber,' he said. He spooned us the history lesson he'd obviously given himself, from sources other than standard encyclopaedias. 'A sort of court or *curia regis*, with roots traced to the reign of William the Conqueror – where three or four choice individuals, persons immensely rich and powerful, exercised the *real* political force in the running of our country. Wonder what that tells us.'

'So what's the emergency?' Daphne asked.

I explained that by breeding and education the earl had escaped the usual vanities of career advancement, and for him all was duty. For constitutional reasons, the powerful upper echelons d'Oc inhabited were faced with difficult times. Just how difficult, for Eliot, I couldn't have guessed, and anyway for personal reasons did not wish to. I was evasive, and allowed the conversation its natural descent into green-room inconsequentialities. Then, almost nonchalantly, I strolled out onto a spangled pavement, in a biting February wind, where under a turmoil of dunnish-coloured clouds I escorted Daphne to her car.

A few days later she sent me the following review, printed in one of her stage monthlies—

Mr Humphrey Jale, a newcomer to the English stage, chooses this of all moments, and one of our most innocent theatres, to demonstrate an arcane political point, all with the aid of anachronism and knockabout. His *New King Palmers*, while it does have entertaining moments, is built up remorselessly from a pen of stock characters. The 'plot' is more the performance of ritual tasks against a larding of historical dates and locations. The challenge to understand what the play is about wasn't helped, in its first festival appearance, by the decision to stage only its second act. Whatever dramatic impact the evening might have promised was undermined by the piece's preamble, from Daphne Hao – director and performer – who stood alone on stage to summarise the *preceding* act. In retrospect this now seems like an apology for what was to come.

Don't misread me. I *can* be persuaded that all is not as confused in Mr Jale's pen as it is in mine. There is probably merit in what it attempts to convey, and good reason to have at the play's engine a modestly gifted rock musician, an entrepreneur, circus performers, a thinly disguised Prince Charles as King, a trio of front-bench Tory politicians – all in an brew of vanity, personal interest, appetence. The structure called on to bear this weight is an unlikely combination of *commedia dell'arte*, the kitchen sink, and the Elizabethan stage.

One imagines the whole concoction was conceived over coffee and cognac as an after-dinner joke. I for one, though I do see potential in that, was not invited to that table. That is probably why the result is shapeless, and doesn't conform to any paradigm known to me (or to any reviewer). All the more puzzling is that Daphne Hao, whose *Number Seven Bus* ran to great acclaim at the Velocipede, should ever have got involved in it. *She* has a career before her. I hope I can say the same for Mr Jale.

—Malcolm Blerby

I phoned Mr Blerby at his office and after several tries finally got the man himself, whose squeaky voice, trembling *en abîme*, retreated into all kinds of unlikely defences once I had pointed out I am better known as Humfrey Joel. I cut short his bluster in telling him that this was immaterial anyway, since he had wrongly attributed to me a play whose ownership and copyright belonged jointly to playwright Leo Dicto – a recluse – and Earl Eliot d'Oc. Blerby, a man not normally given to *any* kind of mix-up, grovelled profusely, explaining that in overhearing my conversation in the foyer after the performance, he had wrongly connected me to information someone had previously given him. He promised to print an addendum and full apology in the next issue of his journal, a publication altogether filled with spite and pugnacity, no copy of which did I ever pass on to Eliot.

In any case he was now exhausted, having shuddered against the splutters of an archaic central-heating system, in a highceilinged room, where wave after wave of privy midnight meetings had taken place. He told me he'd decided to lighten his load and recuperate at Hoe, and had already packed for the journey. Daphne showed interest when I told her about the theatre there – a facility *not*, I stressed, for the staging of plays, but for the training of public orators. She insisted she'd no time to drive down there and take a look, since that Velocipede success Blerby had mentioned she was hoping to add to soon and capitalise on. She'd made strides with her Madame Zeer, clairvoyant, mystic, medium. Zeer's was a no-nonsense appeal to the democratising process our ultimate human condition – death – was certain to bring, and made no distinction between our Neros or Napoleons and the run of plain Jim or Johnny Smiths, whose eviscerate presences had all crowded her crystal at one time or another. As a sort of limbering up, I was treated to a Zeer sitting solo, rehearsing with the dead. This was my very own preview of Daphne's unique contribution to the genre of one-woman show. At a lace-covered table, in a back-room, in a terraced house in Islington, her *MMU* took place. M1 bowls up and inhabits the being of Madame Z, and intones biographically through Zeer the contorted medium. She is a fragile lily, a Mitford, imbuing her sighs with the fading cadences of premature death, yet at times is muscular enough to curse the day she got entangled in the jackbooted politics of 1930s Europe. M2 followed, and was – well, was what? Daphne pursed her lips and drew her cheeks half a dozen times in rapid succession, and asked me to guess – but I couldn't.

'I'll just have to come along and see the show.'

13

Her M2 turned out to be a second-wave feminist whose name I didn't know, who'd died of ovarian cancer. She was more helpful with her U – for Una – who in prototype was the wife of a cabinet minister, a mew not in fact deceased, but who, in the living death the last half-dozen years had brought, had attuned herself to Madame Zeer's receptors. Una Mew had hankerings after the celebrity pages of the glossy women's trash she read, just the thing for sharing secrets she'd acquired in the role of hostess, offering useful insights into the planning of garden parties, aimed, of course, at a distinguished guest list. Slight obstacle to this, and one she'd never overcome, was her partner's impossible ambition, a man who urged her to learn a language (French or German), or enrol for a master's degree in history or economics. He had close cultural links to the EU's Museum of Europe. That, in *his* mind, marked him out as an enlightened European. He rattled on ceaselessly about the great unification project, begun as long ago as the eighth century (according to him), with Charlemagne.

I asked Daphne how she thought she would cope with the enormous physical stamina the performance demanded (all that vibrant air round her, with the waifs of the world's undead tugging at her soul). I also told her that d'Oc, whose threads through European history had left their mark, was looking more than ever pale and ill, and was now at Hoe, where he wanted to rest, and watch from his window as spring unbound its petals. I said what a fine little theatre it was he'd had built there, and again told her – if she had an opportunity – that she should take a look.

Don't think I have yet reached that point of wanting to declare, to put my dummy bridge hand, in all its royal colours, face-up on the table. I did not admit that the name finally chosen for Eliot's theatre – his Thespian Hoe – was arrived at by my mother and me, almost thirty-five years ago. This was not something Daphne needed to know, and anyway, on the afternoon I showed her round, her thoughts were elsewhere. I remember her gazing up into the timber frames forming the roof structure, and wondering aloud at the possibility of bringing her *MMU* to Bath, Bristol, Exeter, and using Hoe for rehearsals. As it turned out, it wasn't her *MMU*, it was *New King Palmers* that had its first full reading here, when only days before she had been on the brink of resigning from the project. That was late spring, at a time when d'Oc couldn't get himself downstairs, and was napping in his bedside chair at two in the afternoon. This we will come to. For now the doctor in Hoe visited two to three times per week. There was other support too (I recall a Macmillan nurse), sent in for longer and longer periods as time went by. Everyone knew that d'Oc was dying.

14

I had hope in Daphne's lone treks back and forth along the M5, and her foray across that western frontier, and watched as she entered theatre professionals – from all over the region – into her address book. The line she drew – in shape a lush, profusely rained-on triangle – connected Bristol, Plymouth and Weston-super-Mare, a geometry inscribed for the hosting of *MMU*. In mid-July I asked her couldn't she do the same for *New King Palmers*. In the toss of her head, in the wrinkle of her nose, in the way she screwed her eyes, I could see the answer was no. A pity, as Bristol was vibrant. Its culture she liked. However, the d'Oc-Nissel-Dicto thing was too big a commitment, and anything that took her out of London for more than a few days was a brake on her career. The solution – develop the play in London….

Well, that wasn't clear cut either, with Epsy impossible to work with, and a man determined to overturn and finally run any semi-pro production he had got involved in.

'Get rid of him,' I said.

'Not that simple. You won't find a better Palmers. Epsy's too good.'

Then finally all these plans were cast in doubt when, on August 31st, Princess Diana, the world's most photographed woman, was killed. Her fateful hour was early Sunday morning, after a high-speed collision in Paris's Pont de l'Alma road tunnel. Other casualties were her lover, Dodi Fayed, and Henri Paul, their chauffeur and security man, whose job was to drive the couple from where they'd stayed at the Ritz. The princess was thirty-six. Worldwide, millions mourned her loss. Official investigations arrived at accidental death, caused by the chauffeur, drunk at the wheel (the said Henri Paul), and a chasing pack of paparazzi. Eliot, when he heard the news, was braced for the eruption of every conceivable conspiracy theory, which did soon follow. One of the most popular held that the princess had been got rid of, with the assassination carried out by the 'Increment', an SAS/SBS military attachment to MI6. But, then, according to d'Oc, the whole story never would be told.

He rose from his sickbed, and on the bright September morning set aside for his friend's farewell exercised his one remaining duty. To the tolling of a tenor bell, a gun carriage drawn by six black horses bore the princess from Kensington Palace, followed by her sons, William and Harry, by Prince Charles and the Duke of Edinburgh, and by the princess's brother, Earl Spencer. She was flanked by a dozen guardsmen in red tunics and black bearskins, marching, arms straight to their sides, while somewhere to the rear, and out of camera-shot, was Earl Eliot d'Oc, whose declining health drove him to *his* death shortly after the service at Westminster Abbey.

There was one package left on his rolltop in London, addressed not to Dicto c/o Daphne, but to Hao herself, with a covering note. His final instructions were twofold. First, his pen strokes were easy to follow, and having made them the play was finished. Second, he'd had conversations with Lucinda Munney, and here was her number. She was expecting my call. I emptied the envelope. Its manuscript I handed to an efficient young woman I hired from a temping agency, and for a whole day kept her confined to my office. I told her to retype, incorporating Eliot's final amendments. With that job done I got her to print off the result. Then, the electronic form of Eliot's final cut I copied to CD, and erased from the DCT disc system. To the new printout, a pile of A4 folios, I added my own amendments, which were heavy, brutal, decisive. I got my temp to retype a second time. Only then did I pass the 'completed' *New King Palmers* to Daphne, telling her that according to Eliot's last recorded utterance this was now the definitive version, but of course it was no such thing – it was my expurgation. His paper version I shredded.

15

I heard that Stewart Grange was going down a storm as Thénardier in a production of *Les Misérables*, in a theatre almost as far east as Ilford, a venue near enough to a Lebanese restaurant that it promised a nice evening. I drove Daphne there myself, having pre-booked the best seats and reserved a table for two. Over dinner I tried to persuade her – more insistently than at Hoe – to tour with *New King Palmers*, out of London, into the provinces. Again that stubborn resistance, and the clincher (or so she thought), for with d'Oc now dead she was under no obligation. I said per contra it was always Eliot's plan to bring his play to public consciousness unobtrusively, by subtle means, its impact timed on a slow burn, from a fuse no one would have noticed I had lit. She couldn't know the play's importance to him, or that it bore my bowdlerising marks, so now I strung her along. The complete work, as formularised according to d'Oc's amendments, seeded within it a message from the British Privy Council to the political generals at the EU, and she knew how busy he'd been in his *curia regis.* She said that sounded preposterous – and anyway, she was busy with *MMU*. I told her to drop it, to abandon *MMU*, a filler piece she could always revive at a later date, a delay that allowed for a new infusion of ghosts, a tactic certain to prolong the project and at the same time ensure extended public interest.

'Now why would I do that, Humf?'

'Because, Daphne, I've got a better plan.' I offered her a deal. She was to drop *MMU*, and in its place assemble a troupe away from London. She'd said herself how vibrant Bristol was. As well there were Bath, Exeter, Plymouth. I'd open up Thespian Hoe, and there, with everything to hand for the shaping and rehearsal of Eliot's play, I urged her to prepare its three acts – the complete thing – for a first set of tour dates. In return I'd got something I'd let her have – a secret history – a slim chapter from the files of the ancient Maison d'Oc. She'd find it pertinent to the Diana case, that event now clouded in conspiracy. It was something she could use for her Channel 4 proposal. She stirred her coffee. Her thinly plucked eyebrows – one of them – the left – twitched very slightly. With careful, almost stage deliberation, something Madame Z was known for, she laid a filigreed coffee spoon into the wild flowers and thorny pattern of her saucer.

'Mail it to me.'

'I can't. Too dangerous. You'll have to call at the office, preferably after hours.'

I wasn't sure she would come, but she did – days after I had given up hope – on a wet, blustery evening, the time five-thirty to six, when Gillian was putting on her coat for the bus, train or Underground. I met her in the foyer downstairs, where the receptionist had shown her to a small leather settee and a pile of magazines, and was herself ready to go. She, Daphne, was wearing maroon denims, a synthetic fur coat, its hemline just above the knee, and ankle boots. I told her some of my partners were out, but there were others who hadn't left, stuck with paperwork or gassing on the phone. I preferred it if we strolled round the corner to a small Indian restaurant, where I knew the management, and it was possible to sit with just a cup of tea. She looked at the menu, with its seafood curries – prawn, crab, pan-fried monkfish – with such curiosity I said we'd eat here later if she wanted. When we got back the office was locked and in darkness, but I carried a key to the back stairs, whose glass door was via a labyrinth of covered alleys (alleys that also served the kitchen entrance to the restaurant). We flew up steps at a time. When she had marvelled at the size and idle comfort of my office I sat her down at my screen and showed her, in its word-processed format, those same pages I had put a line through with my marker pen and on second thoughts had binned. She asked me for a printout.

'No,' I said. 'Read first. If we've got a deal, only then will I print.'

I stood at her shoulder while she read and made up her mind, a short piece about the heir to the Austro-Hungarian throne, Rudolf, Archduke and Crown Prince of Austria, who as the only son of the Emperor Franz Joseph has his official history written and purveyed along following lines—

Extensive education. Travelled widely. Politically, astutely aware of the problems of integrating a ragbag of nationalities into the Habsburg monarchy. Not enamoured of Russian imperialism. Was himself a hotchpotch of liberal and anti-clerical ideas. Alienation from his father, Franz Joseph, was inevitable. Franz Joseph excluded him from government business. His marriage was arranged, to the daughter of Leopold II, King of the Belgians. Young Rudolf fell under the influence of journalist Moritz Szeps, and his radical paper the *Neues Wiener Tagblatt*. Rudolf contributed articles, anonymously. He published two books, and organised a survey of Austria-Hungary, *Österreich-Ungarn in Wort und Bild* (*Austria-Hungary in Word and Picture*). He thought to crown himself King of Hungary. His schemes failed. Frustrated, unhappy in his marriage, he began an affair with Baroness Maria Vetsera, a girl of seventeen. Soon they entered into a suicide pact. One morning in January 1889 they were found dead in the hunting lodge at Mayerling. Clumsy attempts to gloss over events provoked rumours, but officially Rudolf was mentally deranged, and that was the explanation.

But that wasn't the explanation according to the Maison d'Oc.

16
Maria Vetsera

I cannot let the story out in its fullest form, and anyway, long before Channel 4 had been approached, I knew MI5 had put a pockmarked, pallid-looking spook on the case, and that he – unobtrusively or not – was tailing me. To an extent I have had to sanitise the text, though I do not begin it in the style of my *Encyclopædia Britannica*, above, or end it in 1889 with the Crown Prince Rudolf having committed suicide, and taken his lover with him—

I begin rather in the crags and bluffs of a landscape brooding under a leaden sky, and a filthy night of rain. A coachman hunched in the folds of his coat moaned at his secret mission, and paused mid-oath when a reddish-looking ember streaked across his horizon. He watched through the slits of his eyes as it gently arced to earth, and in a pirouette of orange flames cratered the hillside. There it fizzed out abruptly – two inter-twining twists of smoke under an icy sheet of rain.

His coach had been newly retouched, and gleamed in the violet zigzags of light forking through the valley. He thundered on, through the mud and ruts, almost overturning where two enormous boulders – grey, sluggish shapes – loomed from nowhere through the rain. Abruptly the road twisted and rose, fell and rose again, then plunged finally into the forest. He lashed at the horses (for this is a kind of fiction, with all the embellishment that entails), and had as his sole thought his destination – only his destination – and how to accomplish that without mishap.

Borne along with him were two passengers, their embassy the cargo propped precariously between them. They were brothers – merchant bankers both – who despite the wrap of expensive furs shivered uncontrollably. That was because the little flakes of frost that chilled their blood was fear, a new pang for a pair more accustomed to life in the rococo drawing rooms their leisured clientele inhabited. That lumpy sack of cargo wedged between them, all too ghoulish, and greatly inconvenient, was a cadaver – in fact their dead niece, who at seventeen had been pretty, vivacious, and a baroness. Her name was Maria Vetsera, too young and good-looking to die. Nevertheless that loll of her head, as the coach clattered on through all those spooky rain-dark pines, told you how dead she was.

Daphne sniggered. 'Are there degrees of deadness?'

'You know it. You have your *MMU*.'

The coachman's task was to deliver his two bankers and one deadweight to the monastery of Heiligenkreuz, under whose bell tower a sexton and his mate had already knocked the soil from their shovels, and stood waiting by the grave they'd dug. They like the brothers couldn't guess at what it was, this prologue all four mummered in – *or* that the drama was destined to repeat itself twenty-five years later.

But now to Vienna. The year 1889. At that time southern Europe was dominated by the Austro-Hungarian Empire, under its emperor Franz Joseph, whose extents were oppressive to some. In its favour there was breadth of religion, language, culture and economics – those four monsters hard to tame or control. By contrast, other countries the emperor ruled had an unhappy knack of self-mutilation, for even then intractable contours rumpled the cloth, like the Balkans. There were other things the emperor didn't find amusing. A case in point was the one thumbprint grazing his escutcheon, in the person of his son, the Crown Prince Rudolf, whose fads he sought effective means of dealing with, by excluding him from all functions or fiascos in affairs of state. You couldn't be surprised at Rudolf's reaction against this, whose interests were counter to the military education his father had set out for him. His preferences were natural history and literature. One sultry afternoon – or so I have come to imagine it – Rudolf was thinking of how best to resist his father's proscriptions. Activism was one thing, and required effort, while a life wrapped in cotton wool was a misfortune reserved for the effort*less*. With these two at odds, Rudolf gazed into just that limbo where nothing much of consequence could ever be achieved by him.

Our own historical moment must have taught us something of everlasting monarchs, whose longevity their heirs have to suffer while finding a role for themselves. That conundrum, when it visited the Habsburgs, did so on a late January morning in 1889. The emperor had spent tranquil moments unrolling the scrolls of his signature onto one of his crested documents, and had planned for an hour with one of his ladies. Alas that wasn't to be. The shrill of voices, then the sudden sweep of his padded doors, shattered that illusion. His wife thundered in, and had in train the royal physician – a sombre, spindly man whose coat tails flew up behind him. The emperor, who paused to catch his breath, nevertheless had to deal instantly with marital torpedoes fired across his blotting pad.

'Rudolf is dead. Rudolf has shot himself.'

The emperor put away his pen, and was staggered.

Earlier that morning, Rudolf's body had been found in the bedroom of his hunting lodge, in the leafless Vienna woods. To complicate things the prince had not been there alone. In the same deadly pact the corpse of Baroness Maria Vetsera rumpled and bloodied the bedding too – for they'd *both* been shot.

'Then it's clear,' the emperor said. That vixen, in a fit of God knew what, had murdered his son.

His court physician begged to differ, though trembled as he did so. He'd examined, he said, both bodies, and had no doubt that the prince had shot the baroness, then trained the revolver on himself.

'My son is not a murderer,' the sad-eyed king decreed, and that was true – the emperor's son *was not* a murderer.

We pause for the official course of action, when rumours in Vienna invaded every drawing room. The emperor's next instructions were categorical: to prepare the family vault for the prince's body. This was at the Church of Capuchin Friars. The hunting lodge would close, and re-open as a shrine, with a service. After that came the official investigation, which the emperor ensured was headed by Baron Krauss, the top man at that time in the Vienna police. Krauss would report to the emperor, and reporting to Krauss was Baron Friedrich d'Oc.

Krauss took immediate action over the Vetsera burial, which went ahead, symbolically, under an angry, swollen sky, and was veiled in secrecy. It was, potentially, the biggest scandal of European society – just that sort of state dilemma the d'Ocs, with their wealth, connections, and more important a centuries-old diplomacy, were trusted to dampen down. Therefore what history fails to record is Friedrich's velvet glove, and the iron claw that drew it on. Gathered in its grip were members of the press, whose hold on things correspondingly diminished. Even Moritz Szeps, a close friend of Rudolf's, and proprietor of the *Neues Wiener Tagblatt*, couldn't do more than mumble into his pocket handkerchief. What paragraphets he manufactured offered nothing conclusive, with the revelation only that Rudolf – or rather he and his 'paramour' – had been shot dead at Mayerling, a village on the Schwechat River, about twenty-five kilometres southwest of Vienna. The hunting lodge is now a Carmelite convent.

The barons Krauss and d'Oc did a thorough job, and made sure no one was able to say what had prompted these events.

Inextricably bound to them was the emperor's wife, Elizabeth – Empress of Austria *and* Bavaria (and also Queen of Hungary).

One person Elizabeth might have trusted was the ambitious Count Andrássy, who as the most powerful man in Hungary sought to extricate its kingdom from the empire. He was backed in this by Bismarck, the German Empire's first chancellor (1871–90), whose influence on European politics left its mark on the dual murders of Mayerling. Emperor Franz Joseph had too readily bowed to his medic's opinion, even if it made his son a murderer, or worse than that, guilty of the mortal sin of suicide. Against all, he ordered the crown prince laid to rest in the imperial vault – with no post mortem, and no inquest. There was a token investigation, entrusted to Baron Krauss, whose job included the disposal of Maria Vetsera's remains, but of course, only the moment's *realpolitik* drove these things along. The secret treaty of 1877, between Russia and Germany, amounted to a handshake effectively uniting the emperor's two biggest enemies. That was a treaty the crown prince was likely to approve of, and as far as I could see that made Rudolf's suicide unlikely. He'd been eliminated, for fear of what politically he was likely to develop into. Franz Joseph, the prince's father, saw to his removal, with the barons Krauss and d'Oc trusted to do the work and dust his tracks. The emperor's motto was: 'never apologise, never explain'. That served an empire not simply steeped in power and wealth and military might. To Franz Joseph, it was something more ancient and much more permanent than that. It was his on divine trust. If to maintain it meant sacrificing his son, then unlike Abraham his regal hand would not be stayed, and Rudolf had to die.

Rudolf's successor was his cousin Archduke Franz Ferdinand, whose political thinking was more in line with the emperor's, but whose domestic affairs were not as polished. In opting to marry beneath him, any future offspring couldn't accede after him. But then on the 28th of June 1914 he and his spouse were shot in Sarajevo – an assassination sparking World War I, and a final confirmation that the archduke wouldn't succeed to the throne.

17

So now to the nub of Daphne's dilemma. She could not decide on her emphasis, even with obvious parallels between Maria Vetsera and Princess Diana, bystanders distant in time by over a century, yet crushed under the same juggernaut of European politics. I remained passive. Her pen almost permanently poised, she spent days on her Channel 4 proposal, distracted by the headlines, now that conspiracies were added to almost daily. One of the most enduring was the proposition that Diana's chances of retaining custody of her children after her divorce – in defiance of the powers above her – were slim. For that reason she'd compiled a dossier listing her husband's sexual indiscretions. There was speculation as to where that document was, if it still existed. Could some murky investigative journalist unearth it, Daphne pondered? Finally she asked my advice. 'Should I, Humf, reference all this stuff, or leave it to Channel 4?' I said it depended on her thesis. Was she suggesting Diana had been assassinated? If so why? It couldn't simply be for a catalogue of rakish exertion on the part of the Prince of Wales. She thought some constitutional adviser in the bowels of government had pointed out the possibility of a future Muslim claim on the British throne, and therefore both

Dodi and Diana had to be disposed of – the Archduke Rudolf and Baroness Maria of their day.

She asked what d'Oc would have thought, and wondered if in essence this was the purpose of his play, speculating as to whether those clues I'd told her about were somewhere in its court scenes. I said I was glad she'd mentioned our departed earl and patron. I had now been in touch with his executors – or one of them, Baron Maximus, FBA FRSL. Actually he'd been in touch with me. News was, Daphne, you and I have been named apropos of Hoe's future. The house and grounds were to remain fully staffed (no one had been retired). The theatre had a calendar of events impossible to scrap. If Daphne was asking what the guiding principle had been with the earl's influence over Dicto's pen, I said only that d'Oc had asserted something vague like this. On the British left the EU was viewed as a magic business circle. For the right that same political structure was Byzantine in its bureaucracy. Whatever the anatomy was, the legacy for Daphne was time, a venue, and a rolling fee for getting the play onto the English stage. In the meantime I gathered other material from Eliot's family vault, as alternatives to the Maria Vetsera story, should Daphne ask for something else for Channel 4. In no particular order, I'd got a catalogue on Martin Bormann, Charles Bohlen, Douglas Haig, Messerschmitt and Canaris. I'd got the truth about Rudolf Hess. Though for now I kept it all from her.

She enlisted players off the banks of the River Yo, on days free of Eliot's pearl-grey marionettes from Westminster, here for voice and kinesics coaching, important in addressing the House, or live debate in a TV studio. She workshopped scenes she thought would stand alone. I looked on as she booked little city theatres for rehearsed readings, and her plunge headlong into the rites of social chitchat, in a grooming of directors and producers all across the region. Elsewhere she persisted with Epsy and others, taking the circus scenes into public spaces (a terminology I baulked at). Favourite were cathedral steps. On the southeast coast, with its tourist towns, she set up her make-up tent on quaysides. Inland she vectored shopping malls. Then came forays into business, with the marble, fern-hung, fountain-splashed foyers of city brokers, and the flagged walks of St Paul's, and the glassy sunscreens de-symmetrising the blank façades of American banks. One grey Tuesday was spent in the crowds of Covent Garden, which I looked in on. Other occasions I'm too tired to catalogue. For the record, a scene she often chose was the one culminating in the lutenist's song from Act Two, with the cell phone episode (Act Three) also tried out more than once. She handed out leaflets. She formed the Canary Wharf Warehouse, a group of players dedicated exclusively to Eliot's play, with the aim of performing at the Globe. At that time I spoke at length with Lucinda Munney, whose Leader Books Plc d'Oc had chosen to publish his play. Lucinda had got as far as suggesting one of her editors for the project, a man called Matthew Sells, a sandy-haired thirty-five-year-old. I didn't quite hit it off with Matthew, as you will see, but I did enjoy good relations with his boss Lucinda. We met at last, and having pocketed, and later glanced at my calling card, she phoned me, wanting to talk about automating her backlist and re-launching Leader's dreary-looking website.

All plans were dropped when the play had a run abroad, including the Globe idea, which was scrapped. Book publication looked unlikely. Daphne divided her time between London and the Low Countries, Channel 4 and *New King Palmers*. Channel 4 took her to a second round of interview. A panel of grim-faced production pros asked her the hypothetical question what was it she'd *really* like to do? As a written exercise she was told to imagine complete artistic freedom and absolutely no budgetary constraints. She went off, and produced a cast list that read as the contents page of a book-not-a-book but a book for the screen, or someone's adaptation. She was back on her hobbyhorse, but with the renewed vigour of *my* blood in her veins, proposing that even Channel 4 could not escape her usual charge, i.e. of turning the noun *tradition* into a verb. Such was its weight of social propaganda. Her hypothetical piece had the working title *City of the Apes of God*, and these are just a few I draw from her epic *dramatis personae*—

- Duke of Dork, a powerful, connected, immensely wealthy pillar of the English establishment
- Sir Andrew Argue, senior partner in the accountancy firm Fawn Fallow Fawn, dealing with Dork's accounts
- Humblott Gale, a junior partner for Fawn Fallow Fawn, the only member of his firm who has ever met the Duke of Dork, and who actively seeks an accomplice in his attacks on the *force majeure*
- Mal Vole, Fawn Fallow Fawn's bookkeeper
- Sebastian-ho, a strong, virtuous independent
- Ron Cave, artistic adviser to the television industry
- Luce Sterling, a purveyor of commercial artefacts marketed by means of propaganda aesthetics
- Marvin Sale, prisoner to contemporary capitalism, a wage slave

The only critique she received – or comment really – was for her choice of character names, of which she decoded only one. Humblott, his tune doubly smudged (there are two tees in *sostenuto*), under the sustained political whispers of his life and times. Then suddenly all dead plans were revived, and the play was prepared for its UK tour. That left me gasping for air in the madness that followed.

Talk, Talk, Talk

1

Hard-bitten though Lucinda Munney was, she was good at cocktail time, explaining to the minutest point the perfect mix. (So, Lucinda, you use a beef consommé for Bullshots, Bloodshots and Hot Shots? That, Humf, *is* what I said.) These hours of instruction almost always passed in the airs of Bloomsbury, a short walk from her office and her tube station, in a bistro *she* called Scott's. Several changes in management had seen it metamorphose to its present Julep's, which – a lone stray in a cascade through multiple identities – was only the end trace in a long, distinguished history – which Lucinda hadn't seemed to keep track of. That didn't matter. The important thing was its factory decor, which as Scott's or Julep's or anything in between rejoiced in the first great age of the cocktail, with references everywhere to the Roaring Twenties.

Much too did I learn about Sells over our pre-prandials. I distinctly remember Lucinda with a Whisky Sour, her mouth its usual oblong, that resilient woman of commerce sucking hard on the stump of her fag. Myself I just sat there tall on my stool, a Perfect Lady in my clutches – that aperitif shaken gymnastically by the barman, a boy all smiles when Lucinda was here. She told me how little she shared the reservations of her editor-in-chief, who on receiving her *NKP* memo found it couched in just those icy cold syllables that filled him with indignation. Matthew's was not a politicised view of the trade – he operated not exactly *l'art pour l'art*, though he tried to maintain aesthetic boundaries. He couldn't, unlike his boss, abstract himself to a future when the Diana fuss had died down, when the flowers, bouquets, the books of condolence, and those good English homesteaders, lining the streets from the Abbey to Althrop, had left our screens and were out of the news. There was no point, in Matthew's mind, expending time, effort and intellectual energy when no definite end product was envisaged. There was no planned publication date, Lucinda unwilling to say when even that might change.

I was still discussing with Lucinda just how obstructive Sells could be, and was glad of her suggestions when, after a long day at the office, and a platter apiece of Julep's *fusilli* (a house special), we settled in our wicker chairs, she with a Sidecar, me with a Coconut Daiquiri. Matthew, she said, would get used to me eventually. If for the time being I couldn't get his co-operation on the *New King Palmers* book, I should try denting his resistance in nagging for information on the backlist, which she wanted me to automate. Added to that, I should get his views on a revamped website.

All that had constrictions of its own, given the premium on office space. There was a back street off the Euston Road where, gloomily, Leader had its headquarters. Sells shared a huge open plan with other commissioning editors, and had his phone, fax, computer screen and desk space partitioned off cupboard-size, his territory marked by interlocking screens, their dye a seductive purple. His two beaming children gazed out from school photographs pinned with his notices. A portrait of his brown-eyed petite-looking wife sat in an oval frame on his desk. I managed to show him, on his PC, a demonstration database, hard as it was for Matthew to relate an XYZ company selling different grades of widget to the work that Leader did. I said the object was the same – sales – and only the products differed. His phone kept ringing. Often some author in a query over the subjunctive, or when to use 'you and me' and 'you and I', or a Latinisation, or string rules for numbers, or whatever (that 'whatever' being far more important than anything I had to say).

I asked him to book one of Leader's meeting rooms and set aside half an hour, where amazingly he organised a flask of coffee – on a grey mid-morning, metropolis-style – and sat down forlornly (or so I read his demeanour), a small man heading a boardroom table, its polished teak a vast ocean, with its crude reflection – him – a lonely figure dappled in its surface. He fingered then prodded then munched on a jam-centred biscuit, before snapping off his wristwatch and setting it down – all with great theatrical intent – and placed a ball-point in proximity to his notepad – a cue to begin.

I had brought materials with me on my laptop, and began with a sample front page of Leader's redrawn website, a graphic intertext of stylised banner headlines and the company's newly profiled logo – an intertwining L and B – all of which, in deference to his boss's impeccable sense of market presence, wasn't overstated. The whole page took root on a varicoloured background, whose controlling software made changes instantly possible, from staid alabaster to amaranth, through a rosy carnation to chrome to cinnabar, or citrine to murrey or moon or xanthin. For the typefaces similar transformations, over font, colour, point size.

I left him a disc and hoped he'd mooch about and find the design he liked. I pressed him on the backlist, and apart from obvious data (author, title, first publication date, number of editions, etc.), asked him what information its database should carry, bearing in mind there weren't the usual limits (for example a full-blown picture archive *could* be included). It was also important to think about search criteria. Sells looked at me blankly, and wasn't sure that a backlist really existed, at least in document form. The company had gone through so many takeovers and commercial agglomerations that, well, much of that detail was probably lost, especially where works were out of copyright.

'I'll leave that with you,' I said. Next I asked what his project plan and timescales were for the *New King Palmers* book, cue for one of those inky blue clouds tumbling across our London sky, imitating perfectly Sells's disposition. He reiterated that point he had made so bad-temperedly before, that Leader Books had no interest in preparing a work for the marketplace, when the politics made a publication date impossible – at least in the short term. I told him on the contrary Lucinda had given the go-ahead. That together he and I should bring the book to completion.

That was a step too far. I watched him thumb his waistband before producing his cell phone. Did he hope the thing would go off? If so, no luck there.

He had doubts, he said, at the triangularity implicit in what I was now suggesting, and was sure I could understand that ordinarily the editor worked not with the author's business partner, but direct with the author himself. No one had told him the book had no author as such. Nor had it been explained that Marlon Maximus – executor of Eliot's artefacts – had my name at the head of his lists.

'So whose name goes on the cover? Eliot's? Dicto's?'

I didn't know. 'Dicto's a recluse.'

Sells ended the meeting promising that – over the next couple of days – he would give the manuscript close attention. I allowed him the best part of a week, then called. I was no further forward when that phone vacancy he was so specialised in darkened, and deadened his tone. He tried to be polite, expressing his personal view that certain changes to the text looked inevitable.

Patiently I explained that although there might be sound literary reasons for that proposition, politically the idea was impossible. Secretly written into the text was a sign from the House of Windsor to the present EU management team – a message whose wording Eliot had never discussed. I was completely ignorant as to its form or encoding. It meant therefore that even the slightest change to Eliot's final draft had the potential to destroy or undermine its diplomatic purpose (an action I'd already seen to, not that I was telling Matthew). A brief chilly silence in my earpiece, with Sells probably rolling his eyes, and tossing back his head, told me how idiotic I was. But he found the right words, regretful that so much was still to be resolved, leaving as the only margin for progress an introduction to the play, which, because I had been the author's confidant and friend, he assumed *I* would like to write. He warned, however slight that was, anything I did produce he was sure to edit. It was hard to envisage then, but the piece I concocted, and later lengthened and reshaped, is the 'Thespian Hoe' above, in whose process of revision I found it impossible to pin Sells down. He cancelled meetings, was out whenever I phoned, took a week to answer emails, and was open to meetings only when Daphne resurrected the Canary Wharf Warehouse. He might even have enjoyed the bad press she got with its first UK performances.

Sells also contrived one clever evasive manoeuvre, by delegating work on the website and database to one of his juniors. That was an example I tetchily followed, with instructions for one of my technicians. 'The first thing you need to do,' I told him, 'is audit Leader's system. If you think we'll need to restructure it, take a full backup once a week, with daily incrementals.'

2

That first sign of murmurings in the press was a notice in *The Guardian*, an innocuous six prissy paragraphs, whose tailing sentence openly surprised itself with this, and I quote—

> Daphne Hao, whose witty *Number Seven Bus* deserved every last handclap, has chosen this as a next professional step....

Lucinda thought any publicity was good. On the morning the story broke she invited Sells and me to a working lunch at Scott's (or of course Julep's). I had business with a client, whose newly acquired oast house – complete with pond, willows, a picket fence – was home to an extensive image bank, information he and his partner had found a market for over the internet. Lunch was postponed and the meeting shifted to Lucinda's merry cocktail hour, where Sells, unable to enter his boss's spirit of things – Lucinda semi-off-duty – sipped at a beer, and without help demolished a sizeable bowl of pistachio nuts. Lucinda, in fond remembrance of her days in the New

York book trade, had a Manhattan. I must have had a Gin and It, its cherry very handy as I stirred, listening to Sells's freshly cooked objections.

Lucinda knew that one day soon Daphne's production of *NKP* would see itself smothered in a blaze of press and other coverage. She trusted this as the right strategic moment, and was sure that Sells did too, to wrap up any outstanding details and get the earl's play ready for its first edition.

Sells hated to disappoint. To talk of wrapping up, he said, was really jumping ahead. In fact what you'd call progress was more concisely catalogued as what *hadn't* been done. A designer remained a figment. Jacket blurb, not yet written. Artwork (for the front and back covers) – that was non-existent (not even a tentative sketch). No one had thought to calculate an ISBN.

'Matthew, that's not what we want to hear.'

But there was more. Leader had only Mr Joel's word here that the dead author had left things as I said he had, and that no Count de Coq (a not improbable name, Sells thought) was likely to emerge and claim copyright, with that part of the earl's estate contested. Lucinda found that fatuous, and wondered if Matthew needed a holiday. I assured him, as best I could, that the earl's estate had the benefit of prestigious London lawyers, and that all articles of ownership had been dealt with impeccably.

'You'll just have to get down to it first thing tomorrow,' Lucinda said.

'I've got meetings all morning. I'm tied up with contracts till Friday.'

'Monday then.'

There a non-committal Sells made his apologies, leaving half a glass of beer, and setting off apace, late for his train and the distant leafy suburb where he and his family lived.

Talking of contracts, Lucinda's brightly studded girl from one of the temping agencies had managed to delete from disc a draft proposal sent out earlier in the month to one of Leader's TV gardeners, whose finely keened hoe had turned up numerous conditions he wanted weeding out.

'Never mind,' I said. 'I'll get my man from operations to trawl through the backups. We'll find it.'

3

These cold English mornings…mornings tactile, the tingle of radiator heat…world half afloat…in aromas…in all this filter coffee, sluicing round the office.

It's hard to believe the change in weather, but how, Daphne, do *you* cope? You know. With the onset of winter….

Answer: she used her links and her *ad hoc* troupes, and last week fixed her agenda on a group near the Plymouth Hoe. That gave her, for a season, a rented address under the icy winds of Exmoor, or, as she tried to explain with a postcard, an exposed thatched cottage, open beams and grey stone floors (and 'all the funny things they have out here'). Lest I thought her mad, sad, or a nomad, all the rooms were snug, each with a rug in sturdy reddish weave. In the kitchen-cum-lounge an ancient, glass-fronted wood stove, if left to burn all day and night, kept the interior warm and tinder-dry.

Her card came with a cassette tape, both card and tape packaged in a small padded envelope. 'Please have a listen, when you have a mo.' I did – and found there a topical affairs show for local radio, Daphne in triad with a champion worm charmer (all froth and funny jokes), and a disgruntled pig farmer (fuming at his subsidies). In the chair was one of those stolid country folk, more agile mentally, and more attuned to the *beau monde* than Daphne would have thought, for after all what to her was a stage stereotype was not, to the people he broadcast to, a comic dialect necessarily.

The farmer thought Laurel's work with *Palmers* was a pantomime – moot point, as she might have said. She resisted the temptation to lecture him, but ensnared herself in tortured expositions, trying to turn harangues to discussion, and guiding that into the murky journalese of social affairs, thence to the role of politics – an ambitious leap the farmer snorted at. Her other fellow guest was more open to conversation, though having seen the play was still at a loss to read its message.

'The message is,' Laurel said, and reeled off the string of venues where the play was booked for the coming few months. All subsided into belly laughs, and yet, despite these amiable meanderings, the conclusion was that *NKP* was not something you'd expect to take the family to.

Unworried, I pondered that remark.

4

Now to other abstractions. The Leader Books computer system was a constellation of office PCs networked to an in-house server, whose two fixed discs were home to payroll, ledgers and other business software. Our audit and performance checks showed an imbalance in throughput over the discs' controllers, which I appreciate is jargon, but was a situation DoCoTel could easily correct, by the redistribution of data and

processing across the two drives. With that added to our schedule, one of my boys with a key to Leader's machine room had been in charge of full weekly back-ups for almost a month. I asked him to mount his latest tape on one of our machines, at DCT head office, and dump it out to disc. When, later, I looked at it, it showed the following folders, protected by an elaborate mesh of access lists—

ACADEMIC ADVOCATES AUDIO AUTHORS BLURB CDROM CONTACTS CONTRACTS COPYRIGHT CORRESPONDENCE CVS DESIGNERS EDITORIAL GHOSTS IN-HOUSE JACKETS LEADER LEAVE LEDGERS LEGAL LIBEL MEDIA MISC MISSION PAYROLL PERKS PERSONNEL PICS POLICY PRESS PRINTERS PROSPECTS R&D REVIEWS TEAM

There was also a set of files that taken as a whole was *all* Leader's email, sent and received.

Lucinda's missing contract wasn't where you'd expect to locate it in this list – nor did I find it in CORRESPONDENCE. It turned up in TEAM, which in itself had spawned a hierarchy of sub-folders, including one for every Leader employee, including temps (a great many in recent years). In the folder marked SELLS I found, among scraps and odd assortments, and mine a natural curiosity, the first tentative draft of a resignation letter. Needless to say, I kept this information to myself.

5

I met Lucinda late one afternoon for lunch, in a pavement bistro off the Hampstead Road, its bright, reflective outdoor decor – chairs, tables, its sign squeaking in the wind – vigorously combed in a vortex of yellow leaves. Its interior was varnished pine, and a terracotta floor, with serpents, squids, oyster shells and salted seaweed painted round the walls. There was a stabile under the wine rack, where a kitchen boy had hung his scarf and hat.

Lucinda breezed in just as I'd muddied my upper lip in a cup of cappuccino. No strain did I detect, other than those habitual cigarettes, French and pristine at the tips, and very warmly pungent. This was despite her TV odd-jobber round the gardens, a grave Yorkshireman bristling with distrust – at all things London and contractual – who now I heard had girded up his agent in a twelve-point revision of Leader's standard author agreement.

'Ah, well,' I said, 'for the record, I've managed to retrieve your covering letter to it.'

'Thank heaven.' She turned to the menu board – a rambling dissertation chalked in red and blue calligraphy. She debated its leek and mustard crêpe, then un-making up her mind told me how Matthew was still stubbornly difficult. I said that at least he'd dropped his frontier guard, in allowing me a few pages of introduction to the earl's play, a task I hadn't yet dreamed the opening sentence to, though had pored over many of his private documents. Unlike Daphne, I didn't easily summon sparks of inspiration. I was a lesser mortal stalking the correct latitude of mind, in search of a pen athletic enough for a first portentous syllable, the lever to others following—

There was one among many ancient family myths that the Maison d'Oc deemed worth its salt….

'Well don't go round in circles,' Lucinda said.

'I'll let you know, *if* I've made a start.'

She quietly unzipped the flimsy brown document case she always brought to minor business banquets. She covered the ashtray, and my saucer, in a warm new edition of *Sabrina Fair*, a respected lifestyle mag. So what, Lucinda, was here for me? Surely not that cover girl – blonde, golden fleshed, and exquisitely dentured.

'Turn to the arts pages' (somewhere near the back).

Here one of *Sabrina*'s thrusting sub-editors, a Ms Pamela Surrey-Paul, had been threading the cobbled walks through Exeter, a fateful day before a family wedding, and had tired of its stores – quaint though they'd been, after the throngs of Oxford Street (a bazaar she was much more used to). A good sit-down was what she needed. So, what could the city's culture offer a girl like Pam (Pam she liked to be called)? In one of those twists of fate I know I shall one day find unstoppable language for, as I now anticipate a life ahead soiled with curses for innocents like Ms Surrey-Paul, this afternoon's Isca Theatre matinée saw Daphne, leading her band of Cornish trouvères, in a play little known in the metropolis, even though written by an English earl (alleged).

Act One was a village farce the average city girl could just about abide, and that Pam did, if only for the sake of Pam's aching feet. Hers were fledgling sensibilities, and this was a first flutter in a magic summer breeze. Come Act Two, Pam didn't think she liked the innuendoes garnishing the overarching grammar of the text, and explained it as hopeless masculine attempts to smash the frangible iconography engraved in the transparencies of our times—

La lune, la lune,
La Princesse Moon,
Who smiled for the press
On her honeymoon.

A tortured history of photocalls had given the world a multi-
dimensioned Diana, from dumpy bric-à-brac or bride-to-be,
to the bedtime beauty reclined in the satin prinks of an artist's
studio couch. What the author had failed to understand – for
now we stood agog in Pamela's masterclass in culture – was
how social innovation always sought to utilise (or 'subsume
into itself' Pam thought was a better way of putting it) whatever
practical materials came historically to hand. No one or nothing – not even the fashion priests, whose ministry was the
inexorable march of the decades – had the power to impede
humanity's natural progress, once it was underway. This was
why slapstick, put-downs, puerile jest, were only a *surface*
iridescence, a champagne splash over important publications
such as hers. Unlike that beacon of modernity, an earl of the
shires (for so she tagged along with my deception) was not
temperamentally equipped to probe the hidden depths, and
read in Diana's star-peppered status the *cri de cœur* of the
betrayed wife or single mom. If we now saw her life as mytho-
poeic, we did so because that angst-ridden flicker of ourselves,
a forlorn forsaken soul that cast its shadow on our universe,
wanted only that we bend our knees *with* her – Diana, angel of
mercy – everywhere she comforted the poor, or held out her
hand for the sick.

Mythos and myopia, plus a reminder – of the god who

suffered a life of flesh, only to rebirth himself – for was not our fairy princess made of that flesh too, a gal with an eating disorder, born of a broken home? (She was, Pam, she was.) Bizarre it was to think that the Earl d'Ocs of the world had watched, with much the same vantage as staff at *Sabrina*, and seen only a photogenic smile, the gradual shift from those first stoic country-girl outfits – in apricot or navy blue – up through the crazy spectra of international fashion wear, a sugar-pink ensemble or cocktail dress, or those chic little candy-coloured suits that showed her legs to best effect…. Pam said again, how bizarre it was when that was *all* they'd seen. You understood when a passing hobbledehoy good-naturedly overlooked the greatness of a name (who's this Versace then?). Yet here was that hallowed thunder under whose bombarding echo Pam asked us this: was that also to overlook what gem the label packaged?

Somewhere among these paragraphs Lucinda had left blue ovals from her marker pen, where her desultory train of thought superimposed itself on Pam's flirtation with the masses – her streaming cathexis all over the shiny new leaves of fair *Sabrina Fair*. Here we'd got prayers and hymns and mythologies again, and finally the canonisation of Princess Diana, made possible only by that divine and evil end in a concrete underpass beside the River Seine (and how prophetically unglamorous that was!). The tragedy unfolded itself anew. Again we saw uniquely our national flag at half-mast above the Palace roof, the books and books and books of condolence, candle-lit vigils, floral shrines, handy quotations from the worlds of earls and nervous rock stars, and in the Abbey two pale-lipped families seated on opposing sides of the catafalque, and the Archbishop, there to make meaning of her mission. Earl d'Oc's play (if indeed any such person existed) frankly cheapened her divinity, in suggesting that a new Republic of Europe, had it wriggled into life in time, might instead have elevated her as its official head of state, in lieu of the stratosphere she now occupied in the minds of all English people everywhere—

> La lune, la lune,
> La Princesse Moon,
> Her divorce a political honeymoon.

We wept for Diana's boys, all of us apiece, for they and we had lost those tender enfolding arms to protect us – the queen of our souls was dead. Therefore hear ye, skulking cynics everywhere: long live that queen.

God grant us peace.

As we catch our breath, allow me to say there are certain popular misconceptions that I, Humf, am always willing to tolerate – even with so many wailing at an era's end and the passing of an icon. That cathartic moment was upon us, one soon to dissipate as we sought an alternative, a fresh mint and a newly made replacement. I much prefer a substitute frame on a people's unitary outpourings. I think of timely interventions – a repeated saturnalia – a system of regular co-ordinates on the vast planisphere of existence, where we're allowed to weep for that glassy fragility we know our mortality to be.

What I couldn't forgive Ms Surrey-Paul – or the footnote to her piece, written by her boss the editor, a Ms Italics (so to speak) – was its sobbing, internal echolalia, a smothering over the dramatised facts, and her certainty that Earl Eliot d'Oc was a *nom de guerre*, and *NKP* had been decanted into stage receptacles by a freak called Humfrey Joel. That I didn't appreciate at all. Diametrically, Lucinda thought *any* publicity must be good, and suggested I get Daphne to bring her talents back to the capital, where she or her agent might re-enter negotiations for a run at the Globe. Lucinda was going to issue memos. One she'd already written meant Matthew was in for a jolt. Under Lucinda's persuasive cold-eyed gaze he *would* overcome professional reservations. But – we needed Daphne.

We had a crêpe lunch, at well after four. I told her I would see what I could do.

6

Yet somehow I failed to take any proper public action when, my word to Lucinda a kind of guarantee, I did everything I could for the resurrection of Daphne's Canary Wharf Warehouse – to the tune of several thousands. By night my hands were blued in the streaks of sapphire radiant off my computer screen, as I clattered the keyboard, the pursuit often luckless, with historical asides meant as an introduction to an English play refusing to be so framed. Who'd be a writer! By day I sat there helplessly, under the waves of an electrified sky, its dark clouds fringed with a wicked glower of pink. I hadn't begun to guess at the huge momentum gathering against me, with every new venue touched by Daphne's performances – Hammersmith, Kilburn, Stratford, Croydon – attracting weary-eyed scriveners from the world's shallowest collectives. Instance, *In Women*, another pro-Diana 'living' magazine, its 200-plus pages coated in floss, its blocks of type conceived under the same vertigo as suffered by Ms Surrey-Paul, who denounced the play as scurrilous and me as cowardly for not admitting to its authorship. Then again *Goss*, a more sophisticated publication, whose place was the walnut tabletops under the exquisitely moulded ceilings of society people, whose chief luminary had tried without success to establish who the real Earl Eliot d'Oc could be, concluding he must be a fiction for Humfrey Joel to hide behind. All this I could smile at up to a point, until, in the *Sunday Mail Living Magazine*, some quackish sleuth who felt qualified to roam at large in the vistas of my psyche, and there preen himself in its twilit hall of mirrors, offered psychological insight in pointing out that Humfrey Joel was the product of a shattered home. In what private retreats he'd prodded about for his information I dreaded to contemplate.

All this was new, bumpy terrain, with a twisted polemics I found hard to resist mentally, given the distortions it wrought, and the agitation it brought to my life. I did manage, and now as a matter of urgency, the 'final' touches to my introduction – a mere eleven pages – a modest task, yet demanding an enormous effort of will. Its climax saw me scuttling with Lucinda for the cocktail bar, and a long noon breakfast squared off with one of Julep's Irish whiskies. Foolishly I did not think to check on the progress of Sells's resignation letter before putting printed and electronic versions in his possession, both of which he shuffled into his intray, with a tired gravitas, and a sinister smirk.

'I'll be intrigued to see your revisions,' I said.

'All in good time.' He folded his arms and gazed across that huge expanse of office space, with its border controls and territories, its cubicles a chorus of telephone conversations, their accompaniment the hum of machinery as that whirred away among the interlocks of factory-produced furniture. I had other meetings to attend, so left him, a man whose gaze I saw momentarily transfixed on the wintry blue gloaming enshrouding the rectangular window space, a man almost wistful at the life on the street below, where thick-wristed brickies, or gamblers flush from the bookie's, or students in rags, or toothless old unshaven men, slipped in or out of the Dray Horse, an oasis sooty at its façade, and with an interior blooming with nicotine stains.

Later that afternoon I spent a sad hour listening to the proprietor of a motor museum, forcing a smile yet brooding nevertheless in the margins of my jotter, a man finally made to reflect on the excrescences of popular journalism. I had several lucky pencils, all of them newly sharp, and watched myself meander into a wandering system of side notes, their shape and precision one day likely to expand into the full fighting jacket of counter-allegation. I regret that I have left it till now to put the record straight, but with one, plump sideswipe hope I dispose forever of all these tabloid tragedians, their futile headlines a kind of taxonomy for stunted readers everywhere, a collective mind where the specimen (in this case me) finds himself pinned to a slide marked 'family dysfunction'.

So what of this 'shattered home' I came from? That, as I hope I've shown, was more a case of mutually agreed dispersion, geographically speaking. My first father, Martin Keyes, his life already touched on above, graduated with fuss and fanfare with three degrees, one of them in engineering. After a short career in civic construction he moved into electronics, where with the first computer boom he dabbled in systems design, then plunged whole-heartedly into the building of system architectures. He lent his name to a proposed operating system – Keyos. I was an infant then, so mine are only selective memories of Martin and Deidre together. I can say honestly they never argued. What I can also remember fully, and can even name the street, is where we lived – a three-storey house in a leafy enclave somewhere in central London. Its exterior was a dazzling white, even on those gloomy days when adjoining frontages graded into grey, or darkened to a blur if the wind brought rain. Ours was the central edifice, with extravagant cornices, a bold, confident pediment, and Georgian sashes. In these were hung half-dropped scallops, as Deidre had a thing against drapes. They gave the house the aura of slumber through the day. Even our *au pair* said so, and she of course knew otherwise.

Remote is the varnished gleam of my cot bars, which with streams of sunshine through the enormous oblongs of my bedroom window stencilled their watermark on the weft of my bedding. I was older when I began to listen out for the polished cars that drew up outside, the clunk of driver and passenger doors a sure guarantee of the happy adult voices that always followed, and the duple chime of the doorbell. These and other gatherings started later in the evenings as I grew up, spilling out in a flood of drawing-room lamplight into the empurpled garden terraces, and brought up to me all their intoxication in a mingling of scents, honeysuckle foremost, and with the sound of muted orchestras somehow caught in the plash of water from the fountain. *I can hear the sound of vi-o-lins….*

Not all the guests by any means were friends or colleagues of my father's. My mother was a partner in a London firm of

architects, whose company ethos showed its *laissez-faire* whenever my father was away on business. At four or five years old
I went into work with my mother, and remember how its
holiday sense of paradise – to Deidre essential in *any* career –
centred itself in no office discipline at all. For hours at a stretch
a scattering of drawing boards, lunar-bright under their trans-
lucencies, sat vacant, with only a draughtsmen's angled lamp
contorted above them. Dotted round the place were hospitality
rooms, fitted with brick or orange settees, tables for chess,
books, board games, a billiard table, roof lights open to the sky,
and an all-round fenestration with stunning views of the capital.

It's hard to remember, at a perspective of over thirty years,
those shadowy figures passing in and out, the people my
mother worked with chatting amiably, but stalking technical
solutions through mental recreation. I recall being taught how
to make long or short swerves for a cue ball, having Tennyson
read to me – by a clean-shaven tenor, and later by a dramatic
bass, whose beard was long and thick. I won at cribbage,
listened to jazz, fiddled with a Fibonacci sequence, I orated the
closing eight lines of the epilogue to *Pericles*. How often I sank
subs and paper battleships, until finally I was granted a special
pencil and setsquare, and helped to design the perfect children's house – two elevations and a plan.

'One day we'll build it,' I was told.

Then one afternoon a man called d'Oc phoned for an
appointment, impressed by what work he'd seen of Deidre Joel.
He commissioned her to redesign some of his outbuildings at
his newly inherited house in Hoe, in particular the theatre,
which stood in need of renovation, and where so many prose-
lytising speeches have since been rehearsed. After that he

started calling at the house, always in his white Rolls-Royce. It was shortly after that when Martin left for good.

7

Ten days, a fortnight without progress passed in a blank, when all that crept on my earth was an eddy of autumn leaves, swirling round my office. Hints of anything to change that frozen world I read as signs of wonder, usually in an ashen sky, bloated with snow, yet always unwilling to disgorge itself. Lucinda wasn't much fun. Her gardener, in a flap about his potting sheds, let fly with an embassy of specialists, contesting every last contractual punctuation point. As for Sells, if he'd looked at my introduction, he hadn't admitted to it. These were days heavy with portents.

I spent a dark Friday trawling through the latest backup tapes, to discover Sells's resignation letter had gone through multiple iterations, setting off innocently as a 20-kilobyte apologia, and currently a monstrous autobiography measuring 103. Nothing in either of these, or the half-dozen drafts or so in between, made any overt reference to *NKP*, though he alluded to projects 'ethically impossible' for him to carry out. Intrigued to know what pangs of conscience afflicted the average stooge in the publishing industry, I poked about in his email tray, and there found entwined in the usual dross a lengthy confessional addressed to listener Sheena – evidently not his wife (*she* was Arabella, Bel for short). I noted Sheena's e-address – SRMcCall@hiprofile.com. Hi Profile I knew from public relations, used sometimes by us, by DCT. If memory serves (I was there at a meeting a cloudy decade ago) it occupied the three central floors of a steel-blue building, and was part of attractive real estate in Victoria. According to Hi Profile's website, Sheena was in marketing.

Sells poured from a cup brimming with unhappiness, in the recall of desperate moments when Sheena was unable to meet him after work. His salve was her smile, and the anaesthetic procured in a measure of gin, when rather than be dragged into the dejection of his commuter train, his life would recede for a sorry hour, down in the Dray Horse *purgatorio*, where too much fizzy beer would pass his lips, and he played and lost at pool. Retreat into himself mirrored one of those bland hapless heroes he took an airbrush to in that atrocious urban fiction he plodded on with editorially almost every day of his hectic working life, and showed himself to himself as hard-pressed, underpaid, tyrannised by his children, loveless in his marriage, and resentful of my (yes, Humfrey's) apparently carefree life.

What, for Sells, was a homecoming, after the baize or the singles bar? He knew with what enthusiasm he'd massaged his marital home from drab to chintzy, stripping away its insipid pink paper, its pattern of little oblongs standing out in velveteen relief, replacing it with printed trellises and blooms, all from a Laura Ashley catalogue. These wounds he couldn't conceal, Sells a man appalled at the emotional cost of a life with responsibilities. All was an extravagant rite of passage, an evolution he'd measure as a wasted stroll with Bel through an endless avenue of time, the brief affection they had exerting itself through the carpet samples they examined, the furnishings they found to match, and the courage he summoned in an everlasting duel with his credit rating.

After fifteen years that happy homebuilding had deteriorated into the bruised gentility he couldn't bear to open his front door to every evening after work. If Sheena hadn't much sympathised, she was reminded that the tramp of tiny feet marching remorselessly into teenage had brought with it a pattern of morning cornflakes splattered up his breakfast room walls, sweaty palms to the paintwork and window panes (that and all other accumulated filth Bel could never find the time to clean), trinkets exclusively *his* used like toys and tested to destruction: his camera (a gift), a turntable (which he'd hoped to keep, re an attic full of vinyl), a home computer forever performing illegal operations. 'You know, Sheena, I tumble into the hall over a mound of rancid footwear,' a whole shopful of shoes he'd bought in a twelvemonth. *En famille* was gadgets everywhere, gameboys, god knew what, the TV incessantly on, the phone always ringing (not for him). Any day's travail trailed off according to maxims he'd never verbally agreed to, his evenings stunted to bedtime, no dinner cooking, not even the potatoes scrubbed, and a *Lebensraum* in a plea to be tidied and vacuum cleaned before a man like Sells was clinically safe to seat himself.

No litany my resigning editor embarked on ever found a natural end, yet I discovered, embedded in that chaos of his personal life, a dream of his student years. It had become central to him now, though I'd lost track of the prototype epistle, and didn't uncover at all the counter-confession I also might have expected. His bachelor degree was in English (I'm not surprised), a daytime tedium he and his three closest allies soothed away as a cover band – a guitar, a bass, a drummer, and Sells responsible for lyrics and vocals (and sometimes a tambourine) when the venue allowed them original numbers. In those great days the bounds of performance didn't go beyond the college bash or village hall, a point too subtle to dampen the fantasies a disaffected man of industry now besotted himself with, to the point of blowing iridescent bubbles all round his office space. He'd leave. He'd get out on the road. Here were those little iron filings of the soul important to keep in their first magnetic patterning, Sells able to persuade himself that his college quartet, regrouped for business, remained a viable option. Sheena smirked (*I* smirked), and all those bubbles burst.

I couldn't help but feel here in the lyrics he'd penned, in the margins of his medieval essays, and brought with much other personal baggage to Leader's in-house disc system, were the first swollen seeds of his adult misery. A debut album (he insisted this had always been the plan) was projected onto the following song titles—

Hot Night, Cold Woman	Limpy Greeny
Throw Away My Coffee	Rage Test
The Moon-Moon-Moon	Drinkin' Gin
No Appetite	Catalyse Fuse
Nuke 'Em, Ron	Livin'
Way Outta Here	Glues, Booze, Blues
I Mean No	Rockin' Phil More
Socks Off, Honey	Garage Party
Entropy Man	She Ain't Comin' Back
Dog Days, Dole Days	

Needless to add, no official discography lists them anywhere, their grope after immortality left in the electronic dust of his email, a correspondence signed off 'Hugs, Matt' on his part, and invariably 'Feel good, S' on hers.

8

'Feel good, Humf' is how I might react now, cruising for the second time this life in the Milford Sound, and pondering new inquiries, this time into the study of cryptology. I have brought my appointments diary – a solid brickbat sheathed in shiny plastic tortoiseshell – its scope the last five years at DoCoTel. From it I note that on the eve of Sells's resignation our lives were a tired succession of office parties in the weeks up to Christmas. I see him chubby-cheeked in a poppy-coloured paper hat. I see myself, spotlessly shod and as usual sharply tailored, aware before anyone of what that weakened afflatus for his party blower really meant.

Daphne had her programme – very busy – a structure perfectly woven round the urbanity of her being, her outwardness and soft satire her winning ingredients. At this time the limits on scope were the vapid airings found with Corporation radio. She'd attracted those magazines whose permits are doled out selectively for endless talk, the theme one's fascinating life and colourful career. So, what would a belle in the springtide blossoms of her work make of our post-industrial obsessions? Generally these were recurring questions, in her case attached to the dead ideal of the artist as someone specific, but dealing more minutely (at least in Daphne's discipline) with the problems of authenticity, when no one knew who it was who wrote the texts, or why, arranged for public consumption. It was seen as unavoidable when impersonal theory conflated itself with living flesh (or in Eliot's case those ashen remains long having passed through the mortuary). Soon the quiz began as to whose play it was her

Warehouse Co had begun to make notorious. Of course a long legacy in pay cheques is the practical purpose that turns celebrity into mystique, and for that reason Daphne wouldn't betray confidences, saying only it was the late Earl d'Oc who had hired her, who to help the play along had given generously of his facilities. As to Humfrey Joel, why yes, she knew him of course, as one of d'Oc's friends. I was not as far as she knew on his payroll. But that's *all* she said about me.

Others went further, for example the *International Tribune* – you'd think perfectly respectable – a paper listing on its staff one of just many confectioners, her name incised with a chisel, and ringed with stars, and with a photograph long out of date, all of which formed the official visa heading up her gossip column. Her name was Katie Klynch, or a reflexive KK (or so said these tablets of transatlantic print, with a smile). KK had sweeping theories as to our human vulnerabilities, harmless on the whole, but apt to overblow themselves into the fullest European neurosis, when endangered by extremes. I was, apparently, subject to just such stress, not that KK – or may I call her K for short – knew anything at all about my life. No matter. K trotted on, a huge generous soul driven to share her wisdom equably, and at pains to point out that you don't have to travel far into the history of psychiatry and fiction to understand what it all meant. Here with this latest manifestation of that older world across the water you saw how the aged relations lived, crippled with disease.

In setting down the essentials, it was K's first necessity to pinpoint precisely where in the human zoo we were, which most would agree was a rugged geography, a great 'out there' made no less hard to traverse by its confused polarities. For guidance you needed an Englishman – and a particular one, called Coventry Patmore – whose genie once unstoppered let out a mathematics of life, what *she* called a formal metaphysics in a see-saw over an equals sign. This of course served the secondary purpose of establishing her legitimacy—

> For want of me the world's course will not fail:
> When all its work is done, the lie shall rot;
> The truth is great, and shall prevail,
> When none cares whether it prevail or not.

In the long elaborated list that followed, K showed us her acquaintance with all kinds of dualities, from the self-asserting altruist, to the mask of arrogance worn by the timidly unconfident. With wealth went the inner furnace of fear, with its day-to-day flight from the quagmires of penury. Conversely in poverty you found the lust for gold. Where *I* stood K wasn't exactly sure, though having heard from a reliable source I had had no formal early education, what *NKP* amounted to was a show of learning in someone largely unschooled. You must add to this that either I had invented and hidden behind Earl d'Oc, for a similar reason – i.e. a trumpeting of social standing by someone socially undistinguished – or Earl Eliot d'Oc had conceived and cloaked himself in me, as a touch of humility in someone greatly privileged. I couldn't help think of this as shades of that pseudo-romantic, pseudo-urban fiction presses like Leader gave us by the truckload, or through which the *International Tribune* plumped its review pages.

The question K would always ask was why the artifice, why did it have to be that? Did it mean that the average European, in order to find his or her truest identity, felt compelled to don another guise, and if so was this not at the heart of the coming European superstate, a political inevitability, nations forced to seek their otherness in an imperial afterglow – or was this too simplistic? I didn't have K's expertise, amateur or otherwise. Mine was not that easy perspective won through the toils of middle-class America. I had no answer to her rhetoric. What I had was a life – here in these pages – in the delays of my legacy.

And what I knew was how unreliable her reliable source had been, when Deidre in fact did think seriously about my early education. Almost the first thing I learnt was where my father Martin Keyes had gone. She sat me down in the kitchen through whose patio doors I strayed into a lingering glance at the naked shrubs outside, their shadows lengthening up the lawn. Each new reading off the clock or sundial bore with it ominous tidings, news that in my mind is always connected with the lateness of that afternoon, though the season was calm, serene, its palette a velvet of autumn colours. A few flecks of sapphire splashed the ornamental brick edging the patio.

In the days and weeks preceding their final separation, Martin and Deidre had also sat here talking, in a last attempt to merge two parallel careers to one point, plotted on my horizon – impossible, as that turned out. Let me repeat. My name is Humfrey Joel. I was born in a western London suburb in the April of 1958 (the 29th, an anniversary I share with Michelle Pfeiffer and Zubin Mehta. Doubtless others). Having the capacity to know my world – and yes, the Beatles' first LP – by 1963, I could see how clever and inventive, and self-absorbed my father was. He was wedded to progress and social revolution, though not of the kind of *Please Please Me*. Instead he had given himself to those humming binarisms and the march of computer technology. My mother, as practising architect, exercised her imagination not solely in the appearance, function and materiality of spaces, and sometimes vistas, her London firm worked with, public or private. *How* her partnership was run was one of those vital life experiments it was hard for her to abandon, and so, when America beckoned, and Martin was seduced by the lures of California, Deidre let him go. In the initial settlement both agreed that I, at that time unattached by siblings, should have the benefit of equal time with each, and for the first twelve months the arrangement worked: Earl d'Oc had interests all over North America, and frequently flew with me. Schooling became a problem, however, and soon these trips had been whittled down to a fortnight in the summer and three weeks over Christmas.

Not a few days after I had blown out the candles on my seventh birthday, Deidre sold the London house. In its place she bought a small apartment in Putney, and later a stake in a middle-class commune, the place a rook-encircled hamlet. I won't name it, and will say only its location was off a long winding turn from the London-to-Oxford road. We lived there with five other one-parent families, a community served by a written constitution, which included home education – for me and six other children. Lucinda when I told her this rejoiced, as a newly alert reader engrossed in Katie Klynch's misapprehensions. Lucinda was always so alive to the scent of controversy, and had that knowing cocktail smile when I pointed out the fault in KK's sources. That, she said, was a surprisingly bad mistake given the *International Tribune* and its reputation. I don't know by what logic she arrived at this, but the chances were Lucinda could tie up a US book deal.

9

Ten days to a fortnight later one in my gang of seven – one of those pupils in my commune – found herself quoted, or rather misquoted, in a glossy called *Ms Besant*, of a sub-literary genre addressed to women's issues, a tabloid I hadn't heard of till then. There were compensating factors, and for me personally a kind of relief, when written evidence unveiled this latest in a line of victories, with a clear delineation of our sex wars insisting on zealotry first, or revenge, and a sense of fairness later – not that anyone knows hormonally what this fairness is. Her name was Megan Pride (*née* Lane), a child I knew as a redhead, eight or nine, pigtails, a button nose, a little girl prone to wipe her hands over the light-blue denim of her dress. That, depending on the chore, left cooking dough, or compost slime, or any in the range of paints we used, on her newly aired clothing every day. I recall she wore wellingtons and messed about with wormeries – all made vivid, as I now reflect, because she wasn't with us long. Her mother (good at teaching history) re-married, then sold her shares in the commune, and thereafter mother and daughter took their new man off to live on a housing estate.

Amazingly she got in touch with me (Megan, of over thirty years ago!). This was shortly after these *Ms Besant* allegations, a long tedious list of anti-Humf surmises. As I said to Lucinda, once these had squirmed out onto the open page – stuff from the poisonous mulch its three editorial witches had stewed it in – one other consequence was Megan's unblemished conscience, now undermined. She wrote to me personally, brave and agonised apologies, etched in turquoise ink, on yellow scented paper, folded with precision into a matching envelope. She awaited her moment and delivered her missive discreetly backstage, via Daphne's trusted hand, the occasion a one-night performance in Richmond. When I came to read it days later, I could see why *Ms Besant* had portrayed the evil Humfrey Joel as – and this went back to his student days – a man prepared to sacrifice *all* for the theatre. Megan had mentioned one summer holiday the whole of our commune had spent at Thespian Hoe. From that followed a close reading using microscopic plates, with one of *Ms Besant*'s forensic academics finding enough in Acts One and Two to incriminate the author – or me – with the usual misogyny (which begs the question, Daphne, where did she get her script?)—

> I took my fair maiden, / For love I was craving…
> La lune, la lune, / La Princesse Moon…

and in Act Three strains of anti-Semitism—

PALMERS Ah, it's a pity for the old days, Mr Pincher, when your own happy Palmers was young, strong, on top of things. It looks to me as if you let me go too soon. Why, with someone else around, think of the time you'd have for Mr Pluckem! That's the thing about the old days. They're gone….

PINCHER Ah do believe you're raht, Palmers. Ah do, really Ah do….

PALMERS What you need is an assistant!

PINCHER Well, Ah don't know, really Ah don't.

PALMERS Someone young....

PINCHER Mm.

PALMERS And hard-working....

PINCHER Very 'ard t' find, Ah should imadgin, really Ah should.

PALMERS With a sound musical knowledge....

PINCHER Very 'ard.

PALMERS Someone who'd work for even less than I did!

PINCHER Very, *very* 'ard.

PALMERS But why not?

PINCHER You know such a person, Palmers?

PALMERS I probably do....

PINCHER Do you really, Palmers?

PALMERS A delightful boy. Good and honest. No stranger to hard work. And with such a passion for music! What's more I've a feeling he'll soon be looking for work.... You'd do a lot worse, Mr Pincher.... He's just the person, I should say.

PINCHER Well, mah deah, whah don't yer send 'im round, let me 'ave a look at 'im?

A simpler critique is d'Oc's borrowings from the *Oliver!* of Ron Moody's Fagin, and therefore it's another of many asides when I show, in the reluctance of my role – a role foisted on me through my relationship with Eliot – what happened when I phoned the *Besant* editor, pointing out in my best litigious tone that all of the above was copyright material. To *my* knowledge, permission hadn't been granted for its inclusion, in *any* publication (you see what I mean by litigious). *Ms Besant*, I was told, was a highly respected journal, with an important agenda. On the question of copyright, it was a rule of the industry that no permissions need be obtained for the purpose of review – and that applied to *any* work in the public domain.

My riposte might have been that an article whose end was propaganda couldn't be called a review. Instead I said this: 'I have London's best lawyers.'

The second of Megan's two statements, rebuffed by her – they were twisted out of context – 'dealt' with my tendency to shirk responsibility, usually in favour of travel, and exotic travel at that. When that wore thin, impertinent questions pried into my upbringing. It's certainly true that as a boy of ten I listened intently when on a bright frosty morning in front of the blackboard Deidre announced our sabbatical, and a day or two later whisked the pair of us off on a six-week tour of New Zealand. That, on our return, I gave back to the commune as formal travelogue – all a bit hazy now. Day one was damp but mild, an English late November, recorded via my cartridge pen as a drive through tree-hung lanes from the commune out to the London road. Sporadically a shower of yellow leaves glued its strays to the windscreen. The few days after that were a blur of flights and hotel destinations, all in the wrap of the boy's book of wonder I'd taken for the journey, its boldly printed pages having all sorts of insights into the nature of genius, and linking that to the amazing feats of autistic children. It inquired, too, into the possibility of intelligent life in other parts of the universe.

Most but not all of our time we spent on the South Island (the North Island Deidre retired to almost ten years ago). Typical of what we did was a drive to Akaroa, where the near-deserted road threaded a sand and silver shore (the Pacific), while on its other side hills and mountain slopes rolled endlessly on – mile on mile of silky green, wooded intermittently, and cropped by Arcadian sheep. There was a practical purpose to these departures, which I became party to on the road from Dunedin to Te Anau. Te Anau is a lake retreat, where we as tourists remorselessly photographed its domestic architecture. As Deidre explained, a first faint outline she'd left on her drawing board at home was destined to evolve into new housing complexes springing up all over the green fields of England at that time. The developer responsible had in mind retiring ex-colonials, whose last slumbers safe at home were a twilight cradled in brightly painted clapboard, as a reminder of southern climes.

I often reminisced on this, and thought that one day New Zealand would see my return, for the long-term, and perhaps even retirement. I didn't expect, with a first lone pressman camped outside my house, that prospect was quite so imminent.

10

I cannot now clearly recall my last days in England, a little country in the empires of my mind, its remoteness an everlasting night as it crept up symptomatically, then in the lengthening shadows of evening struck with its social terrors. Dark menacing shapes loomed there suddenly, as quick to dissolve and evaporate. I can remember consistently well the petty exchanges, then the crescendo of verbalised threats, precipitating my flight – literally, with Singapore Airlines. Further intimation was an email Daphne fired off from an internet café in Martyrs Field in Canterbury, under the cries and buds of early spring (all views surrounding she described), which I scrolled through on my laptop at home, a machine I had parked on my cocktail bar, and kept there beside a litre bottle of Laphroaig. She was in role, dramatically speaking, rehearsing her newest inclusion in *MMU* (a waif born in earshot of Bow and its bells), and in that guise said

Glad to see our production's causing such a stir,

a view I didn't share, followed by the news that

…alack Globe negs running to delays, so now methinks Kernow project beckons, with summer a-comin' [the summer of 1999]. What chaunce you bookin' Thespian Hoe, where I can do me auditions?

By Kernow she had in mind a working tour of Cornwall, with a band of Celtic troubadours – a point that, diametrically aimed, or so I supposed, inspired further revelations, with an odd pepper of cockney sprinkled on. She'd had an approach from a second-year Falmouth student—

Is thick with me, says 'e, doin' three years' 'ard labour in Theatre and VP. Already plannin' 'is final semester. Bless 'im, 'e witnessed me Plymouth quayside show. Says wouldn't it be nice to close it all art with a tate-are-tate with the author. Name's Conrad Drake. Said I'd pass 'im on t' you.

I noted his contact details, and replied—

I'll get on to Marlon re Thespian Hoe, and get some dates. I'd like to get down there, now that the press have got my London address. Who's this Conrad Drake, and why does he want to speak with me?

'Press' in this instance was a lone reporter, a man I now saw nightly, his hands thrust dejectedly into the depths of his coat pockets. His best option to date was a short walk from the gusty corner of my street, to the ornate old lamppost lighting the line of cars outside my house, a territory he paced to the point of leaving his groove in the flagstones. Sometimes I twitched the lace at my living-room window, or from an aerial vantage stooped to exchange a glance or two. He, tugging at his collar, looked up at me inscrutably. Often I prised apart the slats of my bathroom blind and watched him search his coat for cigarettes. When, with a tired gesture, he'd passed one to his lips, I learned to anticipate the abbreviated action of his lighter, followed by a whirl of bluish smoke as that unbent itself up and away in a tumble of vernal winds. Always I waited until he was out of sight before crossing the street to my bistro, a quaint little Italian place where, if home from work at a decent hour, I liked to have my evening meal.

Then for three nights he disappeared, and possibly a fourth, as I had stayed at the office late. After ten finally, I extinguished the four fluorescent tubes that had flooded my office all day from eight a.m. – a cold harsh light. Somehow I trudged wearily underground, and leaden-limbed raised myself to street-level up the station steps a block away from where I lived. I shambled into the sooty patchwork of my street, and groping with my keys tumbled over the threshold, then climbed the stair to bed. In the morning – which was cold and wet – I succeeded, despite the perfected angle of my shaving mirror, in inflicting a ruddy V asymmetrically on my chin. While searching for the cotton wool, I saw him there again.

An eddy of pale leaves crowned him momentarily, then disintegrated in a breath of wind as, spontaneously, it suddenly changed direction. I watched him make a call on his cell phone, and thought about certain numbers I could dial myself, though the situation had worsened by the time I'd showered, was suited, and was on my way out. Strangely Eliotesque, a Melissa had joined him – she of the *Daily Screech* – a bigbreasted woman camera-slung, and fully equipped with a case of photographic tools. Several shots were made of me, in a hurry for the station, battling to raise an umbrella against the battering wind.

All seemed to be clear again that evening, until, with a lightness in my stride, I strolled across to the restaurant. There, under its soft lights and lulled by recorded lute music, he sat in my usual place, a dish of cubed pineapple and the remains of an aperitif at his elbow. I found a table by the window, its tiny polished surface draped in a pocket handkerchief for tablecloth, where a mess of crumbs and pesto stains, under a glaze of sea salt, had been left with other bits of debris. He joined me immediately, putting down and pushing his business card through the shards of parmesan stencilled half an hour ago around my predecessor's plate. His name was Calvin Poll. His organisation was Harlequin Freelance Copy. Its logo was a pied scarlet and Lincoln green.

Mr Poll I already knew as tall and prone to stoop. At closer quarters, his face was thin and squareish at the jaw, and rurally leathered. His hair, silvered and streaked in outlandish strands of chestnut, he wore unfashionably long. His smile was cynical and knowing.

'Mr Joel. How kind of you to spare the time.'

'Actually I *don't* have time.' To demonstrate that point, I snapped my fingers pertly and summoned a waiter, a willing if sour-looking youth, who watched my mouth and listened very hard to my instructions (here was I, exaggerating every sylla-ble). Not a few moments after that, he cleared and reset the table, bearing in his gift a single serviette and one set of cutlery.

'No problem at all,' said a slit-eyed Mr Poll, who *had* already eaten.

'Then all you want's your bill.'

'That's a bit hasty.'

'What's it exactly you want, Mr Poll?'

'Um, yes, well – problem is, where to begin.' An unlikely innocence had softened his tone.

'Mr Poll.'

'Please do call me Calvin.'

'I have every hope of eating conversation-free. What do you want?'

'Humf – it's what I think *you* will want.'

'All right, Calvin. What do you think that *I* will want?'

It was to do with my sister, Chrissie Keyes.

11

Or I ought to say half-sister. She was the first and only bloom in the second instalment of Martin Keyes's family life – or in melodramatic paper talk, the 'American sibling'. Such anyway was a world of news according to Calvin Poll, a man whose shabby backroom tactics had disrupted the ritual of my dinner gong. There with no sense of how affronted I was he calmly plied the dishonours of his trade.

Sis or Chris, or Chrissie as her mom preferred, graced our planet Earth under the astrological sign of the archer (her birthstone was zircon, diamond in its fire), and was first intro-duced to her English half-brother at only a fortnight old – pink, bawling, cushion-faced. Earl d'Oc had got some work to do, and anyway usually wintered away from home, and that took him from Oregon, where he'd got stock holdings, all the way to Cape Cod, where he and one of his associates had plunged into something in the shipping line. That officially is how he presented his diary, or was how he came to spend a few days overseeing me at Martin's villa, the pair of us having flown and circled together over a steely blue Atlantic, and the US itself, a landmass spreading out infinitely from my window.

And what a villa it was – a kingdom of boyhood memora-bilia, where Martin, a man broad at the shoulders, with tousled jet hair (and so much else I didn't stand to inherit), roamed and romped in the arches and crenellations, or if time allowed chatted amicably with Deidre's friend the earl, most pointedly at poolside. Sometimes I stood alone on the enormous flag-stones laid diagonally, and followed their rhombs from wall to wall. In the vastness of his interiors, in a slant of shadows and naturally cool, I gazed blankly at the same Mexican guitar, hanging on a wall, year after year after year. At twelve I won-dered what was inside the varnished wooden chest at the foot of a stone staircase, and was disappointed to discover thick tablets of computer punch cards, bound with ancient elastic bands (so *no* pirate hoard). I was a teenager when, under the capacious arch of the fireplace, I registered, for the first time, a huge jeroboam filled with dried grasses, and thought how well it looked.

Then there came a kind of detachment in the way I watched, throughout that decade and a half, while the whimsies of third-circle wealth wrought a familiar middle-class Americana all over the life of the man who had been my father – a dollar ideology I had gleaned from movies, mags and jazz bands, not to say the grave authority of presidents and senators, grappling with the cold war, and with an enemy present only as a silhouette. Martin's New World wife was a tennis coach, honey-limbed and hard at the mouth, who in greeting every bright aurora bunched and pinned her reckless hairdo, with its points and wispy vortices, secured at a stroke under the knot of a silk bandanna – all a first discipline that set her on her way, jogging with the sunrise. Martin, I noticed – a man whose powerful upper body glistened under those same friendly rays – did forty vigorous lengths of his pool before his egg-and-muffin breakfast.

Dawning from that penumbral life was Chrissie, with a history all her own, a flower I watched unfold through the rooms she occupied throughout the house. First in that stupendous catalogue was the nursery, of course (it was later a shoe room) – a long narrow gallery adjoining the master boudoir, with an enamelled cot centred on the floor, and a whirr of mobiles overhead. Their vanes were air balloons, and assorted profiles borrowed from the cartoon world of afternoon TV. At three she went to beddy-byes, her brain set sail for sleep on a floating dream of whiteness, in a room whose furniture was foam-filled pillows, with a silken tent shrouding her divan. It was adjacent to Martin's study, who on the magic hour of midnight re-screwed the lid of his fountain pen, and careful to keep that usual boldness out of his tread, looked in and smiled on his cherub's slumbers. At five a whole apartment was assigned to little Princess Keyes – and for the first time she was down on the ground floor, where her bedchamber neighboured her rumpus room. Here – a palace her mom had coloured in with rainbows and fairy lights – a vast overstock swamped her infant troves, with shopfuls of paints, crayons and picture books. From the prompts of childish synecdoche, dried flowers were a forest, and a handful of pebbles the Kansas witch's castle. Her dollies, prams and teddy bears had little houses of their own. And should an adult call, with adult domestic needs, all was catered for in miniature. Wooden pots and pans. A plastic oven with a hob, and knobs and dials that turned, and a broiler. There was a vacuum cleaner too, with a bell that tinkled or tringed as it swept.

When sis was seven, I felt helplessly that had we been full-blooded in our bonding – siblings unalloyed – I might have regretted the sudden loss of interest these transatlantic jamborees had come to mean. I was fourteen by then, moody and self-absorbed, and understood the science of introspection – for me a fruitless gaze on a midwinter vista palely lit by stars. I noted her life of make-believe now extending into an outdoor panorama, with bikes, balls, a pogo stick, pairs of roller blades, a swing, a chute, a brightly ribboned maypole, the full range of junior tennis racquets, and a plastic red wheelbarrow, its wheel a grazed yellow (and spherical), and the family of objects she shovelled in its maw and delivered from niche to niche. When *she* was fourteen I had overcome my misgivings, though now only glimpsed, through a surreptitious veil, the female mystique of Chrissie's early teenage, a private chapter of her life whose pages she kept insistently closed to me, but never entirely out of sight. Such snatches I gleaned saw her dressing table littered with cosmetics – sprays, glosses, all kinds of mascaras, the natural spectrum bottled with her nail varnish – the blue and burgundy festoons across her bed, of jeans or jackets she'd tried but couldn't make up her mind about. There were secret dispatches too, billets-doux delivered through the mail, and somewhere at large a jockey of older admirers.

A few years after that I was summoned to my twenty-third birthday celebration here in that airy expanse of Martin's second family home, where scores of his colleagues and competitors had gathered specially for the occasion, of whom I remember one – a man called McCluskey. He I already knew from glossy flyers that turned up almost everywhere I worked. He was a retrieval specialist in indexed database technology, with a corporation whose HQ was in Phoenix (I say nothing of its logo). He swished away at a last film of ice in a tumbler of lime juice, then gave me his card and told me to send him my company résumé, a little politeness I somehow overlooked, once my return flight had delivered me safely back to the coughs and fogs of London.

The truth is I hadn't adapted well to university life (my university, in a distant northern town), and as a graduate plotted an equally cautious path. The problem was that after Deidre's commune I couldn't adapt to the crowded lecture theatres, or the brash conviviality and social pastimes around the student bar, or even the sheer scale of the library, quiet though it always was. Before long I failed to attend lectures and addresses altogether – even the once-per-semester plenary –

and studied in isolation. Paradoxically, my subject was anthropology. In latter months I carried out these researches under the eaves of a rambling Victorian house, where the view through my small square window was a half-circle of speckled macadam, overhung with the limbs of a pine tree, a spot below me where the other tenants parked their cars.

The regime worked well, and I got my degree. Augmenting that cap and gown were the shares in DoCoTel that Martin, or d'Oc, or one of my fathers, bought on my behalf, and with them a junior partnership – nepotism a final reward for all those years Keyes and I had never had a conversation. One of my first assignments was to Ludgate Hill, where a firm of accountants (in almost permanent metamorphosis, but in those days trading as Pleat Pickwick Pickell) wanted to automate its timesheet system – time meaning fees, fees, fees. As at university, rather than attend unnecessarily lengthy meetings, all a futile waste of time, I delved into how these fees were arrived at manually, then with an analyst on my team designed a computer replacement.

At twenty-three, and a birthday boy, all this was a point of subtle if unexpected conjunctions, which for the first time pressed half-brother and sis into mild exchanges on the royal engagement – i.e., between Diana Spencer and Charles the Prince of Wales, both of whom I'd tugged my forelock to through meetings via the earl. A whey-faced Chrissie Keyes, who now kept out of the California sun, and as far as she could from the tennis courts her mother jogged to every day, dreamed the narcotic dream that press and TV had drugged our respective populations with, with a daily shower of media fairy dust. I could not help but notice that alongside Chrissie's other wall-to-ceiling posters – in span an exotic Hendrix to plain Joan Armatrading – she'd pinned or pasted up the first cycle devoted to the royal couple. Here were those frumpy get-ups, a gauche bambina hairdo, and a pre-society charm as the first mythopoeia surrounding that very doomed life of a princess-to-be. A rakish Charles never shook off that stiffness borne with his breeding and military wardrobe.

Into this a toad-eyed Calvin Poll sought to interpose himself, in showing how fully he knew – his secret sign those pressmen's confidential winks – how much of a scorching I gave my sister all those years ago. She was a girl of fifteen, besotted with House of Windsor memorabilia – tea towels, key fobs, china cups and mugs, jigsaws, pretty soaps, a drawerful of socks, a catalogue of fashion accessories I am too detached or middle-aged to name. I observed with all my old-world weariness that come the end of July, with preparations for the rite itself – an event that took place in St Paul's Cathedral, with a televised ceremony seen by hundreds of millions – Ludgate Hill was not the best location to commute to every day. In a linguistics according to the UK tabloids, this made me fiercely anti-royal, and in particular Diana – a thesis 'fully' scoped in a centrefold piece I had advance warning was about to appear. The deal was a Mephistophelean Calvin Poll, here offering exclusive rights to reply – and what did I think of that?

I told him to find another restaurant.

12

I had not seen Chrissie since Martin's funeral in 1994, though we had spoken on the phone several times since. Ed McCluskey was among the cortege, whom Chrissie was first to thank for the kind words he delivered. It struck me as touching too, Ed's personal recall given public voice in recapping his and Keyes's early computer days, where all that now remained of the problems they'd shared was a wodge of memoranda, a written history of personal professional musings. Incredible to think of that as the last live trace of thoughts they'd exchanged, Martin's office here and Ed's in Arizona.

There were other dark suits I met and shook hands with, not intending to eavesdrop, though that did happen, if only accidentally. First time was in the nave, when somehow I'd obscured myself behind a pillar, and again with impulse later as I crouched to tie my shoe. I formed to a shape easy to overlook, darkly dressed, and smothered in the green shade of a water butt. In both instances, I hushed to the whispers ravelled around me, and got the consensus of what the deceased's ambition had been, and how in the end he'd failed. Lurking in all these undertones was a thing the company referred to as 'Tripos', the name a chilling invocation of Martin's bachelor degree – his BSc (Hons), Cambridge. This later incarnation was, I discovered, a trademark title for the operating system a world of interconnected computers would one day use, an endeavour beaten into second, third place, nowhere (not to overlook Steve Jobs) when citizen Gates and his Microsoft took the laurel, the plaudits, and almost all the cash. The shock of it killed Martin Keyes, and so deprived me – a disaffected son – of any last opportunity to cross that internalised Atlantic always existing between us.

13

Days after that liaison with Poll, where a good bottle was wasted, and I aborted my ravioli, the *Sunday Herald Express* carried the centrefold he'd promised, its long diatribe denouncing my anarchistic, anti-patriotic youth. The case was all but proved, in the bolster of contemporary photos, showing the world a shifty Humfrey Joel, now seedy and middle-aged. Take a look here, at how suspiciously he keeps that coat collar turned up against intrusion – or was it the wind and rain? Well what about this? His peevish glance through the glassy front of Carlo's restaurant, a posh, swanky place for toffs. Not a surprise perhaps, with Melissa out on the pavement, constantly clicking away. So on to the clincher – two eyes burning with menace through the slyly parted slats of his window blinds. So that was it!

In the days that followed, a horde of hacks and paparazzi commuted between my office, my doorstep at home, and whatever performance of *New King Palmers* Daphne had underway. The result was a barrage of idiotic headlines and a scrapbook heady with *non sequiturs*, the choicest of which amuse me only now, here in the South Pacific. Instance the *Sunday Mail Living Magazine*, whose editorials clung to those atrocious schools of therapy—

Humfrey Joel, a pathetic little man who never found it in his heart to love…

or *UK Today*, the voice of political reason—

…curious to note that here in our enthusiasm for all things

European, Joel can think some tinpot little Englanders in the end will save the day – one last cavalry charge…

the contrast to which I chortle over now in *Goss*, whose rare intervening print, stitched between galleries of sumptuous colour plates, has all but a blue rosette for watermark on every page—

> Humfrey Joel, a man of his country, or another affront to common sense? Know this, Mr Joel: the shires are unanimous, and treat scandal as scandal – you who dare to suggest our future king confuses treason and the national interest.

Nor did the odd affirmation help, as in the vaguely liberal arts and culture survey (not known to me till then), calling itself *The Protean Times*—

Two cheers for democracy!

A comprehensive list of other journals adding to the clamour is as follows, whose summaries of Eliot's play I show as best I can: *ArtKart* (gentlemen playwrights should really wipe their specs before they venture out); *Celebrity* (for we see in its author how ultimately self-destructive spite and venom are); *Bazaar* (sad Humfrey's earl-y play); *Lifestyle* (we find it isn't *de rigueur*); *Fourth Wall* (it's Laurel but is it moral?); *Proscenium* (dear oh dear); *Broadcasting News* (when all's said and done, we much prefer the Morton-Dimbleby axis); *Club Scene* (a Diana stripped of what she most was: human and humane);

Escort (don't go to this one bearing arms. You'll kill someone); *Culture Now* (hey, mom, a provincial type has just crashed through the plate glass); *Peninsula* (can't see the point frankly); *Megalopolis* (like blood sports it's not our cup of cocoa, but aren't there *important* things to debate?); *In Women* (it's why we have to say the war is never won); *Hi!* (like it's like wild); *Lady Jane* (the inscrutable Humfrey Joel!); *London Lit Bin* (do we really have to write this stuff up?); *Logos as Factum* (no lack of opportunity here, all lost alas to confusion); *London Lit Online* (global resistance creeps into the theatre); *Feel Good* (feel bad); *Operatic* (Signor Berio might have had a field day); *Practical Public Relations* (it won't exactly help with EU integration); *Psychic Times* (*is* Humfrey Joel a living recovered memory?); *Writers' Rostrum* (yes, we think he is); *Zine Dream* (and so, actually, do we).

The conversation got to the Other place, and was given amused gravitas by Baroness Barr of Quintin Kynaston – or Serenity, Earl d'Oc's niece. She was known to a TV public for her pacific, liberal views, and had spent a political lifetime in the fight against international money laundering. For the benefit of her fellow red-benchers, she examined these deceptions with her usual sharp analysis. She addressed the House circuitously, via the Lord Chancellor – or so I'm told – he with a wry smile and an elbow to the woolsack. She remembered Humfrey Joel as a shy, polite young man, more inclined to listen while others debated, rather than enter the debate himself, and not given to treachery and betrayals against the people he loved. She couldn't imagine I'd written her uncle's play.

14

I phoned Chrissie at her office in New York, where she worked in the *parfumerie* trade, long having reached a giddy cliff-top, and making easy rungs – just as Martin had predicted – up through its tiers of middle management. Her secret was, you didn't need to think of it as high-gloss or an occupation. With that as a maxim Chrissie led her team, a group of ardent people. Like her they set about their work with unassailable vitality. Headquarters was a dove-grey building in a street in the lower sixties, off Madison Avenue, where you sometimes saw, under the wash of autumn skies, windows tinctured with azure – a phenomenon I once idly noted from a handful of brochures sent my way.

In answer to my probes, she remembered a despondent-looking newspaperman, one of many roughish beasts who swam in and out of her launch suites. 'You know, Humf, showed no interest whatever in our product lines.' Ostensibly sis was a target for his how-to-be-successful column, a new direction for him, and a copy of which she never subsequently saw. It demanded all kinds of biographical information, collated in a novel way over several pages graded into tick boxes, attached to which was a list of stupid questions: Would you say your attitude to science / movie stars / the stock market / fast food / royalty / Wall Street / French cuisine / the free market / casual sex is a) friendly, b) indifferent, c) hostile; what about mother, father, siblings?

What mess had oozed out from this into all corners of our world of reportage had not prevented *Practical Public Relations* from broaching *its* explication, its best minds approaching that task equipped with blunted instruments (Fleet Street's surgical toolkit not having had an overhaul in decades). One surprising result of all that hard work was a Sister Keyes and Brother Joel, who by the uniqueness of their nativity 'would seem' to emphasise both the repulsive and attractive poles in the special US-UK relationship.

Astonishingly that gave Matthew Sells just the courage he had so far lacked with the various drafts of his resignation letter, which now as he kneaded them together, into a single unitary whole, assumed the metal of invective, and ended in an article published by the *London Review of Books*. His premise as professional in our industry (that 'our' was his word) appeared to be that no sane person ever invested in 'literature', and therefore a buoyant book market was wholly dependent on selling the public important names in authorship, making *his* function (at least in his Leader days) no more than minor, if well-rehearsed, in the service of a controlling cognoscenti. These latter, a laboratory-coated gentlefolk, determined what those names would be (long string of Booker winners he could point to, as gore in his palms). Somehow the tactless Humfrey Joel had blundered in on this, adopting as his ruse the fictitious Earl d'Oc (a name not appearing in any peerage listing Sells could point to), or a vehicle by which a naïve and hapless playwright – or rather his ragbag *New King Palmers* – stood to be packaged, marketed, sold. Thanks for the compliment.

Sells next took his forensic brush to that eleven-page introduction I had last seen under a pile of paper debris in his intray, and pointed to infelicities that had seeped from my pen, as evidence of the deception I was trying to bring about. Regarding the d'Ocs' involvement in the Vetsera cover-up, I had written this (about the coachman, transporting her corpse)—

He lashed at the horses (for this is a kind of fiction, with all the embellishment that entails), and had as his sole thought his destination – only his destination – and how to accomplish that without mishap.

What by chance I'd enclosed in innocent parentheses, according to Justice Sells was damning and incriminating. He issued an open invitation to historians everywhere, asking of this –

The emperor had spent tranquil moments unrolling the scrolls of his signature onto one of his crested documents…

– *did* Franz Joseph really authenticate his letters in that way – and would anyone like to comment on that crest?

Nor is it satisfactory for Humfrey Joel to disavow authorial ambitions (as he frequently does), when he had written passages like this –

I was shown to, and read, one of Princess Diana's many chroniclers, his 'true' revelations a muddled exercise typographically, a world of orthographic gaffes, and so many missed opportunities punctuation-wise…

– because it's clearly self-contradictory. And it was no good trying to pretend that the play wasn't mine by forgetting the sequence of scenes—

For the record, a scene she often chose was that culminating in the lutenist's song from Act Two….

One last, conclusive point came with that made-up name again, when Eliot d'Oc was almost an anagram of DoCoTel, the absent 'I' being precisely that (the absent Humfrey Joel). I would have to say, Matthew, that is ingenious – yet what kind of a friend would I be in revealing Eliot's real identity?

Lucinda assured me that none of this should hamper the project in any way at all. She also told me Sells now worked for a tiny house in Banbury, its specialisms numismatics and military history. I made the mental note that if ever I was passing through I would put a breeze block through his window.

15

My first suspicion that Leader *had* lost interest was Lucinda's polite deflections whenever I called (she was chairing a meeting, or stuck in a subway, or attending a family funeral). Nor did I make genuine progress with Sells's replacement, a spiky-limbed ladyboy with limpid brows and a preference for black: black tights, black skirts, a black Alice band. My eleven-page introduction to Eliot's play he failed to grasp as anything other than a copy-edit exercise, arguing endlessly over the proper place of em and en dashes in today's publishing world, or whether for example Baron Krauss deserved the full dignity of that leading capital B, a leap into the upper alphabetic register a democratic age really ought not to connive at. I asked him, do I *look* like a socialist? Prior to me, his brief had been twofold: celebrity chefs (much time he wasted in TV studios, or dashing from dinner to dinner, the venue small fashionable restaurants owned by his TV authors); and popular science, where selected book titles were: *Really Fermat's Last?*, *The Golden Mean Explained*, *Cryptography, From the Vigenère to Fast Computers*, and *Pharaoh's Mathematics Man*. After those heady heights, his heart really wasn't in my project.

It dragged on, yet with Daphne emailing daily I saw an escape into Thespian Hoe. I might have to thank her, I said, for a few days there, a jaded Humf looking on in holiday mood, *NKP*'s first mistress hard at work, cracking whipcords or sparking the dark blue air over the heads of her troupe. All good in principle, though getting away at all involved some clever bedtime subterfuge, now that the press was camped outside and watching every move. I called one of my hand girls and watched from the window as she emerged from a taxi (a taxi throbbing taxi), a girl silken with cleavage, in a skirt that rode the firmness of her rump, and the mask of midnight crafted in her mascara – innocent prey as she wriggled across the sidewalk and through that jostle of press and paparazzi, they with their hoots and catcalls, she with her boots and hand tools.

Huge favours in £10 rolls did I ply her with, helping her shed her footwear, then escorted her up the stair into the disrepute of my bedchamber. Here I eased off her only flimsy outer garment, then sat her down beside me in the fringe of my bedside lamp, we two stately, there among the satin pillows heaped across my mattress. I showed her the bottle of Bacardi, where the popcorn was, how to master the TV remote, or if she was bored some fashion magazines I'd got. Her instructions were, not to extinguish the light, which must remain low, until after the midnight chime. In the meantime Humf slipped out and groped through the damp night and darkness, scaling his back fence and wading through the neighbour's sodden grass. I stepped out smartly into the next street, where that same taxi throbbing taxi waited. At seven a.m. on the following day, my decoy left – dishevelled, damp from the shower, and void of make-up – yet wiggling her rear for the press (cue for further caterwauls). I checked my watch, then slumbered on to the croop of wood pigeons going about their chores at Hoe.

16

It was almost my birthday, which made me recall the first time I was here for that event. I was twelve. For that occasion Deidre had brought the commune with us, asking me to script, with Eliot's help, the legend of William Tell, as a forty-minute act. My classmates had the job of putting it on, and were given Eliot's newly refurbished theatre. There was interest from some of his weekend guests.

I was given latitude with the source text Deidre had chosen – a libretto after our music class. I ascribed to the tyrant Gessler a 'vast' empire, touching the Alps and stretching to the Loire. That idea I'd arrived at from the canton skiing holidays Deidre took me on, and the interest she had in Swiss chalet architecture, and our drives through France, where she considered (and rejected) relocating the commune. Some mothers weren't opposed, but a consensus was never reached.

Tell I made mercantile, at odds with the price rigging and rules of trade Gessler ran his empire by – this an evil man but blessed with a dark-eyed daughter (Matilda). Matilda has fallen in love with Arnold, a Swiss patriot and shop steward in the barrel factory Tell owns and runs. Gessler sends his squaddies in for the rescue, who pillage the countryside and deflower its elder daughters. With Tell's help, Arnold and Matilda flee into hiding, an act of provocation a tempestuous Gessler must correct. His soldiers embark on indiscriminate swathes of genocide, laying waste the land and shattering the Swiss economy. When Arnold hears that his father is one of those slain, he swears he will have his revenge. Meanwhile the cantons come together to throw off the yoke of Gessler's penny-pinching empire.

Unrest rises to its climax a few months later, in the market square in Altdorf. It's the anniversary of Gessler's rule over Switzerland, and the people he has long oppressed are told to doff their caps to images made of himself placarded in the streets. That, predictably, is a step too far for Tell, who has arrived in Altdorf with his son Jemmy, and is busy trading barrels with a salter. He refuses to make obeisance, at which point Gessler appears and orders Tell to shoot an apple from Jemmy's head. When Tell succeeds, the next bolt in his bow is aimed at Gessler, whose execution is the catalyst for Switzerland to rise up in rebellion. In an instant, theatrically speaking, a whole nation throws off its oppressor, and begins work on a new economic infrastructure, founded on clocks, confectionery and a liberalised banking system, all of it underpinned by an awesome sense of independence.

Eliot's guests for Humfrey's birthday weekend arrived under an inauspicious sky, its dark crystal a collision of muddy-coloured clouds, in a rage with the wind, the rain intermittent, and brief glimpses of the sun's rays. The hills were hyacinthine in a rapidly changing light. Thespian Hoe outdoors was a filmy green to the water's edge, where our mooring's tan-coloured lifebuoy appeared a dark shade of orange in the gloom. Some folk came up by the River Yo, though mostly people came by road or rail, with the prime minister chauffeur-driven (here in a rare conjunction with his chancellor). I met them both under the fringes of a sodden, dripping wisteria, Harold in almost permanent conflict with the wind, coping to keep his pipe alight. These were difficult times for him and for England, with unemployment rising, and the unions disputatious.

Eliot had his open palm to the small of my back, and propelled me forward gently, where in that parliament around me I explained what meaning the legend of William Tell had now, now that I'd reinvented it. Inadvertently the chancellor had planted his feet in a last remaining clump of pwimwoses, though remarked wittily that had the convergences of history given *us* Switzerland's neutrality, *his* job wouldn't be quite so hard. It began to rain ferociously, so we trotted indoors, where the three of them hid themselves in Eliot's study, and I returned to my birthday cards. One was from Chrissie, which she'd made herself, from a photograph of her and her ma, dwarfed by and in the shade of a Sequoia, with captions added in red and blue crayon.

17

Daphne arrived, then for a reason I never understood returned immediately to London, then arrived a second time, disappearing again after three to four days auditioning for parts.

'Don't forget Conrad Drake,' she said.

'When's he coming?'

'Day after tomorrow.'

I had to postpone that meeting when, with Daphne's arrival a third time, it was with press and paparazzi in tow, who unbeknown to her had hired a transit van and followed her little black car, down the M5 and beyond. One of Eliot's old retainers, who still came in to cut the grass, helped me get away, taking me by motor launch – under cover of darkness – up the Yo to Middle Hoe, a busy market town where the local trains connected with the London line. Daphne assumed – and I didn't enlighten her – that I was heading back to work. Not so. After a spate of newspaper stories speculating on Humfrey's nights debauching a Soho tart, my partners saw it as in their interests that I stay in hiding, not emerging till the next public scandal had paled mine into history. Needless to say, I couldn't get hold of Lucinda.

I spent what was left of the spring and summer months decamping from one rented cottage to the next, where wadded with leaflets and listings, and testing the limits of operatic disguise, I followed Daphne's vanguard over the wilds of Kernow, from theatre to quayside to open-air performance space, and on to a tour of England (itinerary below). First was an outdoor illumination, where I came as a sandy-haired curate, all good will and beatific grins. In a private hut in Tavistock, I arrived as a visiting Pole, tetchy and intractable, an émigré commanding very little English, and tweaking everlastingly the goatee I had grown. In a civic hall not a few miles from there, that goatee had bloomed Viking-style, a large man garbed in a tee shirt, and noxious with cider. In St Ives I chose a 1950s tuxedo, a starched shirt and cummerbund, and having gelled my hair and put on an outlandish pair of spectacles I hired a limousine to take me to and from the night's performance. Once I went as a newspaperman myself, and was asked by another drudging in that trade how one began, writing up the sensational Madame Zemlinsky.

'Hablo un poquito de inglés,' I told him, and immediately went off to order a paella.

A good vacation I enjoyed – a country summer that tanned my flesh and bleached my hair – though of course all avenues mazing the human conurbation are measured to an anti-climactic end. I drove back home in a hire car through a piquant wind and the mists of autumn, and stole into my office late on a Saturday night, that bright beautiful city below me boozing or sexing itself, or tucked up safely under the waves of floss oozing from every TV. On my desk were the usual memos, my diary – a hundred days crossed out, cancelled – and an album of postcards Daphne had sent from her Cornish expedition. The first I picked up, and fingered nonchalantly, pictured a dark-looking gig entering Looe Harbour at sunset, under a pale yellow sky, with dwellings in miniature crowded together on a tree-fringed hillside. One had to feel sympathy for that solitary craft, as it scythed its way through a depth of shadow massing in the evening atmosphere. Another, from the same place more or less, bore the legend 'Banjo Pier' – that pier a large, circular, brick-and-stone lookout, wreathed in purple flecks reflected in the water. Hereabouts ore was once shipped and fish were landed for the multitudes.

I had skirted that coast myself, in flight from one sleuth or other, and now remembered vividly a day in Polperro Harbour, where under its pleasure boats nestled together, their colours – reds, whites, blues, a tawny – the water was liquid rainbow. These were the features two passing tourists wanted me to photograph, the pair as props for foreground, urging their camera into my innocent hands. They'd have, they thought, as a backdrop, those pastel-painted cottages banked up the terraced streets – and of course, I did my best to oblige. Here too Daphne drew my attention to something I hadn't seen – for in taking the ferry you chanced, among other things, on what was once a dwelling owned by Daphne du Maurier, tucked away riverside in the shade of half a dozen beech trees. Nor did Daphne overlook less celebrated souls, marvelling, as her homage to china clay, at those who worked its industry, where now there were only abandoned pits that the skies had filled with rain. She reserved something similar for tin, with a chimney in silhouette atop a hillside.

On the reverse side of a card from a dreamed-up 'Roseland Peninsula', its central motif a crenellated tower, and plentifully soaked in sunshine, Daphne had written: 'I woz 'ere.' ''Ere' was a wooded coomb, with subtropical shrubs. In Truro she had photographed the honey-hued houses in a district known as Lemon Street, and in Trelissick Gardens she and her troupe staged all three acts enveloped by camellias (I was there, as a curate).

I was about to stuff the whole wodge into my jacket pocket, yet paused with a card that showed me Helford from the air, its river snaking through a gently undulating countryside, and again with a laurel maze at Glendurgan, and yet once more with a large rock in silhouette that Daphne had selected at the mouth of a cove in Kynance. She posed for tourists on St Michael's Mount, and in boarding a ferry (the *Scillonian III*), someone posed for her. 'Drank here,' she said (the Admiral Benbow, whose interior heaved with nautical artefacts), 'and here I almost shed my cloth and danced to the moon' (a stone circle, of lichen-coated granite). Logan's Rock was cliffs and a sandy cove under a purplish theatrical light, in whose Minack

Theatre she received three ovations plus floral bouquet. There were caramel sunsets, spits of land, a sooty reddish orange sky, a hillside fort, shoreline surf, a terrace of tiny cottages, Fistral Beach, wind farms, an ancient Mesolithic site, and two different views of St Enodoc's Church. On every quayside, human actions looked out at me eerily frozen by the camera (fishermen half-bent over their nets), and in other instants ferns, brooks, stone walls, late sunshine, rickety fence posts, churchyard crosses with intricate scroll- and plait-work. Every time I shuffled the cards distinctive rocky outcrops found their way to the top.

All that nostalgia soon had its oppositions, when from an envelope I casually unsealed – addressed FAO Humfrey Joel, and less than a fortnight old – a letter from Alexis Jeepe, that blond, bouffant, incisive *News Insight* host, whose nocturnal apparatus was a late-hour scheduling and the might of the BBC. Would I be interviewed, he asked, about this intriguing play I'd penned, now the subject of so much media furore. I emailed him promptly, pointing out that his premise or terms of reference were wrong, and that provided he gave me advance notice of his questions, I'd be pleased and proud to talk about Eliot's play. When, some days after this, his list of questions arrived, there were so many superficial assumptions underpinning them I insisted he couch them in more objective terms. Jeepe's only reply was his live conquistadoring some nights later, when his viewers were gravely informed that the reclusive Humfrey Joel, though invited to discuss his work, had declined to do so, and so instead a panel of arts *apparatchiks* would do that job for him. The first was a hideous feminist. The second was a seedy male, an academic blessed with a roving vocabulary but no matching agility of mind. The third in this trio was an up-and-coming *farceur*, who therefore spoke good gospel. Their conclusion seemed to be – and they were by no means unanimous in this – that I had somehow garbled the whole postmodern ethos for the sake of some very public deception, this being a blurring of my own identity with that of Earl Eliot d'Oc (who informed critics agreed was a fictional character). All I can say is this: postmodernism is already a garbled ethos.

I called Daphne frantically every day at Thespian Hoe, until by some miracle she returned there briefly and picked up the phone. We agreed I had to get away.

'Next week the circus moves to Tewkesbury,' she said. 'Meet me there. Oh, and try me on my cell phone.'

'I have been. You must be out of range.'

Players Played

1

The thoughts I'd had on Eliot's 'note on staging' located that as the first possible cipher penned for his friends at opposite ends of the Tunnel. I had changed only the wording, as that would eliminate whatever crossword clues were there. I'd kept as his play's setting the King's court, and pilgrimage to it from Harlesden, NW10. That was not a part of London I had passed through – and I don't know that Eliot had – though according to my London pocket guide I lived in an adjacent grid reference.

I left untouched the opening scenes' emphasis on the hunting season, in its flirtation with an England approximated to the late twentieth century, the chronological congeries I shared with the play's co-authors. I left intact the visual pun – that imagery and costume culled from the court of Gloriana – having reasons of my own to reprise and underscore its symbolic meaning. I was in agreement with the d'Oc-Dicto focus on King Chads's as a life circumscribed by precedent, which as dramatic backdrop was the concretisation of the tradition and ritual our half-modern state is rooted in. It's a debatable point that the English are a reflection of their two worlds – the old and the new – with significant numbers besotted by pageantry – staged as that is – and therefore open to confrontation by their polar opposites, those resurfacing periodically with stern republican talk and contesting loudly anomalies like the Act of Settlement. This might have been down to d'Oc's personal relationship with the Prince of Wales, but paradoxically it's King Chads only who sheds his courtly encumbrances, the one royal who has faced up fully to the crisis of his reign, and has formed a plan to steer his future heirs through the mires of political change.

Or is this d'Oc encouraging his friend to retire into private life, with the monarchy dissolved? I don't have an answer, though it's worth noting that, conversely (as now we're back to the play, back to *New King Palmers*), his Chancellor and Defence and Foreign Secretaries have slid at the same rate in the opposite direction, as *they* take on the exteriors of a Cecil or a Walsingham (Eliot's examples). They cannot see those who elect them into office as anything other than economic units, where politics is a trade in human flesh, amorphous populations bound to a mercantilism newborn as a corporate English feudalism, and held to it by demands on the waged. Fully blinkered at the close of the third and final act, the scheme they concoct is no more imaginative than the many like it our history is littered with.

That apart, the play I am happy to attribute to the Eliot-Dicto partnership – not that I gave Daphne any information to the contrary, of this or any other change.

O Fortuna….

2

I rattled off a golden mint for the Bangladeshi driver I hired, in the dead of night, to drive me west on the motorway, then up – with no stop for coffee or *petit pain* – on an A road skirting Swindon – through the yellow limestone and deserted streets of Cirencester – out on a further stretch of motorway – remorselessly to Tewkesbury, Plantagenet battleground. I review these notes from the haven of Remuera, halfway round the world, and don't care to check that I have remembered that route correctly. I said goodbye to my chauffeur by the Old Baptist Chapel, and he, bewildered and newly enriched, scratched his head and rubbed his chin, with the assuaging words that if ever I should need a car….

'Go now. Loose talk costs lives. Get on back to west London. You've family, I guess….'

I made my way into Church Street, and stood at the half-timbered frontage of its Bell Hotel, where Daphne had kept to her quarter-hourly vigil, and appeared in the porch presently, in a long coat over her pyjamas. With formality, I lightly kissed her cheek. She led the way and lit the stairs with a pen torch – an ascent with gently creaking shrieks at a bottom, a middle, an upper step. Her room was a single, and it meant I had to sleep – after an hour of rebellious talk – hunched in a chair by the writing desk, a cold, troubled drifting in and out. There followed that same repetitive pattern till a dawn greyness filtered through the thin fabric of the curtains, which after restless denials I drew back on a twitter of birds – on a morning filled with sunshine. I watched and waited for Daphne to wake, but she stretched only, arms and legs luxuriant. I cast round the room, at her bag un-zipped on the floor, half-emptied of its clothes; at the few watercolours hung on the walls. The one above her bedstead showed a pew and stone wall in the Saxon Odda's Chapel, just a few miles away, as the hotel brochures were yet to inform me. Another was a sweet bay (*Laurus nobilis*) in a Mediterranean setting. There were tea-making things.

'You okay, Humf? You were behaving very oddly….'

'Ah, no, yes, good morning! You first for the shower. I'll go and book a separate room.'

I breakfasted on boiled egg and a slice from a granary loaf, toasted and lightly spread with salted butter. Daphne I expect had grape juice followed by a bowl of muesli, and an Americano coffee. At eleven we had our first secret meeting, at a dark table in a vacuumed corner of the bar, where we were served tea and finger biscuits. She showed me her itinerary, resumed yesterday, Wednesday, three nights here, then thirteen days in a zigzag straddling middle England, her run for the month ending in Southampton – fourteen performances in total. She explained, the theatre here had a proscenium arch, with a full fly tower and counterweighted system. She'd business there in twenty minutes or so – I could join her if I wished – a short walk to the High Street, and a building I couldn't miss: its brick and window frontage, its modern façade, its two glass doors, doubled etc. I'd last seen full rehearsals at the end of the Epsy-Ibert era, personnel she had since replaced by a motley gathered west of Hoe, through a network of regional theatre groups. Her troupe she'd baptised La Trouvaille. Her first problem had arisen, to do with her present Zemlinsky, who in a caterwaul of hoots and whistles was treated to roses thrown at her feet at each curtain call in Hereford. Since then she'd begun to overplay her part. I wasn't there for Daphne's corrective, a session with just these two – director and directed. Instead I set out, at a few minutes after noon, when I saw, on the pavement outside the Abbey Hotel, a man in a battle-grey fedora and a raincoat almost to his ankles. The brim of his hat lifted briefly as he lit a cigarette, revealing, in a glimpse, a sharp nose, narrow eyes, a pocked complexion. I saw him again that night, in the theatre foyer queuing for his ticket, his presence unnerving enough that I left at the end of the second act.

I told Daphne I thought all that old trouble had started again, or hadn't ended.

'Don't worry.'

'Easy for you to say.'

But. I liked the new way she did her hair, and the fact that her loss of weight, and my gain, didn't impede our new rapport. I paid for the rooms wherever we stayed, insisting that hers should always have a king-size bed and garden views.

3

To an extent she had tamed Madame Z, whose name – Michaela Anchovy – had been listed seventh in the programme notes, and had risen to third. I gather she'd abandoned minimum pay and the farm shop where, for eighteen months, she'd worked, that being an accredited organic in a prime location off the road to St Just. It sold sides of beef and local wine. After an hour's speculation Michaela joined those first few to enlist in Daphne's band, still to be birthed as the raffish La Trouvaille (Daphne mentioned other lucky finds, or see below). Anchovy agreed to the tour on the strength of a campervan, which was owned by Melvyn Fish, and on a strict driver roster split between the three others she shared it with, who were Star (the said Melvyn Fish), Lady Michael (Astoria Abricot), and Erato Electric, whose slim role saw her double as servant, reveller, courtier, and so on (Letitia Columbine). Daphne drove her little black car – I don't remember, a Fiat – and offered passenger space to the simpatico Chads (Monty Gargoyle, a retired vet), who supplied regular payments in the hundreds, the first coming when she scrutinised a bill for thirty quid, the small price to pay for having shattered the sleep of Penpillick, where in a cobbled yard she'd had the exhaust fixed. Daphne, who went for frequent walks in the woods, wherever we went, was forced to sit in the prompt box, with her A4 script now secretly under my stamp, when a prompter wasn't otherwise available. It was a necessary task, because Gargoyle – once a vet to the farming community – had a tendency to forget his lines.

Since Hereford a reinvigorated Z had begun to overdo her dealings with Palmers. She was unbendingly forthright as to how she saw him, as a man of easy prey. The full epithet, as one of Eliot's jokes – not I imagine fully appreciated by most audiences – is Palmers Ltd, as I must have said, and was played by Andrew Venezuela. Palmers is a pro-monarchy entrepreneur, and is a loud advocate of the most ambitious of Chads's initiatives – viz., the social rehabilitation of lost young men like Star, who are without education, without obvious talent, and without guidance. Z, with her little tent and trestle table, and never far from her crystal ball and her Tarot cards (her Rider pack is courtesy Trouvaille company coffers), sees *him* as material too. By now she's managed to allow her sneers, looks and asides to degenerate into pantomime, and didn't appreciate the trek into Tewkesbury, *before noon*, to have these faults pointed out. And didn't Daphne know, the van on its campsite, plugged into the main and topping up its other fuels, was a good half-mile off the bus route, plus her laundry didn't get done, or not on its own. I was asked to look for signs of improvement in Friday's performance, and got to the box office a few strides ahead of Taylor Ess, the name I heard uttered by that spook in a fedora, here to collect the ticket he'd previously booked by phone. Nervously I took my seat, and did my best to follow Z closely through her opening scene. Ostensibly that is centred on Palmers, the tall, neutral-sounding Andrew Venezuela, stuffed to the gills with moneybags, and keen to launch his business partner Star on the next phase of a glittering career. As that involves first flirtations with royalty, I thought it possible there were elements of dialogue the earl had reshaped for his *éminences grises* across *La Manche*, so I had reshaped again. Instance—

1 REVELLER To be honest, I'm getting fed up with all this Republic talk.

2 REVELLER I'm surprised to hear you say that – you always spouting off opinions. There's a rumour going round that the glorious Republic has already been born.

1 REVELLER What, you mean Chads has sold his shares in the Royal Household Plc, and retired to one of his methane farms….

2 REVELLER Nothing quite so dramatic. You have to read past his divorce, or what is said in the better sort of rag. Some are hinting he's reached an accommodation with the EU.

1 REVELLER That's all wishful thinking. I can't see His Majesty's Government ever agreeing to hand the whole lot over – Crown Jewels and all. Those blasted bureaucrats in Brussels!

LANDLORD What's your opinion, Mr—

PALMERS Palmers. The name's Palmers. Here's my card [*hands him business card*]. Personally I can't imagine the

King, what with all his generous initiatives, ever retiring from public life.

1 REVELLER I don't call unveiling a few plaques here and there on a wind turbine, or a field blooming with organic courgettes, or stocking his bathroom cabinet with herbal remedies, 'generous' exactly, *or* much of an 'initiative'.

Every eleventh note has been sharpened by me (sorry, that should read 'every eleventh word is replaced by a well-known phrase or cliché'). I have Letitia Columbine to thank for much of that approving laughter I heard rumbling round me in Tewkesbury's Friday-evening audience. Oh, and by the way, Daphne, Michaela had damped the melodrama—

3 REVELLER Why are you so sure he's carrying so much cash?

ZEMLINSKY Because he works that caged canary strictly COD. I've followed them from Harlesden: every day that fat man just gets fatter.

4 REVELLER My Uncle Ollie had an illness just like that – made him balloon up something chronic. How d'you know it ain't that?

ZEMLINSKY Look, the only medical condition Mr Palmers there suffers is greed. You'll never see him out of that coat – it's custom-made and stuffed with euros.

I have insight into the life of the commercial adventurer, and can understand why she'd like to relieve him of his cash, the euro a good speculative currency, and not a fit mechanism for the Union's second leaguers. In her train are the two tabloid journalists, whose narrow interest is the King's divorce, and the casual observation that with the departure of Princess Moon, and the last of her wardrobe off in some pantec, the vacancy Z should fill is that of Astrologer Royal. A violet light picked out Anchovy centre-stage. That proposition she thought about without, this time, recourse to pantomimic introspection. A more important truth was the one expressed by Andrew Venezuela, who said he found it hard to play Palmers as someone blind to the merit of cheques or bonds or credit cards, the role demanding stamina, lugging all those moneybags through Acts One and Two, and to his nemesis in Act Three.

The republican debate I cannot begin to contemplate in a European context, and after the show rather than slip back-stage I left by one of the fire exits.

4

I left Daphne sleeping on Saturday morning, her bouquet of lilies still in the silver bucket the hotel had provided. The champagne bottle, now empty, was on its side on the writing desk, and beside it was a flute upended (mine). I showered and left without breakfast, and found an internet café a few streets away, on the site of a water mill in an early stage of renovation. Its interior, cramped, whitewashed, and modern in its lighting, was supervised by a curly-haired soubrette, helpful if verbally not forthcoming. I paid my due in coins at the desk, and was placed at a station near the window, with a pass code she clattered in on my behalf – an impressive precision of key-strokes. I was allotted twenty minutes, enough time to read my email, though I hadn't expected the machine to be as slow as it was. A thin mist had descended on the river, where from a mooring a small boy expertly skimmed pebbles across its surface, from a pile he'd crammed to a bulge in his trouser pocket. The next time I looked up Taylor Ess was standing outside at the window, in his long coat, and fedora, the brim of which he pushed up half an inch, his expression the granite fixity of calmness and hostility. Slowly I returned to the screen, where in a loss of self-control I checked the delete box on all my mail, a situation I retrieved only at sight of the tailing Taylor Ess, merging into the gathering moisture, and disappearing completely under a thickening mist. Cheltenham was ten miles away, and Worcester fifteen. I got back to the hotel, where Daphne was packing her things – meticulously, she folded her snazzy pyjamas. Her next run – two days, and two performances – was in Stevenage, and after that Bracknell, but that didn't start till Monday. I told her the earl was stalking me from the grave.

'Humf, whatever's the matter!'

'I want you to drive me to Cheltenham.'

'Cheltenham! What on earth for?'

'It's not the medicinal waters.' I explained it as my best obfuscating tactic apropos of Ess. From there I'd don one of my disguises – I'd be a curate, with a flannel jacket a size too small – and get a train into London, where I was needed at the office. Gillian had made provisional entries in my diary, which I needed to look at. 'I'll see you in Bracknell. Don't book your usual poky room. Eliot's left you plenty of money.'

I visited the Holst Museum, and there on the top floor, in the maid's bedroom, I changed my clothes and put on the wig Daphne had sifted from her props department – sandy wisps in a parting on one side. On the train into London I read from a Gideon Bible, whose October recommended readings were exclusively St Matthew – 'And why take ye thought for raiment?' (6:28). I hurried from the platform after my train had pulled in, and on a blur of ill-shod feet, cascading ever forward, I rushed across the concourse, a cleric with a Godly mission. If anyone should ask what my business was – well, I'd a string of excommunications urgently requiring attention, and somewhere in someone's bedsit I'd been asked to perform an exorcism. I dodged out into the damp London air and ducked into a side street, where for an hour I stood in the moted gloom of an antiquarian bookseller's. I lost myself in a study of ancient AA guides, quaint introductions to the roads and motorways of England. I never stopped glancing through the window, suspecting Ess would appear at any moment. He would pause, take stock, just yards outside on the pavement, me in my gospel raiment (see above), and in that minatory presence casually produce his next cigarette from its crush pack, catching my eye as he worked the flint of his lighter. I know, I needed to pull myself together. I thanked my patient bookseller and wished him God bless, and headed for a department store, where I bought brightly coloured woollen socks and a deodorant, trophies I took up with me on the escalator and handled with great devotion as I sat with a cup of tea in the café. An elderly lady with a shopping bag on wheels shared my tiny table for two. I assured her St Crispin – feast day the 25th – had her podiatry interests very much at heart – she'd slipped off a shoe and systematically massaged a livid-looking bunion on the inflamed first bursa of her hallux. I kept to myself in the next few hours, and in a rustic tavern in Smithfield devoured a pre-heated pie, smothered in salt and sauce. On the last bell

I tottered out, my cheeks aflame with Museum Ale. With a newspaper over my head, and a patter of rain drumming *ostinato*, I crossed to Finsbury Square, where I fumbled with my key. I let myself in. In the dark lobby, in DoCoTel's depressing city office, I cast about, at a loss, disorientated, stumbling for the stairs.

I ascended those dogleg flights to my office, and on easing open the door was mindful not to turn on a light – yet. I walked to the window and saw, on the far side of the street, under a misty orange glow, a large powerful bike cocked on its stalk, tilted at a precarious angle in the gutter – and a few feet away its leathered rider peeling off his gloves. I closed the blinds and switched on my desk lamp. A brief history of phone messages, the last of them tinkling in the ether yester-day p.m. Someone put-upon and lowly had transcribed them, in a hurried hand, to my pad: Bernauer (twice); a silk trader in Spitalfields; a plastic surgeon; a PR specialist, Stonetrax Records; a golf pro with 'seminal' ideas for holiday destina-tions (a wrong number, surely); among them all Lucinda Munney…. She, it seemed, had an aged, ailing mother in sight of the final milestone, a frail widow living on the ground floor of a rambling house in Ledbury. The gilt and mirrors of her dining room had dulled in the reapplication as bedroom (the problem, stairs) – all this under Lucinda's filial protection. She'd seen notices for Eliot's play, and out of professional instinct had met it on its rumble into Edgar Street, Hereford, the occasion of all that enthusiastic applause for Anchovy's Madame Z, a reception that had so rankled Daphne, who now asked me to call her by her professional name, Laurel. Lucinda thought it a merry entertainment of spectacle and satire, and said what a shame the publishing had fizzled out. I'd remember to call her back.

I tore off the top sheet and stuffed it in a pocket, and next turned attention to the diary, whose provisional entries I put a diagonal line through, and left the book open on my desk. I switched off the light. When I reopened the blinds that Tolkienesque rider – a dark presence, offspring of the night – was still across the street, gloved, helmeted, and now astride the saddle, and in conference with someone on the pavement. A cigarette was lit. A diffusion of blue-grey smoke swirled around their heads, and dissolved. A purr of the engine coincided with the merest charcoal of exhaust. The bike as it pulled away – as I should have guessed – fully revealed a man in a long coat, a fedora. He glanced up at the unlit building and roved systematically over its façade, its symmetry of windows, its blank pattern of rectangles, aware, perhaps, that someone in its mesh of glass and steel returned his gaze. He lowered the brim of his hat and paced to the corner of the street, and there paused for a last look back – a long few seconds – then calmly strode north in the direction of Shoreditch. I retrieved, in its plastic sachet, the CD I had wedged between two manuals on my bookcase – *B-Trees Explained*, *The Case Guide to Communications* – that medium the digitised mausoleum where, with the aid of a temp, I had immured d'Oc's last surviving testament of a would-be king, of a man called Palmers. I checked the phone for rogue messages – any that might have escaped my secretary's pen – and left as quietly as I'd come. I chose a late-night club – jazz, revue, that sort of thing, saxophones and stand-up – and once safely inside found a table in a remote, unoccupied alcove, where I dined on a platter of haddock and sauté potatoes. Into the small hours I read from my Gideon Revelation—

'If therefore thou shalt not watch, I will come on ye as a thief, and thou shalt not know what hour I will come upon thee.' (3:3, and so on.)

Come the first leaden wash of dawn I counted from my billfold a generous tip for my driver, insisting he manoeuvre his cab several times round every elevation of my house, as I assured myself the resourceful Taylor Ess hadn't yet tailed me here. I went in cautiously by the front door, in a miasma, a ripeness pervasive everywhere. Days had gone by, with the kitchen bin not having been emptied. I completed that and other chores, and packed a bag, and called in at the tobacconist's for a bundle of Sunday papers. I read the pullout reviews on a train to Reading, disguised as a college professor, and pored in feigned interest over an excessively long essay – its linguistic currency clichés heaped one upon another. It was penned, I noted with the greatest scepticism, by the 'first' name in the turgid world of English fiction, a man addicted to *Lolita* – Lo-lee-ta. Oh but never mind – '…each man kills the thing he loves' (*Ballad of Reading Gaol*, and here *was* Reading). I escaped these sub-literary clutches in dispatching that rotten paper cargo to a road cleaner's truck. In a fast-food place I asked the shrewish girl at its counter to show me her *Yellow Pages*, thence got on the phone to the concierge at the Coppid Beech Hotel, Bracknell. A taxi took me there, and with the formalities dealt with I secluded myself in the suite I had booked.

I phoned Daphne, or now as she insisted Laurel. She was

changing, and rapidly. She and Monty Gargoyle were already in Stevenage, where Old King Chads and New King P were set – or not exactly set – to deliver that garbled Eliot-Dicto state dispatch. Its important landmark was a first parabasis, or an address parabasis-like, to a southeast citizenry, with its two performances Monday-Tuesday. Now, however, Melvyn Fish and Michaela Anchovy had had a falling-out. Anchovy in the role of Z considered herself the show's central attraction, a pretty gypsy-looking girl, unassailably self-aware, her allure the mysterious combination of presence and deportment – all in the way she dealt her cards or degaussed her crystal ball. Fish, or Star, had nothing much to do throughout the play, other than show how talentless he was, and in the end everybody's dupe. Even one of my partners could have played him. I.2–3 is a good example of that, the setting a stage-lit morning in a Restoration inn, on the road from Harlesden to that unnamed place of masque, Muse, revelry, of boarhounds and the boar – though for me it is Kent or Hants. Star appears briefly twanging his guitar (unplugged) and singing to himself, still blinking off the drugs of sleep. A hearty Palmers steals his limelight and settles down to a solo breakfast, one of those simple visceral pleasures undermined by Madame Z. She brings him a lucky charm, and offers to read his Tarot cards, all a prelude to her fortune-teller's tent, where she plans to fleece him of his cash.

ZEMLINSKY [*Holds up a card*] It's all a matter of chance. Look at this [*the card is the V of Pentacles*].
PALMERS What am I supposed to be looking at, precisely?

You can see he's a sceptic.

PALMERS [*Scrutinising card*] A beggar woman – barefoot – outside in the snow…. [*Begins to eat his breakfast*]

ZEMLINSKY [*Holds up another card, the IX of Cups*] Ah, now what have we here! This is you, I believe….

PALMERS [*Takes card*] It's a passing resemblance, I suppose.

ZEMLINSKY [*Snatches card back*] Oh come along! It's more than passing! This is the card of success – and *I* should know.

PALMERS You're well qualified, are you?

She is. She's about to become the new Astrologer Royal. That's where Palmers shows a little more interest, revealing he too has business at Chads's court, though we're still not told his business is espionage. Her coaxing earns her plaudits in the local press (I mean Anchovy), though it doesn't ever work with Palmers, who declines to visit her tent (and I mean Madame Z's).

What *of* that local press? In the driven triangles Hereford to Southampton, the easy gratification provincial hacks seemed to offer – if written to formula – was important to La Trouvaille, if scoffed at by a sardonic Melvyn Fish. The least empowered onstage, Fish was obsessive in his styling and an autodidact off it, habitually reclined in an outdoor chair, in fingerless gloves and a trench coat. The tour when it opened coincided with his reading of *Emile*, Rousseau's treatise on education. After so many hundred miles that had been replaced by the small library of books he'd acquired on the method and other schools of acting – Adler, Strasberg, Meisner *et al*. This he believed qualified his dismissal of Anchovy's successes, with analyses intuitive in their grounding. He offered as proofs the parts he doubted she could play. The parts cited were Shakespeare and Shaw (Cleopatra, Mrs Warren). His pronouncements risked mutiny on the part of two at least, for in parallel with the studied inquiries Fish went through in forming his ideas, it was Anchovy or Columbine who swept the van or did the washing-up. I was party, in the days that followed in the Coppid Beech, to the secret auditions Laurel oversaw as possible solution to these petty dramas. These had reached their climax – a bustling female pert in her offstage persona, and deadly in her smiles – over the two days they had trouped in Stevenage. I kept a lookout. Laurel entered the hotel car park after midnight – in fact in the small hours of Wednesday morning, having de-toured at Virginia Water, where Monty Gargoyle was cheered into the boarding house run by his nephew, and still trying to learn his lines. I carried her bags. I ran a bath. I read to her in bed. I was able to tell her that breakfast kippers were a hotel speciality, and the manager here had a deep interest in amateur dramatics. He'd begun, or was about to begin, thrice-weekly rehearsals for a village-hall production, which must have been *An Inspector Calls*, which we wouldn't be here to see.

5

We were offered a late breakfast in a small abutment off the dining room, about which Mr Godolphin had left his staff with specific instructions. The napkins were starchy stiff and an irksome apricot in colour, and had been laboured into oyster shapes. The cloth was an adman's dazzle of white, in a flood of autumn sunshine. I could already feel its warmth on my back, my place at table facing inward from the garden, inward from the window. There was toast in the rack, without crusts and cut into golden triangles. When he appeared, Mr Godolphin personally poured our coffee. He was slight and lightly framed, with greying hair and a faded red moustache, and anxious to share his stage experience. She humoured him. He said what an honour that had been. Her interest turned to the fruit bowl, an object he passed in her direction – large, knobby, glassy, green. Perhaps there was something else he could help her with.

'Name it,' he said.

She thumbed the flesh of a clementine, but instead chose an apple, its skin a speckled yellow, and in three slow incisions quartered it on a plate. In a few moments more she'd removed the core and accepted his humble offer, i.e. use of his card room, where shortly after one o'clock she assessed a replacement Madame Z, with Godolphin also reading, and a reluctant Humf asked to revive his monosyllabic Star. I said I couldn't understand why it wasn't the latter being replaced. Ah, she said. The crucial factor was Fish's van, and those he shared it with – a trio likely to revolt at the thought of organising digs and travel by public transport. His loss meant the loss of all four.

The rival Z was young and flaxen-haired and arrived in a smock and maidenly white, and was pink and adenoidal, a girl in a permanent search for tissues – a presence hardly more unlike the Romany Michaela. Her name was Amy Dettol. Godolphin explained the rules of pinochle, and sat at a table balding in its baize and thickly discoloured – the place where he and his cronies played a weekly hand. Amy had a two-seater studded leather sofa, but immediately stood when Laurel handed her the script.

'You, Mr Godolphin—'

'Do call me Ham!'

'I'd like it, Ham, if you could read Palmers.'

He conjured it with gusto, midday on an English country road, where pools of yellow stage light will have made it unseasonably hot. Palmers and his protégé have broken their long walk south and are sitting at the roadside, about to eat their lunch – or rather only Palmers is. Star is off his food. A lack of career prospects has blunted his appetite.

> STAR I was thinking….
> PALMERS That's no good on an empty stomach.

The deluded Simon Star was promised a brilliant future, but the wealth and fame he was told are his due haven't materialised. Palmers – who *is* hungry – evades the issue, but refuses to be pessimistic. When Madame Z appears, she soon dupes Star into having his fortune told. She is typical of Tarot mystics, in not so much a foretelling of his future – her trade is rather the gnomic, generic niceties likely to recall his past. Her predictions are retrospective in the summoning of family misfortune. She has a need to feel their vibrations through a trinket he has handed her – a ring—

> ZEMLINSKY Ah, an early tragedy. A death. Someone close.
> An uncle, or brother, or could it be your father?
> PALMERS *You're* supposed to tell *him*!

Some further chicanery follows. In warning against the vagaries of fortune she produces his defining Tarot card – the Nine of Swords. That, I can tell you, is a bed of lamentation. As, portentously, Z departs, Palmers offers his youthful charge a more pragmatic forecast, with news that very soon he'll be playing in a highly salubrious venue.

> PALMERS Now! If old Palmers told you your fortune, it'd go something like this. Assets – not worth much now – will suddenly realise great value: keep writing those lyrics. And forget the pubs and clubs – that's the other thing. From tomorrow, you'll play for the King. That's a little something I've been working on.
>
> STAR You're kidding me.
>
> PALMERS Straight up.
>
> STAR The King of England?
>
> PALMERS He of the shire horn. He of the divorce suit. He of the tabor.

I can't imagine fantasies of this kind ever translated into actuality. Only think of it – something tantamount to new old crooners – or an old new world of glammed-up pop and rock stars – dragooned into public events of suspect motivation, something specious in the binding of our nationhood. I for one couldn't ever foresee – as it just won't happen – a galaxy of popular entertainers paid to perform in the Palace grounds, or even on the roof, as a doff to the real, reigning monarch, Elizabeth II, not even on her golden jubilee. That's just *one* example. It's as I said: all in the common weal is a bed of lamentation, where in this and other devices you'd have to question Eliot's rationale.

The novice Amy Dettol didn't share my doubt, and must have wanted the job (all I wanted was to quit the country). She said how much she enjoyed, as a true hallmark of science fiction, those clever conflations of time, the point at which Laurel looked at her dejectedly. She advised she take in, and she articulated it slowly, a full live performance. Godolphin asked could he come too?

Laurel gave him that option, and went on ahead, and said she'd leave us tickets at the box office. So then later, in a gloom of garden illuminations, in a smattering of rain, Godolphin led us other two to one of his hotel vehicles – a high-sided car his lackeys used for trips to the local wholesalers – and presided over Amy's squeeze into the back. First, a bag stuffed with other bags, and a small crate of tinned tomatoes had to be rearranged. I was ushered to the bench seat at the front. We set off on a sedate drive into Bracknell, Godolphin's opportunity to elaborate on what an ingenious plot he had found *An Inspector Calls* to be. I told him *New King Palmers* promised something else. We parked, and having strolled as far as the theatre door I said I must return to the car – my wallet had somehow wriggled free of my back pocket. Curse these trousers. He gave me the key. I delayed for as long as I dared, and retrieved everything, notes, cards, a pencilled aide-mémoire – here in my jacket all the time – and returned to the crush room minutes behind the final call, and no sign thankfully of Taylor Ess.

'All okay?'

'Found it. Sorry to keep you.'

Amy snivelled throughout with her tissues, and applauded lustily at each punctuated climax. Godolphin would have loved to play King Chads, sure he could learn the lines and wouldn't need prompting. Laurel, at three that afternoon, semi-towelled from the shower, was emphatic about the green room, and now demanded I repeat her instructions into the bathroom mirror. I caught and returned a smile, noting that only mine was salacious. I offered to dry her back. When she was dressed I massaged her shoulders, and said several times 'Into the green room Amy Dettol shall not pass.' Instead I found the public bar (still no sign of Ess: relief), where Godolphin was shown ambassador service, and got a tray of drinks brought to our table. Laurel joined us briefly for a glass of soda water, and must have sensed – as all of us sensed – the truth as Amy now knew it. I recall eye contact strenuously avoided, as La Trouvaille would not be her next employment. She cut a forlorn figure, and told us which scene from the play, had she auditioned *that*, was the one that might have shown us her potential.

'Amy, which?'

She named it. I remember which it was – the busy street outside the Rose and Crown, in a small market town somewhere in southern England, a scorched Eden of inflated house prices, with a large clumping populace still outside that covenant. Zemlinsky is sitting with a client. Palmers and Star enter at the other end of the street, where Palmers bumps into his past employer—

PALMERS Old Pincher? Surely not….
STAR Do what?
PALMERS If that's who I think it is…. Oh but look. There's that fortune-teller.

Star is lost, his gormless look more than ever accentuated, but politely waits for Z, Z in solemn debate as to the personal finances of her current client. As a summary of where this now left us, the following couplet occurred to me—

Where Amy thought it should have been Dettolian,
Instead is a comic drama deemed Anchovian.

Star gets his turn. He sits. He cannot hide the stupid-looking awe of a man about to play for his king.

ZEMLINSKY He's at his estate, I hear.
STAR He's down for the season.
ZEMLINSKY Ever played for him before?
STAR Nah.
ZEMLINSKY Um, well, can't say I'm surprised you're invited.
   I knew I felt *something* in that ring.

And so to Palmers, a man well adapted to the entertainments business, through a career begun as apprentice to Pincher and his partner Pluckem, for how well I know the nature of business partnerships. That, those decades ago – and sweet is nostalgia – was in the sale of sheet music, from an infested Dickensian shoppe in a re-imagined Dean Street. In the grammar of popular economics, prospects have taken a downturn – Mr Pluckem is infirm, and trade in the metropolis has shifted into a realm of strange abstractions, in a departure from cash and tangible stocks.

PALMERS What went wrong?
PINCHER Bizniz wuz 'ard. *Very* 'ard.
PALMERS That explains the pay!

PINCHER Tarms wor bad. Couldn't get a rate, 'cept 'rageously 'igh. Banks closin' in. Everyone wantin' 'is pound o' flesh. I see yuv med it up though, Palmers.

I know that shakeout. It happens all the time in the shadow world of commerce, with good royalist strongholds called on to absorb the ensuing Diaspora. Palmers shall not acquaint himself with other such interests relocated here, a dyed-blue town, with its settled domestic life, its council chambers run by gunsmiths, the elected mayor a respected family butcher, and the Pincher-Pluckem duo in its entrepreneurial death throe.

PINCHER You got bizniz 'ere, Palmers?
PALMERS With my partner over there, who's got a bad weakness for fortune-tellers.
PINCHER Nahs lookin' boy.

Zemlinsky's trade is dependent on cultural stereotypes, where masculine creativity owes its inspiration to a Muse, with some of that energy expended on ornate chiselling in an idealised plinth. In her probe for information, she flatters Star as to what creature of Parnassus is presiding over his toils, and is delayed when asked to explain these allusions. Star not only lacks talent, he has no education, and the response to his ramblings is an implied detour—

STAR About this Muse thing....

That was not in her plans, so hastily she attributes his aesthetic to a radiant Erato, an aside that plunges him into a fog of adolescent contemplation. At the same moment, Pincher is a very nervous businessman, in need of Palmers's reassurance that Albion will never be a republic. He obliges—

PALMERS Talk is all it is.

Anyway, I digress. A quiet, reflective Amy Dettol was driven to her bus stop, and so far as I knew got home safely. Godolphin offered a nightcap, but with a matinée at two Laurel had dual performances the following day. We made our excuses and went upstairs to our respective beds. Laurel, finally, was tired. I slept fitfully. At dawn I showered and dressed. I retreated to the landing, closing the door quietly behind me. In the recess that lit the stairs I looked out through pearly refractions, a grey morning light grazing the drizzle dripping down the window. I experienced the first in a series of powerful sensations, certain that this – our pseudo-vagabondage, our life on the road – couldn't last much longer. Then I had pangs of conscience concerning my absence from work.

It was my task, Laurel having driven and dropped me there, to visit Melvyn Fish at his fleeting new address, or zone 7A of a holiday trailer park. His plot was a short walk from the shower block, where at ten a.m. he emerged, book in hand, and a razor and shaving foam, and with a striped towel slung on one shoulder. Two of his companions were washing up their breakfast things, in the adjoining kitchen block, while Letitia – large-framed, clumsy, garrulous, a very open, friendly girl – was at the roadside trying to hitch a lift. Laurel had seen her, and I knew would drive her back to town. I couldn't see where Fish's reading had taken him, and that as a possible opening to the difficult conversation ahead was one I abandoned, when towel and paperback were thrown together in a heap.

The fine mist the dawn had brought had thickened here in the valley, a blank vista flowered with little red and yellow tents, their pitches not too distant from the van. He invited me inside, where by now the beds had been folded into the benches where we sat, into the tables we put our elbows on. The floor was smeared from the lacklustre mopping someone had given it. At the rear was a two-ring hob and a camping kettle. He offered a mug of coffee.

'Ah yes – black, no sugar. Thanks.'

I cupped it in my hands, cold and meditative. Star, or rather Fish, at a remove from the stage presence I knew him by, had less of that round-eyed boyish innocence the lights, the make-up, the distance from his audience imparted. By contrast his features were sharp and angular, and his build athletic. We chatted amiably. He told me he'd worked in the laboratories of a powdered soup manufacturer, a life he thought he'd return to if La Trouvaille disbanded. I said, and the lie was prophetic, that our group ethos *was* under threat, as already a malign fraternity of critics had sharpened their nibs, and a skirmish – if it couldn't be confined to the trade press – threatened to violate the Saturday and Sunday supplements. The long-term effects could be deleterious, as I knew Laurel had plans for a tour of the Low Countries, and on her glorious return a conquest into Edinburgh. He'd heard nothing of this, he said. I resorted to the illusory ploys of team participation, where the body politic cements itself – its internal relationships unbreakable – in face of attack from outside. I thought by that I'd impress on him the value of good personal relationships with those he worked closely with (meaning Michaela). We shook hands, and I left, and much as Letitia had done I stood at the roadside, traffic looming in the fog, waiting for Laurel to give me a lift.

6

I missed the matinée, and for that matter the evening show, but witnessed dramas of another kind on Friday morning. Laurel had a report file stuffed with papers, and a pencil tucked behind her ear, and spent an hour in the internet café trawling through her news. She made phone calls. I met her for lunch in a sitting-room eatery tucked up a cobbled yard – a beamed fireplace, horse brasses, tables prone to jig, a cold stone floor. 'Matthew Sells' was a name she knew (through me of course), and now one of his authors, garlanded of Leader days, had launched himself via the Oxford Playhouse. His books were biographies. He'd been given a weekly column, with moniker, in one of those upright, moral, politically minded journals, whose editorials were a perpetual flirtation with predictions of ruin. His lampoons featured the venal goings-on in Westminster, a wild growth and rampancy of paragraphs printed under the call sign 'Satyr' – that a linguistic conflation apparently. It was a batch of these that Satyr had adapted as a tableau for the stage. A triumphant first night ended with him and Matthew in a drunken return to the old college quad – libations and motions to the moon, the moon and its horns etc. – and a good long piss up somebody's wall. At a still later misspent hour they chortled over that 'farrago' dignified as *New King Palmers*, part pantomime, part social electioneering. Matthew I can hear guffawing loudly at its ludicrous mission and its barred path into the closed bunkers of Euroland. That I surmise was followed by Satyr's uncontrolled, maniacal laughter, under the influence of barroom raconteur material, fodder for his other great talent. In this I can't help seeing parallels – or perhaps 'reversals' is a more accurate geometry – with the close of *NKP*'s Act One, with its last scene in Chads's court, centred on the minstrels' gallery. Some hapless lutenist sings a bawdy song, but makes the mistake of setting up his stool in earshot of the King's Musician, a classics man. He, the true artistic heir, shows his disgust in forcibly expelling his upstart rival, who serves only as forerunner of the lesser talent Star, and in such a grudging way—

> KING'S MUSICIAN Don't dare show your face again! [*More moans and jeers. King's Musician struts to middle of floor and kicks away Lutenist's stool*]
> 1 COURTIER Such a show of petty feeling….
> 2 COURTIER And frankly surprising. Is this the man whose saintly masses choir the angels of heaven!
> 1 COURTIER Whose madrigals…
> 2 COURTIER …sung in a quincunx of trees…
> 1 COURTIER …and from the King's high windows…
> 2 COURTIER …over the King's marble floors…
> 1 COURTIER …have bewitched the world's ambassadors!
> KING'S MUSICIAN Yes! And for this! A world that glories in Philistinism!

That's the end of Act One, which as garbled parody found its way to the Oxford Playhouse (and so garble I in a thank you Matthew thank you Satyr). I should preface all other excerpts in stating my awareness of accumulated gossip in the UK's theatre undergrowth, and the impossibility of staging *New King Palmers* without a surrounding buzz of speculation. I personally have overheard really quite rational people – hard-nosed impresarios, money-driven publicity agents, the cynical, the career-minded – in an exchange of views on Privy Council machinations. I have listened in on the fabular as to the co-ordinated impress of a quirky English earl, and where in the text you'd identify his message. And now that Matthew and Satyr had let our secret out, *everyone* had an opinion. Only I knew how fruitless their search would be, though I suspected Taylor Ess knew it too, and about that I'd be hearing from him soon. As for Laurel, she liked the attention, and always gave local journalists her one trusted line: she couldn't possibly discuss terms and conditions of commissions she'd accepted. Her parting shot was always this: that Eliot belonged to a stratum of society that took its secrets – in his case state secrets – with it to the grave.

'Do *you* know, Miss Hao, what the message is?'

'We've all been taught by now – the *medium* is the message.'

I got up for a late egg breakfast on Saturday morning, and amused myself – in a mild sprinkle of sunshine, the world gem-encrusted after the most colossal English downpour – and strolled in the hotel gardens. Even the remotest corner here, a bench under the maple tree, didn't escape the earl's tentacular reach. I was joined by a lank female, Germanic-sounding, fifty-ish, who said she was a delegate at a two-day therapy convention. The paper in everyone's thoughts was a reformulation of FM Alexander, to the benefit of desk-chained office folk.

'You know diss?'

'I know the name.'

She'd read the local press, and was intrigued by the play now running at the arts centre, which she thought she'd go and see. You know, she'd said all along the Europe thing was better served as an Anglo-German pact.

'You'll have to be quick,' I said. 'The last performance is tonight.'

Before that was the Saturday matinée. Laurel and troupe were ushered out promptly on the stroke of its conclusion, their temple's newly emptied space making way for an after-noon youth group. Exercise there was dance and mime, yet everywhere you looked, or rather listened, the talk was of *NKP*, or more pointedly how to acquire a text in order to crack its code. It was here in Bracknell that the first of our scripts went astray. That was Monty Gargoyle's – an A4 word-processed document numerously thumbed by him, and bestrewn with annotations he'd made himself – on the reverse sides trigono-metric diagrams of exits and entrances, and how these varied theatre to theatre. The loss had implications for the last night, in the transition or fading of scenes, out from II.1 and into II.2.

It is simulated night. The stage is a cloak of darkness. Laurel likes to joke, and is always alert to material for her memoirs. She hears coughs, splutters, the creak of theatre seats, chocs in cellophane wrappers *un*wrapped. The curtain rises on Star, or the lights go up, depending on where the mélange is thrown together, and is then served up. The prime ingredients, bad taste and moral indignation. He, Star, is dozing in a room at the Rose and Crown – a chair, no bed. His guitar is hanging up. There are fresh manuscripts arranged haphazardly round him, placed for ease of exit, or the moment Fish has to pick them up. By now I'm tired and regretful of the whole sorry set-up, and want to go home to my ma. It's rain, rain, rain, wind, rain again.

We don't ever see the resemblance of sunrise, only a seductive twilight. The process has been rehearsed to the point where the sound engineer is known as Mr PhD. Gradually the crash of waves to the shoreline is awash through the auditorium. It's supposedly emblematic of Star suspended in partial wakefulness, and conscious as he dreams. We know the precarious, chance, aleatory lives of artists. We are asked to believe in Star's encounter with Madame Z as momentous, as the catalyst of private revelations. He has reflected much on the structured integration into his life of a Muse, and thinks he'd quite like one. She is not, it turns out, the daughter of classical antiquity as suggested by Zemlinsky, but appears to our audience so: her hair is in dreadlocks; she has a ring through her nose; there are safety pins in a rising ladder up one earlobe; she wears a loose smock with tight leggings; is shod in Doc Martens. We can't call her Erato, she's Erato Electric, a ladette of Star's inner-city origins. She cannot be seen as she starts to sing, but soon the dimmest of lights is directed to the mouth of a sea cave, where she sits. The song is lyrical, but distorted through a vocoder, or some more recent piece of electronics, as is the chorus, for all of whom Dicto penned some polite anthology verse—

CHORUS
When the Fates are all confounded
And the Furies all beguiled,

229

The silver ship of Erato
Will turn to leeward reconciled.

Mr PhD dealt a wonderful range of sea waves, first in a series of crescendos, then in a final diminuendo, while Erato humming, and Star strapping on his guitar, retreated into the vulvar darkness of her cave. On a fading of sound and light they disappear offstage, and this is a nightly occurrence, the two seen with an arm entwined each round the other's waist. The lights come up. Between acts the stage has been set as the King's cabinet room – a long table, democratic chairs, Chads's autocratic throne. The loss of Gargoyle's personalised script was not, in the absence of the extra information he'd inscribed on it, responsible for the King's delayed entrance – for how I remember that damp last night in Bracknell. It's a grandiose appearance, with the sovereign perturbed at something, that something given expression in a flourish of his household accounts. Gargoyle knew exactly the point to stride onstage, and didn't need his script to remind him. Nevertheless the pause was long – too long – and those in the wings I am told got agitated with him. He paced into view, impatient as scripted, belated as not, the spell not fully recovered even in the way he tossed his documents onto the table. Laurel looked on. Gargoyle sat on his throne uncomfortably and took up his papers. He read them perfunctorily, and rather casually tossed them down again. He tutted, drummed his fingers, crossed, uncrossed, re-crossed his legs. Laurel's sigh of relief I know was palpable when at last he uttered his opening line, just at the moment the prompter in the prompt box uttered it too—

KING Oh, for heaven's sake!

He told me later, Gargoyle in a check shirt and mustard-coloured waistcoat (I handed him his first gin and tonic of the night) that he attributed his loss of concentration to the theft from his dressing room, with just a hint of gloom and desperation in his voice. His triangular conception of Star's exit, the King's entrance, and the stage at its angle to both, was an automatic model eluding him tonight – and no, he protested, he hadn't forgotten the line. He'd be talking to the prompter later. Later still, one reviewer interpreted that stutter as the clear signal of Eliot's coded communiqué to come, and picked out the following lines as a further clue (discuss)—

CHANCELLOR Sire, I am late! [*Flourishes accounts*] I trust you've found a moment for these?

KING I've tried very hard to *avoid* a moment for these.

CHANCELLOR That won't look good – not to parliament. I cannot press the case strongly enough. Our enemies are the worst breed – they gnaw away from the inside. They've long eyed these chambers. Power, Sire, the very organs of state…. It's only a matter of time – something has to give.

KING Yes, yes, yes! I hope we're not going to have the Republican lecture!

I'm told he recovered his equanimity on the Sunday drive to Farnham, Laurel on a back road followed by the van, and plodding at a steady forty mph in a fury of windscreen wipers. Godolphin had wished us a fond farewell, insisting on his card room as venue for a private showing of Laurel's *MMU*, and a guest list he'd be honoured to devise. She left him an email address, and promised to keep in touch. I rummaged in a box of perukes and periwigs, and chose an outlandish Purcellian hairdo. That I complemented with a pair of wrap-round sun specs, and so disguised went cross-country rail routes all round the southeast and into London, having rehearsed – a bit hastily – the nasal drone of a Greenwich Village dropout. The washroom off the Paddington concourse was drenched in the scent of urine, though I was pleased to see, peering forward gingerly as I examined myself in the mirror, the beginnings of a two-day stubble. I downed a slug of espresso. I walked through Marylebone. I caught a bus on the Euston Road. It disgorged me, with one bedraggled pensioner, in a street several grids north of where I wished to be – by which I mean the office, Finsbury. I bowled up to its plated entrance as the afternoon dusk had begun to hum in the parks and trees. I looked guardedly round, and let myself in. Unexpectedly one of my partners, his office door ajar, was frenetically busy under the localised glow of his desk lamp.

'Oh, hello there, Guillaume.'

He recognised my voice, and betrayed not the slightest shock at the eccentricity of my appearance, pacified that grumpy Humf had torn himself from an afternoon of role-play, from the drawing rooms of Primrose Hill, in urgent recall of work he'd got to do (or some such). I gently closed the door of my office and walked to the window, and saw the street empty below, and a pale, quartered moon at a dizzy angle hung above the roofline. No sign of Taylor Ess. I began to foresee, the sense of relief conditional, a new ease of movement around the country, without the necessity of travelling incognito. That, my friends – and don't think I don't know – had reached a new plane of absurdity, especially today. My scalp itched – however did they wear these things! Distantly a phone began to ring – to do with Guillaume, I guessed. I looked at the pad on my desk, and read through its mild proliferation of notes since my last appearance here – the same hand, a varying pen, different coloured inks. An Anatole Haddock wished to know if I'd kindly invest in an urban regeneration scheme. Someone who'd seen Bernauer's light box asked would I be interested in building him a time machine? When I have a moment. Esther from Perdita Lines Ltd was selling blinds, and wanted to show me a catalogue of discounts. Improbably an Ariella Quince, a big name in real estate, had said how surprisingly easy it was to relocate to New York. Thanks for the tip, Ariella. I'm bearing that in mind – you just never know. And there was this: 'Call Lucinda Munney.'

That phone, which had stopped, began to ring again. I turned to my diary, and repeated the procedure as before, cancelling new appointments. Then the phone on my desk rang, an object I glared at, confused, incredulous. Cautiously I lifted the receiver, and for the second time today spoke to Guillaume. Somehow he'd got to grips with the arcane inner workings of the internal exchange.

'A call for you,' he said. 'I'll patch you through.'

'For me!'

'Mr Humfrey Joel. Good afternoon – or I should say evening.'

'Who is this calling please?'

'I trust you've had a pleasant excursion.'

'*Trust* these days I find is in very short supply.'

'We have some unfinished business, I think.'

'Who's "we"?'

I matched the cold, calm, diabolic basso, as it measured out its syllables with polite, malicious intent, to the flash of fierce green eyes I had seen close to in Taylor Ess – it was Tewkesbury, I think (it's all such a blur in my mind) – he in the act of lighting one of those endless cigarettes. I had the pleasure of listening to a long, detailed account, with asides aimed at garnering my sympathy, of the pains his technical people had gone to, remotely, secretly, accessing not only the computer equipment here in my office. My secretary's too, and the servers locked in the DoCoTel machine rooms – each had had a thorough audit. Yet, the missing manuscript hadn't been found.

'What missing manuscript?'

'Oh come come, Humf.'

A quite affably rendered, leisurely description of the interior of Eliot's study showed that d'Oc's computer was included in his survey, with well chosen objects singled out for mention – the year of the earl's *Who's Who*, the inscription on his paper-knife, those ghastly vials of nail varnish the last of his temps had left behind.

'Still nothing,' he said, and that was very perverse.

'I suppose that means you've gone through my house too?' A mere sigh I got in response told me that was the case. 'I'm surprised you haven't trashed the place.'

'We are not barbarians.'

A gentle rap on my door, and the door opening an inch, was followed by the hush of Guillaume's voice as he wished me goodnight.

'Don't work too hard.'

'Goodnight, Guillaume.'

'Goodnight. Oh, by the way, did you know? Bernie's taking early retirement. Or, er, natural wastage actually. We're lining up a grad, as replacement, at less than half the salary.'

'Thanks for letting me know. We have a date for his office bash?'

'My word yes. Jan the 5th or 6th.'

'Good then.' For his leaving do and the gift to go with it I would order a pair of yellow stockings and a box of cross garters, luxuriously wrapped, and with a handwritten card: 'Some men have retirement thrust upon them. Good luck, Bernie.'

When I returned to the phone, Ess had hung up.

7

The next show was a one-off in Farnham on a frosty Monday night, at a performing venue I avoided, instead meeting Laurel in an obscure freehouse she'd found in the Bourne valley, the Bourne a river you can fish – chub and barbel (I was told). There was a five-kilogram carp trophied as a photograph behind the bar. She was amazed that whatever I'd said to Melvyn had brought a new *entente* to the campervan quartet, with Michaela back from the brink of revolt. Her antagonist had brought his self-taught intellect to penetrate the problems of the play itself, a trinket glazed anew under the secrecy of Eliot's cryptography. Further, his regard of Monty Gargoyle reached a plateau, for our ham in the part of Chads was a man of waffling solidity when it came to the exercise of electoral rights, the man a committed voter and evangelical as to the duty all of us must perform at the ballot box. As to profession, he'd once been a regular fleeting face of afternoon soap opera,

English TV-style, a shop floor he'd escaped with urbanity and bankroll still intact, before he retrained as a vet. He knew the casting – how to look casually comfortable in tweeds, aghast when a teenage daughter turned out in *that* get-up, or how to show sorrow at unexpected scripted deaths, conversely joy in the holy union of marriage, the resultant offspring etc. There was something else Melvyn thought he knew, on his plinth as La Trouvaille's authentic *éminence grise.*

'Oh, what's that then, Laurel?'

On the night of Gargoyle's performance aberration, and an entrance some had feared for, he changed his tone for certain lines, or was it only Star who noticed this? The scene balances a dejected King Chads, resolved to ignore the excesses of his household accounts, with his impatience for his hunting boots, footwear one of his vassals – a fool but not a Shakespearean one – is supposed to have fetched. Affairs of state are dull. All Chads wants is the great outdoors. First to appear is not the vassal with his boots, but his Chancellor, Sir Ossie, brandishing his own copy of Chads's accounts. He is terrified of public outrage should this document leak to the press. It reveals how the King's spending is lavished on delegations from the EC, just the right concoction, or just the incendiary of glee, for a Eurosceptic press. Sir Ossie's sermonising conceals the truth of his xenophobia, his only point of oneness with the tabloids—

> KING I don't think public perception, or even popular opinion, is as wooden as you think – at least if you'd only succeed in keeping those wretched tabloids out of it.
> CHANCELLOR That's never as easy as it sounds. They *always* worm their way in.

KING Well I've banned them from here.

CHANCELLOR They'll find a way, I promise. And what if they get their hands on these [*flourishes accounts again*]? Just listen. [*Reads from accounts*] 'Thirteen thousand jellies, tarts, and custards. A thousand sheep…' [*No response from King*] 'Five hundred stags.' 'Three hundred porks.' Ditto 'veals.' 'A hundred and four oxen.' And what's this? An 'unnumbered quantity of chickens.' And 'quails, pigeons, seals, porpoises, swans.' This was a single meal!

KING Yes, yes, but it's not as if I'm entertaining friends.

Moreover his ex's wardrobe is costing him a ransom, while *her* popularity soars. The point is, Fish says, Gargoyle has denied this scene the professional aplomb, that boyish mischief in his voice, we all expect. What does it signify? According to Melvyn, Gargoyle knows his European politics better than anyone in our troupe, and has been clever and coy enough to deflect attention off II.2, as the sign this isn't the kernel of Eliot's message.

'So where then, according to Melvyn, *is* the kernel?'

Chads questions his Chancellor as to the propaganda initiatives set in train to re-launch *his* profile, the only one being the scheme with guitars and chord books, whose first direct result is the arrival of Star at court – and Fish thought that had a lot to do with it. Disappointingly for Sir Ossie – for it now emerges the scheme was invented by him – the King is not at all interested. The Chancellor reveals he has also appointed a new Astrologer Royal, a post Chads thought had disappeared with the divorce. Sir Ossie encourages him to embrace this and other populist ideas, for the good of his reputation. With that in mind they visit the minstrels' gallery, where Star will embark on his debut performance. I told Laurel I remembered, from the 1980s, when I was down in Hoe, being puzzled at the intensity with which Eliot studied a recording of a televised Royal Variety Performance, made on the night before Guy Fawkes, in 1963, when seniors from the House of Windsor were guests in the audience, grim-faced if caught on camera, thunderstruck when told to rattle their jewellery. It's the next scene, II.3, that Fish boldly declared as the most fruitful for study, and urged those with a will to decode its priestly political testament that it's here they should start their probing. I kept to my charade, and didn't like to say that the best linguists and mathematicians, drawn from the civil service, or pledged to secret if commissioned from private industry, had by now run the entire text in every conceivable sequence, in every involution, through a suite of computer-hosted algorithms, in search of that elusive pattern. Ess knew that *I* knew it wouldn't ever be found, or not as currently performed.

I predicted personal loss for myself, and made Laurel walk with me the short length of moonlit riverside outside – willows, a bend, a ghostly pallor in the water – and the ensuing long trek to the cheap hotel she'd booked for the night, its electric sign sad and depressed against a wintry sky. There was confusion over the number of duvets, and a supplement we'd have to pay, but the room was ruthlessly clean. I dozed off to the bark of a fox, and on the morning of the 27th woke with a stiff neck and a backache, Laurel having paid the bill and left. I shopped in town for a haversack and fancy dress, and togged myself from head to toe in denims – a flat cap, jacket, a pair of faded jeans – and got myself a pair of boots fit for a bin round, colour oxblood. I immersed myself in a book of cockney rhyming slang on a coach to Winchester, a journey I spent seated with a straight-haired teenager, she exuding the sickly scent of the bubble gum she chewed, and plugged in to a high-pitched whine, its scalar ramblings up and down buzzing in her earphones. I met, or saw her again in the cathedral, in strangely resentful homage at a metalwork canopy (eastern end) marking the shrine of St Swithun. I noted the dog-eared paperback – *The Trial*, Kafka – unceremoniously stuffed in her rump pocket. No Taylor Ess tailing me. Should I stay, break bread, drink coffee? At midday I gnawed on a shop-bought pork pie, and launched into rigorous mental computations in the study of a local bus timetable. The culmination of that was a final setting down in a leafless lane in Compton Chamberlayne, where I looked for the A road west, and there dumped my haversack verge-side and stuck out a hopeful thumb. Involuntarily I counted and categorised the blur of vehicles passing by, indifferent – cars, vans, haulage – and rose to a heady number I somewhere insanely recorded. I had left myself to an exposed dip in a winding, undulating landscape, a half-hour hike from the last smoky hamlet I had trudged through, an outer fringe with scrub and no trees, and behind me a hill of ochre-coloured fields. Rain, in foamy sheets, wrapped its tenderness round me, and only in that drenched state did anyone take pity – a youngish man in a flatbed truck, his cargo a V8 engine, excessively secured with ropes and chains.

I climbed in. He asked where to.

'Not as far as Taunton,' I said, whose Brewhouse was the tent of Laurel's next two showings, tonight (which stealthily I'd miss), and at the same time tomorrow (I'd attend that in the guise of rabbi, not that I knew it yet). We set off in a scud of wiper blades slicing into the rivulets of rain, and a wash of oncoming headlights ballooning into the windscreen, he with a fixed smile and inscrutable gaze into the oily vortex ahead. He told me about his V8 engine – that large lump of machinery just a few feet to our rear – and his plans to have its valves reground in a barn workshop the other side of Shaftesbury.

'Oh then put me down there,' I suggested.

He asked what work I did. I said I was roadie to the band the Fictile Splints, a four piece specialising in electronica, a name that – to my astonishment – he'd never heard. Perhaps that was because our major following was Welsh, as in fact we were on the road to Swansea. He remarked quizzically how off my route I was.

'Oh that,' I said. 'That's the boys – they're always at it.' I'd lost them at the diner in Stonehenge – a joke they'd played at unpredictable intervals before. They'd driven off, see, when I'd gone for my afternoon shave, just yards away in the cold gloam of the public bathroom there. He didn't imagine that was good for business.

'It's what they're like,' and anyway it gave me the opportunity to visit my Bulgarian aunt, Lenochka, at home in her tiny cottage in Crewkerne, a place she inhabited with a mobile populace of old, young, middling mewling cats – strays all. I demonstrate thus how tempting it's become to dream these fictions. In proximity of that address I summoned a station taxi, and in a change of costume regaled its driver with similar untruths. I insisted she drop me – in a moisture of gathering dusk – at the closed gate on a remote field abundant of pink-ish-looking sheep, way out on the agricultural hinterland of Hoe. I swished through wet grass down into the Hoe valley, and there followed the dark winding river, unlit under a moonless, starless, clouded sky. Somewhere a pheasant cackled. An owl hoo-hooed. Under cover of darkness I skirted the periphery of a quieted d'Oc estate, its perimeter walls, hedges, fences in a shadow of moving shapes, in a ragged line round the gardened hectares I had mentally mapped as a boy. I knew the ways in, up from the riverside, in a zigzag of muddied, wooded paths at a remove from the landing stage, that planked rectangle accessed by a gate I had last seen unlocked for Harold and Woy's awwival, though they surprised the earl and arrived by car. There was a small, circular, shingle-roofed outbuilding, not visible from house or river, whose lock I had learned to pick, and picked again tonight. Inside was a gas fire. It lit after several stabs of the ignition button, though the reddish blue flame in a glow in its squares of mesh puttered out as the canister emptied. I spread out my damp denims, and left the haversack, and made my way up and around the house – an Elizabethan ramble – and beyond to the stable block, where Eliot kept his collection of vintage cars, a fleet now reduced to a lone Ford Prefect, a left-hand drive he had used round Zürich during the 1950s. The keys had always hung in a wall-mounted cabinet, in an order of preference systematised by a double row of hooks. *Its* lock I couldn't pick. Instead I forced the door. That one last set I found intact, on a leather thong with handwritten display plate – registration WGK 597, that modest green Ford he'd allowed me to drive once when I was twelve. It started eventually. I nosed up cautiously, not to the main gates, which were certain to be padlocked, but to a service entrance crossed by two massive bolts, my covered exit into an unlined lane flanked on both sides by tall, twiggy, leafless hedgerows. Moodily, I began the drive to Taunton.

I parked up in a cul-de-sac off the Glastonbury road, and made my way along Whirligig Lane, on under a church tower, with gilded cockerel at rest in the still air on the axis of its vane. I swung round into a small if palpable drop in temperature off the River Tone, and there arranged myself unobtrusively under a dripping maple tree, across the street from the theatre. I waited, then followed her to her car when, in the wake of stragglers after the throng, Laurel trotted down the steps and set off at a brisk pace, buttoned and trussed against the autumn night. I caught up and found her seated, belted, about to turn the key. I rapped on her window, softly. Reluctantly – with an anxious look I'd never seen in her before – she opened it an inch or so, then more fully when she recognised the figure bowed beside her.

'Humf! What on earth are you wearing?'

'Oh, that….' I'd got on a grey knitted beanie, an assassin's cloak, and a pair of *mafioso* shades. 'I'm trying to look inconspicuous.'

'Well you're not trying hard enough!'

'Um, yes, must get round the shops tomorrow.'

I told her I needed a copy of the script, as a matter of urgency, but didn't say what for (I intended printing it off in the morning). Her address over these two days was a holiday cottage halfway to Minehead, a sideline run by the Brewhouse lighting engineer, or rather his wife Gerlinde, who had a coconcern in Burbach in Siegen-Wittgenstein, a part of Germany Laurel assumed I knew well.

'No, Laurel – haven't been there.'

Never mind. She'd drive back in after breakfast and meet me here. 'Ten o'clock. The bandstand. Vivary Park.'

'I'll find it.'

She wiped and left a smear in the condensation on her windscreen, and on the muffled coaxing of clutch and accelerator lurched onward into the rustic night.

8

Wednesday. The bandstand. Thick fog. Laurel in her yellow scarf. She handed me a computer disc, a development I am sure could not have been photographed. Other news as follows. Still in her Madame Z makeup, Michaela had begun to receive marriage proposals, in notes sent backstage, or vocally as the night's applause began to fade. Melvyn too had attracted a following, for the new theory he'd devised, one based on scrupulous insights into the play's inner meaning – its political secrets he alone was honoured to purvey. According to him, Star, and not the new king Palmers, is central to the plot, 'plot' being shorthand for 'political architecture', despite the limit on the lines he speaks. Fish has rationalised it thus, 'voice of the people as no voice at all', in the buffeting he gets, in the crossfire of high-low arts wars staged around him. That, he says, is emblematic of the degeneracy by which a unifying culture spreads itself, its means media and commerce, that remorseless cocktail of our age, and a medicament convenient in the remedy of whatever state-based chauvinism the UK presently suffers. The success of revolutions is in the rise of ordinariness, the dilution – into a single, homogenised whole – of state and parliamentary diversity (a chip, apparently, d'Oc was prepared to barter with). Supposedly the theory proves its authenticity in a short sequence from II.3, which takes place in the minstrels' gallery, where Palmers is showing off his protégé to Chads's court. There Chads feigns his delight in Star's modest accomplishments, much to the displeasure of the King's Musician, who represents a pinnacle of civilisation, and one the earl is complicit in sweeping away, a sacrifice necessary for the deals and accommodations now taking place.

> PALMERS So, so gratifying – when the papers are all so full
> of his melancholy, after the royal divorce.
> FOOL [*Reads from scroll*]
> La lune, la lune,
> La Princesse Moon,
> Who smiled for the press
> On her honeymoon.
> *Exit King's Musician, upset at the success of his rival.*

I said I would meet her backstage before tonight's show, and went off with my disc. I searched for, and found – after several shop and café inquiries – a small, cramped data bureau in a back room in a residential street, a drive or bus ride out of town. I stepped in and hesitated momentarily, casting round at the chaos of open filing cabinets, teacups perched precariously on piles of output paper, the place not bigger than a stationery store, its jumble of computer accessories having the look of someone's afterthought. The abrupt cascade of a toilet flush was followed by the efficient appearance of a slightly built, shortish, bearded man – the proprietor. He took a position under a tower of envelopes, gummed manila bound by the hundred in a cellophane wrap, packaging that had begun to turn opaque at the seams. I produced my disc and asked him to print its one, solitary file – if that were possible. He thought it was, with a smile. A rack with boxed laser cartridges, which wouldn't suit my purposes, launched me into specifics about what I did want – dot-matrix type on tractor-feed paper, the more yellowed with age the better (that sort of arrangement). He stroked his beard methodically. A thought occurred, and while he rummaged in a cupboard I said there were certain amendments I needed to make to the file, and for that he sat me down at an office PC. I lit on lines randomly, and changed as much as I could in the short time available. For example there was this, from II.4, one of the journalists talking to Madame Z: 'So you see stick with us and we will get you in.' I modified it so: 'So you see stick with us and who knows where else we can get you an in.' When I had finished, my unsuspecting partner in duplicity produced an ancient-looking machine, for which he admitted it took some ingenuity in the search through his archives, to find an appropriate driver. The eventual outcome was a wodge of faded-looking paper, one further corrupt text to add to my other. I paid him the paltry sum he receipted me for, and went on a minor shopping spree.

These I added to my wardrobe, from a dealer in outdated couture and specialist in fancy dress: an ankle-length coat, the colour of midnight in the Levant; a leather cap, with a peak; stout navvy boots; a cane without a ferrule; a false Marxian beard, still moist from its previous wearer, and finicky to set in place (I tussled with the mirror). In a quaint, fashionable bistro, busy with pasta and avocado starters, I printed wine and coffee stains onto my newly aged script. For that I chose

I.2, 3, 5, 8, a Fibonacci series, where arithmetically Scene 13 is II.7 (in case you are looking, Taylor Ess). That (II.7), as I don't doubt we shall come to, takes place in Chads's cabinet room, where he has called together his ministers regarding policy on Mack the Metric Martyr, and how best to mobilise his yeoman's sense of natural justice, where as ever England stalls in its eternal dialogue with France. I tapped my way through the town's crowded streets, in that look of reverence for the written word, and didn't abandon that artifice even in the remoter byways where I had hidden the earl's green Prefect. I drove back to the estate, where I spent a little less than half an hour in my temporary shelter, the chalet, careful in the nonchalant arrangement of that final batch of falsifying papers, this latest revision of an already travestied Eliot-Dicto script. I adjusted my hat. I twiddled with my beard. I set off for the theatre, fully prepared to lend what little support I could for the freshly minted theories Melve (as we called him) was sure to have come up with. Palmers *is* the music business, a cash-driven excrescence. Star has a GCSE in carpentry. Chads is the fossilisation of an Anglo-German aristocracy. In his ministers is the bluster of parliaments Europe-wide, deprived of leadership and vision. These combined are the new feudal apparatus anonymous moneymen have put in place, a scheme devised somewhere on a yacht (champagne, sunny days, sea breezes etc.).

Everyone remarked how well I looked, and not on my dress code, though Laurel promised to lend me a biographical sketchbook on the subject of English eccentrics, a proposal telling me how little she understood the emergence of Taylor Ess. I didn't have time to explain, braced as I was for a new bout of textual exegeses from the troupe's amateur sleuth, Melve with his Machiavellian deconstructions. A bright lad – misguided, if on the right lines. Alas that pleasure was displaced when the fantastic inflations onstage found a parallel in the live world of capital. We fall through the cracks in that Fibonacci patterning above, in a jest of arithmetic fate has resourced from II.4. That's where Madame Z is briefed by the two journalists, full of their own underhandedness in placing her in Chads's household. She knows the sinister undertone belying their prissy duetting, but doesn't flinch from business (the business of business is business), Z producing the document the Chancellor was careless to let her have. You know it. It's the one we've seen, with its 'thirteen thousand jellies, tarts' and more. They try to wheedle it from her without the nicety of payment in exchange. Dicto's grounding in the equations of television stereotyping makes of her a shrewd match for the hounds of News International, therefore Madame Z isn't to be duped. Palmers and Star, out on an errand, witness the transaction. Real banknotes were used – they had to be counted before and after each performance. Tonight the stash was sixty euros short, and that remained consistently the case till a fourth or fifth reckoning, when mysteriously the figures balanced. Accusations hovered, if none was ever voiced. I drove back to the chalet after a nightcap of lemonade and lime juice, and noted with satisfaction the violation of my privacy. That jaundiced, bistro-stained script had been removed. Laurel had instructions to pick me up, on the following morning, outside Hoe's one-room post office. On that I slept soundly.

To Thursday then I came. I record, and remember it vividly, as one of those short caesuras in the brief and brilliant life of La

Trouvaille, whose next professional engagement was at a theatre in Southampton. From there I looked to a ferry crossing over La Manche, or escape to the continent, but instead went through the less exotic business of signing us into a hotel, if not quite free of that delusion – trains, planes, buses south, my identity permanently changed. Sun-soaked, sun-blocked, I'd so easily embrace the hobo life, as an ambiguous Englishman people talked about, resort to resort, in every nightclub or casino. I inspected the two rooms and the plumbing and Jacuzzi in the apartment we were offered, and noted the neutral view – a grey sea, a grey sky, ferries in and out, a tanker low on the horizon, the blink of orange lights. The astute and compact Monsieur Zigzig, our hotel manager, echoed those first thoughts I'd had, saying how very highly convenient it was for travellers.

'What do *you* think, darling?'

'We'll take it,' Laurel said.

'Permit me – Madame has made a *very* good choice!'

Roughly the suite's two halves were split-level, separated by a double pine doorframe (no doors), and were adequate for nuptial romps and the daytime work it was possible I could do. The desk, which I cleared of its brochures and postcards, served reasonably as my office, with phone, writing materials, a kettle, herbal teas and sachets of instant coffee, though the transformation wasn't immediate. On her day off Laurel had a yen for country drives, meanders in wooded vales wet with fiery brackens, in the thrill of winter sunshine she remembered had been forecast – and in this I humoured her. Not till the Friday and the first of her three performances here at this south extreme did I get on the phone, in a position (at last) to speak to Lucinda. 'Dial zero,' I was told, for an outside line.

That and the number from my address book set me free in the hum of the Leader Books exchange, where after an interval I was connected to her office.

'Humf!'

'Lucinda, hello.'

She was fulsome in her praise for Laurel's direction of – and let's be honest, Humf! – a bizarre, spasmodic, zany, oddball bit of theatre – or what could you call it really?

'What would *you* call it?'

'Never mind! Lots to tell you, Humf.'

Successor to the lamented Matthew Sells had now also been replaced, and in charge editorially of all new acquisitions was the much younger Debonie Gamble, who on her own initiative had driven to Bracknell and seen the play.

'You should have said. I would have shared my peppermints.'

Debonie so looked forward to a black coffee and croissants in one of Leader's conference rooms, and would book it up, pleased to entertain me there – of this Lucinda was sure – any time next week. I specified Monday, and on that point was not prepared to negotiate, knowing very well how briefly I had stalled Taylor Ess with that last little gift I'd made. I imagined the amended manuscript I had posted down at Hoe had, by now, been optically scanned and digitised, and put through computer algorithms up, down, across – in fact in every direction. An acrostic I had given Ess and his office, and a point to ponder, occurred in II.4, and read like this, in a feminisation I expect will raise a frown with film buffs— 'Whooped 'em again, Josie!'

   1 JOURNALIST We have overplayed our part.

   2 JOURNALIST Everyone does, eventually.

1 JOURNALIST Melissa as good as incites napalm.
2 JOURNALIST Just on showing I exist!

I had also to call at my office, where I planned to put word about that I was now at that delicate stage of closure on a deal, my client a vendor whose gaming machines moneyed his empire into the farthest reaches of southeast England, a man who'd be seen as a worthy addition to my portfolio. That, however, was subterfuge. The reality was, there were figures I had written into II.5 I'd begun to regret. Laurel had problems there as well. The scene is Chads's cabinet room. The visual joke is the King, garbed up as medieval monarch, yet hobbling left to right with the aid of an NHS stick, one of those calibrated alloys the dependable Gargoyle always arranged a setting too short, with the resulting curve to his spine a further slight on his sovereign dignity (Monday, Debonie, you'll appreciate exactly what I'm doing). Monty attacked his role with operatic gusto, and is supposed to have fallen off his horse (as Chads), but in actuality (as Gargoyle) had not renewed the medication controlling his gout, and for the Friday matinée instead required a wheelchair.

'The hours I ran round trying to find one,' Laurel moaned.

The Chancellor offers his sympathy, but it's a bad-tempered Chads he ushers offstage. Sir Nigel arrives with fanfares, announcing unashamedly with what success he resisted closer alliance with the EU, having driven himself, with commendable English insularity, between the warring tribes of Gaul and Teut. There follows much anti-EU bile. There is, too, personal disappointment, and political frustration that Princess Moon – in shallow, soulful celebrity – has allowed her name and social rank to be linked with treasonous talk of the republic. Enter Lady Michael, Secretary of State for Defence, reading from the morning's tabloid leader – a catalogue of Chads's household accounts, in particular his spending on the EU. It's a crisis, and Defence thinks the only answer is war – it's the Englishman's duty to march on Gaul.

The Chancellor, in a more measured analysis, nevertheless concludes that Lady Michael must be right. He summons the Fool, who in turn brings Palmers before them. Palmers is given a diplomatic mission, and earns his first plaudit in revealing it was Madame Zemlinsky who leaked Chads's accounts to the press. The Chancellor pauses for thought. He issues a plan. Palmers, in a dangerous undertaking, must make formal contact with the UK's most famous metric martyr, a man called Mack, and hand him a document. He must also pledge the dispatch entrusted to him is for Mack's eyes only, and is one that he himself will never, in any circumstances whatsoever, read or even skim. He swears, but of course as a street-school entrepreneur will not keep his word.

> CHANCELLOR It cannot fail, Mr Palmers, so long as you leave the statecraft to me, and do exactly as I instruct. Just remember, what you're being charged with is of the highest national importance.
>
> PALMERS I will, Sir Ossie, do my very best.

A series of chance interventions drove me to our room in the hours between Michaela's customary matinée encore, an afternoon grey with fog, and curtain up (so to speak) that same evening, under the appeal of Eliot's feeble, second-circle epigraph, which I retained at the head of each text I had expurgated: *O Fortuna, in excelsis*....

A lemon-faced tycoon with a glazing emporium had taken the honeymoon suite in a remote wing of our hotel, and over a champagne breakfast cooed his affection at everything his wadded spouse showed her amusement at. There was a play she'd read about, this *New King Palmers* showing here, with its director Laurel Hao in this very building, apparently.

'You shall have everything you want, my love!'

At a cake and cocktails hour, and an invitation sent through the hotel management, my partner in deceit plunged into a salvo of vigorous handshakes down at the bar, where in a rain of smiles she parted with two complimentary tickets for the night's performance. I estimate at the same moment I, Humf, was staring out to sea through a firmament of ocean lights, in a failure to put my papers in order. She returned exhausted, in a mouthing-off counter to all that enforced politeness, with a resentful summing-up of her new admirers, Mr and Mrs Bravure.

'Tory fools!'

'Oh now Laurel don't!'

'It's all right for you, Humf.'

'Let me massage those shoulders. Here.'

I feared for the newlyweds, and what an aristocrat of the *ancien régime* would do for their sensibilities. I had pause to wonder how, or where, an accidental, gouty English monarch – a man wheelchair-bound! – would rank in their devotions. You must please understand, I am just the locum, with limited choice as to the medicines I dispense, and therefore ill-placed to predict anything. As it turned out I put away my writing for that day, and was shown, over a late-night cognac, how not the King, not

his ministers, not Palmers, not Madame Z, not even those rep-
tiles of the press, were truly the butt of all those costume jokes.
Bravure told me what a very musical mind he'd got, a man for
bathtub imitations of – in a gargle up and down the scales – his
favourite showbiz crooners. He offered me a sample, or the
rumble of its climax, with a heartfelt *Pack up, let's fly away!* Of
course I applauded, *Bravo, Bravure!* Mrs Bravure, a stout lady
and a new convert to the culture of gated communities, clasped
hands together limply, and sought out the ceiling under the light
flutter of her eyelashes. Bravure couldn't say what it was these
youngsters, with a proletarian lyric, and electrified guitars, were
after exactly, but was very glad those histrionics of the opera
house had at last been put to rest. We now had generations, at
home in, rooted in, the chaos of the twentieth century, all so
much more enlightened than their predecessors. I told him I
would ask Daphne (as I knew her), or Laurel as he did, to
dedicate Scene II.6 to him, *and* to his 'good lady wife' (as I think
the terminology is). That's to say the moment in the minstrels'
gallery when the King's Musician, a man who writes pavanes,
masses and madrigals, is victim to a spate of Renaissance melan-
cholia. He has seen his rival Star royally favoured above and
beyond himself, a stratagem Bravure seemed also deceived by.

> KING'S MUSICIAN It's all on a par – paltry rhymes, trite
> verse, idiotic entertainment…. *I* sweat blood in the pro-
> duction of masterpieces, yet all the King wants is saloon-
> bar karaoke. It's not as if I get paid, to speak of!

As cautious Englishmen we approached the play's politics with
care, Bravure reaching for his wallet on mention of that sub-

ject. With a large wooden gesture he ordered me a second cognac. He was a donor, he said, and he fundraised, and in retirement planned to engage further with affairs of his constituency. It boasted a motorway, farms, a forest, lots of light industry, and a daily troop of commuters into the City. His MP, friend and confidant was the backbencher Toby Emerald-Hamm – perhaps I knew the name?

'Ah yes, the outspoken Eurosceptic.'

From his wallet Bravure produced his business card, and asked Laurel, rather Daphne, might he have hers?

I watched the ritual exchange. Mrs Bravure was enchanted. I downed my cognac in one. Toby, we heard, would be told to come and see the play, as he'd absolutely love it.

'He'd better be quick,' said Laurel. 'The tour ends tomorrow.'

9

To my amazement that golden-tongued MP arrived with a small entourage early the following morning, Laurel's final Saturday. I woke reluctantly, and found her up and dressed, blowing dry the chestnut red she had said she would dye her hair. I shaved and showered, and put on one of my plainer disguises – a good cut in the casual trouser leg, and the kind of cardigan worn by patriarchal heads in old commercial houses. I followed her down, in a tread heavy with the night's narcotics, then on into the breakfast room, where Mrs Bravure was coddling her protector, endlessly stirring his tea. Emerald-Hamm *et al* exploded into the capacious hall adjoining, where one in that group tapped the barometer, remarking on the variance mere separation of adjacent English counties accounted for weather-wise. Bravure swapped the glee of his sausage and scrambled egg for that of his political mentor, one for the other and back. Laurel poured a glass of grapefruit juice and ladled a spoon of yoghurt onto a plate of blueberries. Me, I sank down in a seat at a distant table, and erected as barricade the breakfast menu, where I studied to its last full stop the stony territory of its punctuation. All to no avail. We were heartily introduced, Emerald-Hamm, his blond boyish hair swept flamboyantly off his forehead, repeating *ad nauseam* 'So you're Daphne Hao!' He had heard so much, and all of it positive.

'Pleased to meet you, Mr—'

'Toby, I insist!'

'Toby, this is Humfrey Joel.'

'Once in a while, it's nice to get out.'

'Couldn't agree more, Mr Joel.'

'Well I never!'

Again Laurel promised complimentary tickets, and in return was invited – 'you too, Mr Joel' – to an address he'd pencilled in for five this afternoon, with Monsieur Zigzig, very kind of him at such little notice, agreeing to open his conference room. Those free tickets were for the matinée, whose audience demographic I see I have noted down as fit-looking senior citizens, blue- or silver-haired and rosy with smiles – with no resurgence yet of Taylor Ess. I couldn't imagine he didn't know what it was I had left him at Hoe – another of my duds. 'Very funny, Mr Joel.' Emerald-Hamm had arrived with two of his defenders, broad-shouldered toughs casually understated in their dress. Toby – a man generous with his handshakes – was impeccably turned out, the suit slate grey, of bituminous sheen and pinstripes oversize, the shirt silk, the cravat yellow, the hair bouffant. From my seat at an angle to his, and several rows below, I paid careful discreet scrutiny to the twitches and grins crossing his face with each comedic landmark. At I.1, with talk of the Republic, he worked the mote from his eye with a corner of his handkerchief. He frowned when Madame Z spirited from her Tarot pack that fateful V of Pentacles, a chance card preordained in the edicts of Eliot's editorial pen. The fizz of restrained laughter shook his shoulders on the electrified clang of Star's new chord, and with the tragedy of his Muse. The King's accounts were a hoot. His falling from his horse he acknowledged with gentle laughter. Critics of the Left had found equivalence in the economies of thriving provincial towns and the cost of the Princess's wardrobe, a proposition Toby remained inscrutable at. Not so the Chancellor's risible statecraft, nearest stimulus yet for the contempt all our Emerald-Hamms held their party's frontbenchers in. At II.7 his laughter was a loud visceral smear, at the point where the topic in Chads's kitchen cabinet is Mack the Metric Martyr, and how to mobilise that English stalwart in the perennial dispute with France.

The plan they hatch, in acceptable, stage exaggerations, involves secretly supplying Mack with arms and ammunition, and showing tacit support for the continental sorties he and his brigands have in mind – as the kind of transgression costermongers murmur about, at least in popular stereotype. This is all outlined in a communiqué a puffed-up Palmers is licensed to deliver to Mack and his band. It's one of those pitifully English, Machiavellian strokes, whose end is supposedly ensured in one other little scheme, timed to run concurrently, with Madame Z tricked into reading a forged memo from the King. That second document expresses Chads's private concern at the accumulation of power Brussels exerts on his own parliament – information his three foremost ministers would gladly see leaked to the press. You will forgive me, Mr Dicto, please, when I say how true to his typecast Palmers is, a man for cash incentives. He disobeys instructions (of course), and once left to himself immediately reads the memo officially meant for Mack. We, in the audience – and strange curiosity was registered on Toby's face – can't be sure this isn't a further layer of trickery, one dreamed up by an educated coterie, moreover a coterie mismanaging His Majesty's government. You have therefore to ask, could Eliot conceive of an inner core of senior ministers, gifted men astride the British establishment, operating in such a narcissistic vein? They can't believe in simple class-based propositions, foremost that a stratum of plebeian adventurers was likely to challenge accords they had reached. Palmers, Mack, Madame Z – the whole ragbag – are deluded into comic raillery against the status quo, and by their impotence are key to its preservation – bread, circuses, saturnalia. It must therefore have been disquieting for the po-faced Toby Emerald-Hamm – as I remember him photographically – to follow the opportunistic Palmers Ltd, at II.7 remoulding himself as middleman, the enterprise the lucrative arms trade, not usually the preserve of little men like him.

Tumultuous applause.

I collapsed into a long, ardent hug with Laurel back in our hotel bedroom, a man on a seaside retreat connecting nothing very much. Then with great strength of purpose I put away a slug of vodka I'd found in the fridge.

'You okay, Humf?'

'I'm fine. I suppose we'd better face it.'

She combed her hair as I put on and closely knotted my tie. Together we trod, tentative, our footwear weighed with doom, down to the conference room, where Emerald-Hamm had gathered an audience of Hampshire martinets. Monsieur Zigzig ushered us through the open door, with a thumb and forefinger twirling his monstrous moustache, that fecund cultivation topping the slow contraction of his smile. Before I had taken my seat those plum-coloured lips pursed to a Gallic pout, and there were tempests in his eyes. His honoured guest of the English upper echelon resumed his oration, a carefully plotted eloquence, and a trumpeting of good honest home-steader appeal for EU withdrawal, a thesis he put without xenophobic self-negation. Mumbled approbation. On then to the 'facts', which I do my best to paraphrase—

English civic life is founded on flexible employment laws and funded pensions, and is fundamentally at odds with the EU's inward-looking command economy, a structure saddled with high taxation and centralised state intervention. By contrast ours was a global pattern of trade, underpinned by a burgeoning financial services sector, and booming hi-tech. The state planners of Brussels, whose aims were at variance with English individualism, regarded traditional free-trade liberalism, and the dice-throws of capitalism, with the deepest suspicion, and had already shown their preference for a unitary state with central powers. That was the essential conflict.

Monsieur Zigzig quietly closed the door and returned – I don't doubt fuming – to his hotel duties, the chef and waitress high on his list. Mr Bravure, whose business was bound in the red of continental tape, stood enthusiastically and asked a non-technical question (answer: restatement of the paragraph above). I withheld my approval and looked on neutrally, and only once gripped her hand – a gentle caress – when Laurel began to fidget. The meeting broke up after six o'clock, when on the dinner gong she marched me back upstairs. The restraint of her indignation calmed the spike in her voice when she pointed out the little time we'd got until the final performance. Tonight the tour ended. She changed her blouse – a sunset-coloured cotton for a sober grey silk. She took a lint of cotton wool and anointed it with No 5 Chanel. That salve she applied to the lobes of her ears, to her clavicles, to the shaven flesh of her underarms. She buttoned up. She didn't know what the relationship was exactly, and asked if I planned a return to work, or would I please travel with her to Scarborough, where for three nights she was putting on her *MMU* – I mean, what's it to be, Humf? I didn't know. Later I discovered marriage had entered into my thoughts and fantasies, a little sprite flitting in a pool of moonlit midnight blue. That subject naturally filtered into later conversation through the momentous events not usual between Acts III and II. It's Michaela spanning that interval of darkness, first in a rounding off with the King in his private apartments, thence with the King's Musician – a spiteful, jealous genius – all in the shroud of secrecy. We now officially embrace what all along was the melding of fact and fiction, with certain preliminaries shoved aside in advance of a first marriage proposal. Neither Michaela nor the King – I'm sorry, neither Madame Z nor the gouty Monty Gargoyle – is in Chads's apartments at the start of this particular piece of chicanery. Instead the Chancellor is there with the Fool, preparing to receive Madame Zemlinsky, ostensibly to brief her before her private audience with their sovereign. He, against all principles of patronage, etiquette, or any other construct, has agreed to have his cards dealt and read by her ('Your Highness, shuffle, cut.'). Sir Ossie is careful to place that forged memo I have mentioned above in a prominent if not too obvious place. When, finally, she does appear, there's a brief preamble to her meeting with the King, where Sir Ossie outlines vaguely Jungian concepts, all a ruse on his part, his purpose being to suggest that Chads's outdoor pursuits, and Zemlinsky's researches into the almanac of human destiny, are bound by the same mystical rite. When left alone practical obedience reigns, and she reads the memo, just as she's intended to do, though not entirely according to plan. She waits patiently. She surveys her surroundings, which are studded with an opulence she likes. Bored, she runs through her Tarot cards. She checks her watch. The memo seems to her of only marginal interest, on which she's casting eyes when the Fool re-enters.

> FOOL Madame, I am instructed to inform, the King will see you now – if you'll only step this way [*goosesteps offstage*].
> ZEMLINSKY [*Nonchalantly replaces memo, and for a few seconds considers what the Fool has said*] Lay on, McFool [*goosesteps offstage*].
> *Re-enter Fool, who pockets the memo. Exit Fool.*

End of Act Two. I have reliable witnesses to Michaela breezing into the communal dressing room, where, in relief from the lights and the weight of her costume and makeup, she threw herself onto a couch. She cooled herself in the flutter of a fan that only days before she had found on a market stall, in a clutter of oriental dressing-table things. That action grew more vigorous when a steward pointed to certain deliveries someone had made backstage – a bottle of supermarket champagne bound at the neck in blue and pink ribbon, and a handwritten note sealed in a pale green envelope, addressed to Michaela Anchovy. She slit it open in some trepidation, and in a mixture of flattery, embarrassment, rage, read a long, detailed prospectus, ranging over income and career solidity, and including photographs. It had been penned by a sad middle-aged man who'd watched every performance since Bracknell, now pleading for her hand in marriage.

No one has said how, on this last, sentimentalised occasion, she launched herself into Act Three, and I couldn't be there to judge for myself, preoccupied as I'd become with that fury of paperwork – newly scribed sides of A4, under manufacture every ten minutes – up in that shore-side cell of our hotel suite, where the wall lights dipped and dimmed, and the sound of distant traffic seeped through the closed windows, sometimes a foghorn. I did attend the farewell party, with its toasts, blowers and streamers, one an avuncular Monsieur Zigzig hosted in his conference room, where the ebullient Bravure paused only briefly from his bottled beer and cocktail sausages, and wondered aloud what had happened to Toby. That doyen of little Englishness failed to appear, from the first popped cork to the final *thank you and goodbye* (Laurel, very slightly tearful). We discovered the reason at a subdued breakfast table the following morning, Sunday, the sky serenely blue, the view from upper elevations copper bright under a glitter of autumn sun, just an hour before our departure. Emerald-Hamm had not been alone at dinner in choosing, the menu impressively varied, chef's coronation chicken, but *had* been singled out for a pallor to the cheeks and a first movement of gloop, come bedtime, and the beginnings of intestinal inflammation. That magma swelled in its purgatorial earth, and climaxed on a writhing intense enough that at dawn a team of paramedics nursed him from hotel room to private hospital, which he left a day later, frail but in recovery. We commented little, and said goodbye to Bravure and his wife. Laurel drove me home – a quite pleasant saunter, really – where I found doors ajar I knew I'd left closed. I told her yes, I *would* come to Scarborough, and ghost-like Laurel disappeared. Alone, I submitted to a parabola of phone messages, an auditory curve that eased itself to a vibrant hum, thence to a troubled silence, as I couldn't fathom which, if any, I'd reply to.

10

That bit of business I wanted to do at Leader Books, with its expertise in making reputations, fell tamely from my schedule. Having teased with a pirouette, it scudded off and quietly met its oblivion. Sells's latest successor was pinpoint in her paper targeting, a girl improbably outspoken, younger even than Laurel, and pleasant to deal with. She and Lucinda had bantered on about the play, both having applauded Daphne Hao's 'masterful' production, as it's now historically described. That revision of the script I had so carefully planted in Sells's resentful little cosmos had been retrieved, printed, read and reread – and let's be frank, chortled over.

'I am so glad you liked it, Melody.'

'Debonie. The name's Debonie.'

'So sorry. Now then, Debonie….'

An angular stroke of her pen showed how that had dealt with the first of her tick boxes, good augury in the disposal of her time, which she was dangerously over-generous with. A flask of coffee was brought to our meeting, and on the same trolley a platter of prawn-and-lemon-zested sandwiches, with plates, napkins for two.

'These are delicious.'

'Yes – do help self. Well now, Mr Joel – Humfrey—'

'I like that informality.'

She was blonde, dimpled, infectious with her smiles. Patiently I listened. She rattled off names of half a dozen newspaper and magazine columnists, a roll call of satirists known to have bandied reconstituted jokes from *New King Palmers*, a play the elites of Wapping had quoted back to the elites of Westminster. There were some she mentioned that everyone – including me – had heard of – I may even have soiled my hands with the newsprint of their wares. She announced, with an aplomb I didn't like to dampen, that Roy Plateau, an award-winning BBC screenwriter, had been persuaded to 'write us' an introduction. This was all innocence, I know, yet so ill-advised.

'Us?'

'Why yes. It'll help with sales,' the next of her boxes waiting for a tick (Melody, Debonie, no better than Matthew Sells, mi-re-do – you can see how this descends).

I am loath to explain again that Eliot's final text (or under my hand his final palimpsest) cannot be tampered with in any way, a passion I stoked with ludicrous animation, as I carefully registered the tone of her bewilderment. If Leader wanted a responsible adjunct to the Earl d'Oc communiqué, well, these papers in my briefcase, an evolving opus courtesy the play's

appointed memoirist, were our mission's best introduction –
as, with respect, no television hack had quite the capacity.

'His adaptations of Henry James are highly regarded.'

'Need you say more? Doubtless Mr Plateau is expected to be
named in the New Year's honours.'

'As a matter of fact yes.'

Lucinda had told her the death of my 'friend' Earl d'Oc – a
man I held partly to blame for the ruin of my early life – was
what had suggested to her certain opportunities regarding the
play's publicity. It was because of my boyhood experience that
I, Humf, had lavished, in a satire on the English system of
patronage, the d'Ocish mystique of EU and Privy Council
politics, though I wasn't about to admit it – least of all to her. I
fumed remotely at her plan, and told her her boss could not
have dreamed an insult more barbed, knowing what I was now
having to contend with. Briefly I touched on the presence of
Taylor Ess. She retreated hastily.

'Sorry. A misunderstanding. What about these papers?'

I unclasped my briefcase and made a show of searching for
its only contents, then handed her a wodge of A4.

'These are photocopies.'

'A precaution.'

'It's all – *hand*written!'

'Yes. I don't get to use the laptop. Laurel, or Daphne, plugs
in everywhere we go. Lots of email.'

'I'll bet! That girl's in demand!'

'Always.'

'And *so* talented. And what a team, husband, wife!'

'Ah, no,' I said, and there I had to correct another of Leader's
misconceptions. 'We're not married.'

'Oh, I thought…. Look, anyway, I'll get this typed up.'

'Do.'

I sulked, and related none of this to Laurel. Then with the advance of winter I settled on a regimen of dawn showers and frugal breakfasts, and rehabilitated myself to two or three days of office life, my only pressure a stint of paperwork and several pointless phone calls, and plans for decamping to Scarborough. The story I gave my secretary was a fantasy centred on a blueprint for the digital revolution as embraced by that resort, and the backing for it I had forced from the Lord Mayor of London. Over an eggnog aperitif and a lunch of toasted cheese I had shown him certain museum artefacts. These, as I stated it, proved there had been a positive response when similar public duty was asked of one of his predecessors, at which he accepted my handshake. Having set that little trail, with its cold clues halfway to nowhere, I hired a roomy black sedan, one I chose for its sumptuous leather and the purr of its radio – a Blaupunkt. I programmed the buttons before driving to the leafless vale where Laurel had her basement flat. I found her at her kitchen table, the fingers of her free hand in a tight twirl in her hair, her hair newly cut to a precise straight fringe, and dyed a nutty red, while the other hand clawed at a pencil. Nor had I seen her before in a skirt so short – grey flannel, at its waist a broad black belt.

'Is it me, Humf, or are you early?'

'A little bit maybe.'

Rehearsing, as I guessed, some Channel 4 amplification, she informed me the project we had now completed didn't depend on the earl's money alone. Latterly La Trouvaille was paying for itself, with the sum Earl d'Oc had invested still thirty per cent intact. I watched her at work with a pocket calculator, its display opaque under her desk light, set down next to an open notebook, its columns double entry. I didn't know just how early I was, and I didn't want to stay. My attention roved over the receipts, evidence I hadn't seen before. In this present exercise she had clipped them in large batches to the playbills she'd collected. There must also have been a factoring in from the stubs of her chequebook, or rather the company's. From everywhere history calls us back.

'Why don't we leave all that to my accountant?'

That she hadn't thought of, even as an option, but now that it was she swapped the calculator for the hand mirror from her purse, and dusted up her make-up.

'You've recovered,' I said.

She had, and was looking young again – or *too* young for me (again). I helped with her bags. I drove the first leg, in blind obedience to the lefts and rights of Laurel's navigation. When we reversed roles, the return service terminated meekly, the map infolding in my lap as I began to doze or sleep. Our notional midway was a roadside house in a small hamlet on the south shores of the Wash, a rambling, ancient family pile with severe-looking gables and a garden overrun with children's playthings. From our room above, the view was a gnarled grey pear tree and a forlorn, bailless wicket. From the hall downstairs, the prospect from the rear sash featured an inflatable pool, its water shallow, slimy, and a virulent green, and littered round it a dormancy of bikes and trikes. The garden edged a flat vista of arable waste, and at its border loomed, in wintry silhouette, an assortment of plastic apparatus – a slide, a see-saw, swings. Our hosts, late thirties to forties – a man thickly bearded, his pinafored wife, strands of hair across her face – obscured the secret of their progeny (numerous) only until our departure the following day, whose seven a.m. was loud with hoots and spats from the wilderness below. In one sluggish grope I found my watch. In another I saw that Laurel had folded back her quilt and left her bed. When I got downstairs for my egg – a monumental double yoker frying on the Aga – I saw through the kitchen window a scarfed, bonneted Laurel pushing a six-year-old ever higher on a swing. I stepped out-side and followed her trail, a dewy tramp of footsteps in a swish through the grass, and met the bright smile on her face, the girlish colour to her cheeks, with a rare smile of my own. A spinning ball in a spiral of coloured hoops arced above our heads and was instantly put to rest in a pool of mud a few strides away.

'Give it a kick, mister!'

Two tousled boys, nine and eleven – one in loud red checks, the other a blue bomber jacket – grinned at me expectantly, the pair vying in an ooze of energy at the makeshift goal where they'd put their pullovers down. Gingerly I toed the ball, and with an ominous-sounding squelch levered it to firmer ground, where with little finesse I gave it a punt in their direction.

'Bravo!'

'Why thank you, Laurel.'

'What a dad you'll be!'

'Breakfast's about ready.'

Our long straddle north resumed in a thin mist, against which I tested every intermittent grade of wiper blade, swipes fast, medium, slow. Destination was a holiday cottage I'd booked by phone, with directions I had taken, perfectly lucid then, if inconclusive now. With ease we drifted miles north of the North Bay, into a moorland fringe, on a ribbon of grey road into the bleak, endless grandeur of rain-swept hill and dale. At every turn-off I pulled in tight to the verge and looked up imploringly at the signpost, its designation one, two, five miles down a track not the one we wanted.

'Let's head back to Scarborough.'

'What good would that do!'

'We can ask someone.'

'We can ask someone here.'

She was right, of course (I am just a bloke. I cannot think). After a half-hour of tetchy conversation, I pulled up at a village green, a grassy triangle remote on a dusky summit, its landmarks a horse chestnut tree, a bus stop, a drinking trough, a phone box. Only other signs of civilisation were a glum-looking chapel and a rickety village hall, the latter a rain-dark timber structure with a square of yellow alight in one of its windows.

'I'll ask in there,' Laurel said.

I drove across and pulled in a few yards from the door – it was ajar, and three-quarter framed in a blur of interior light. The squeak of a hinge – its origin a farm gate, or a pub sign – chorused a gust of wind and a twisting sheet of rain, as Laurel stepped outside. She dipped her head, she turned her jacket collar up. She reached the threshold in the same stride as another, a man whose age I couldn't tell, in a dark blue greatcoat, and with an umbrella he'd ceased to use against the storm. They stood talking for brief moments before he ushered her inside – a sudden ballooning of light, a glitter of rain vectored in every direction. I expected her to re-emerge just a few minutes later, with road numbers written down or memorised, but that was so protractedly not the case I resorted to the radio, and listened, cocooned in a throb of studio voices, to a discussion of the modern vacuum cleaner. The news followed, in summary, and after that a lukewarm analysis of the past twenty-four hours in politics – the point I switched off, to a twiddling of thumbs before she returned. I opened her door as she dashed through the rain. I turned the ignition and put the fan full on. She shook her wet hair, unsure of how to break the news – pensive, and pale.

'What kept you?' I said, that attempt at irony feeble, even for me.

Actually, an incredible coincidence. Inside that windy building she had stumbled on rehearsals for Leo Dicto's *Cinderella*, an adaptation he'd been asked to pen in 1979, with asides at the Callaghan-Healey Winter of Discontent, all now a monument commemorating the playwright's tragic demise in a house fire, earlier this year.

'House fire!' How had we not known?

The shock of it focused our concentration, and with the few notes she'd scribbled down we found our way to the cottage, a small, isolated place, half a mile up a muddy track, in a parting of trees. It appeared without warning, a bluish sheen to the slate of its roof, and its four rectangular windows blanketed in darkness. We parked up. Confidently, I rattled the flowerpot found on the back step, where the landlord had left us the key. Once inside I groped for a light switch, which stubbornly would not work – abrupt tiredness, dejection. I had a fob light on my key ring. In the diffusion of its beam I patted my way to the fuse box above the front door, whose buttons I reset (to no effect).

'Electricity's off,' I said, as Laurel knew already. With a rattle of drawers and cutlery, she scoured the kitchen for candles.

'Any luck?' No.

'Oh then come in here.' I'd opened the door on the living room, where the cold stone of its fireplace was already laid with paper and kindling in the grate, and had in its compact ingleside a small stack of logs.

'Now the search for matches.'

Power was restored too late for the making of our beds, whose sheets, quilts and pillowcases were stacked on a chair, their presence unveiled in a brief foray of moonlight, which appeared through a parting in those furious clouds racing overhead. I slept well in the circumstances, and trod down-stairs at six a.m., to a pallor of ceiling lights softly aglow in the hall and in the kitchen, which dutifully, systematically, I turned off. I made cups of tea, waking Laurel as she'd asked – at seven, about. She'd got some days of rehearsal as prepara-tion for her three nights of *MMU*, at one of the little theatres. I drove her in each morning and wished her luck but didn't stay, instead setting out on evasive little trips. There was, as I quote from my diary, the Anglican church of St Martin-on-the-Hill, which I'd read of in a leaflet, said to house works of notable pre-Raphaelites (Rossetti, William Morris, Burne Jones, Ford Madox Brown). I walked to the old town. I ad-mired, lingered on, the Regency and Victorian terraces in South Cliff Promenade, and wondered would a hotel here have suited us, rather than that rustic cottage where I'd not yet found a corkscrew.

We put up with it, floods through the back door etc. Neither of us remembered exactly Leo Dicto's house address, one of those details swollen to full-blown guesswork when Laurel got back one day with a paper she'd picked up. She left it on the table, folded open at a half-page article reflecting on the life and work of that 'esteemed' local author, now that his friends in amdram had pledged to honour his death, rehashing his 1979 *Cinderella*, of course as the pantomime season loomed. I suggested there might be drafts of covering letters to him still on the laptop, and that proved to be the case – so after all we did have his address. We drove out, in a rare break in the weather – a placid sky with shortened bursts of sunshine – and trudged gloomily in the burnt-out remains of his little moorland house, the grey stump of a front elevation, the roof gone, just a few charred rafters angled in the open air. She'd come in her long black coat, with an ornamental enamel pinned to the lapel. I looked on sympathetically as she walked round solemnly, her hands deep in her pockets. I detected the glint of moisture in her eye as she toed bits of domestic debris underfoot – the scorched lid of a tea caddy, the remnants of a toasting fork (things like that). The truth of Dicto was always his bluff, professional Yorkshireman exterior. We knew him as a man disappointed with the outcome of his career, and that made him difficult to deal with – by phone or in person. For that reason Laurel had kept contact with him down to the barest minimum, a decision she now regretted. We hugged. Her lips, I note, were pale. Tenderly I stroked her hair. I made a gentle point of Taylor Ess's hand in these events, and stressed the impossibility of reaching a fixed assessment of him.

'You see, Laurel, I am in a quandary.'

I understood more starkly than I was able to show how ruthless all of it was, this determined pursuit of Eliot's finally approved manuscript. I didn't dare tell her its whereabouts was something only I knew – the ruins of that old stone cottage where as a boy I had hidden my cigarettes, a niche in a weed-strewn gable, with its rusty sheet of corrugated iron. Into my little crevice I had placed, in its polythene sachet, the disc with d'Oc's last testament, a deposit I'd exchanged for a weathered treasure map, with its *Yo-ho-ho*, which like that Ford Prefect was of great nostalgic value. I couldn't know whether Ess was an agent of the Crown or the State, or which of these institutions I, as citizen, should guard against more (*'Debout, les damnés de la terre…'*). There were so many possible scenarios. If, for example, the earl's purpose had been subversive, and his intervention in the play was spawn of an ancient Habsburg dream, his treason against the Crown was hatched by the revenants of central Europe. In that case my stock was high with the Saxe-Coburg lineage, because of the actions I'd taken. This, you must know, I would never admit to. If on the other hand the earl had been a fully assimilated British monarchist – as with all converts, that made him more trenchant than the rest – his shadowy negotiations pro the next king I had reck-lessly interfered with, in which instance my escape to the South Seas I am planning for now. Assuming all these little intrigues were in favour of the Crown, was our next sovereign signalling a willingness to retire the House of Windsor from its public duty, with his lands and his real estate fully realised as commer-cial concerns (so paving the way for a republican takeover)? Or was the opposite in force, with tradition and anachronism still permeating all aspects of national life, the Crown the ultimate symbol of a people divided against itself, with its grades, privileges, exclusions? My problem was I didn't know the answer.

'I can't possibly say, Laurel, where this leaves me. Or which side Taylor Ess is on.'

'Humf, this is madness! Take me back to London.'

So to a gloomy journey home, with a wrestle for the radio, the thing finally turned off when we failed to compromise our choices – respectively, a drama with cut-out characters and sodden climaxes, and for the driver the dry discussion of spherical geometry. I dropped her at her door without elaboration, claiming a tight deadline for the return of the car to its hire firm. I got in after midnight finally, to a catalogue of phone messages, the latest a few hours old, advising how touched the sinister Taylor Ess had been with photographs recently received – notably, of a sooty moorland ruin and its two visitors earlier today. I phoned Laurel immediately, impossibly late. She was cleaning her teeth, about to go to bed.

'Nothing untoward?' I asked.

'You *any* idea what time it is?'

The place hadn't been torched or trashed, and there was no sign of missing papers or computer discs. Of only slight significance was contact she'd had from Toby Emerald-Hamm, who was interested in a private viewing of *New King Palmers*. He'd got in mind his estate in Wiltshire, and an invited audience of young Tories, who according to him would need to know the perils of convergence. I tried to resist, and got hopelessly drawn in, and for the sake of La Trouvaille, and what proved its last hurrah, put off the buying of air tickets. Instead I spent pleading phone hours pearling the likes of Michaela Anchovy *et al.* Then I was told that Conrad Drake had applied for the job of usher, and hadn't missed the opportunity of listing Daphne Hao as one of his referees – and with Laurel busy with a rejigged cast and rehearsals, could *I* write the reference?

'Conrad Drake?' Did I know that name?

'You do. A student, remember? He still has hopes of quizzing you on *NKP*.'

'Ah, now that you mention it.'

I feigned the weight and insistence of IT commitments now that I was notionally back at work, and avoided Hamm and his family estate – a large wedge of rambling downland listed on his letterhead as 'Barnadine'. I sent her off alone into his wide valleys and limestone landscape, and did not appear until a week before Christmas, when this final resurrection was due to be staged. I found the place easily enough from Laurel's directions (I read sarcasm in her play and rhetoric of detail), and was shown to a gravel parking bay by a youngish retainer, a man-boy dressed for the farm. All was a crepuscular grey and gothic-looking in its four o'clock dusting, but this was not the abhorrence that made me break my stride. Two lackeys in Ess's pay and mould – brimmed hats, long coats – did not allow me to reach the capacious porch and studded oak door, but quietly escorted me to a line of bleached flags running round the side of the house, to a door, thence down a timber flight of steps to the Barnadine cellars. Not since I'd been a boy had I read Edgar Allan Poe. Ess was seated among the wine bins, at a makeshift table, lit sketchily in a dusky cone from a shaded bulb above.

'Sit down, Mr Joel.'

A chair was put in place. I felt the gentle levering of my shoulder. Compliantly, I sat.

'What's this all about?'

I will not say what awful interrogations passed, except—

'Tut. You think we are stupid.' I knew, my various absences had tried his patience. That was at its thinnest now that we had reached the point of Eliot's final draft, the one I had thieved, and a thievery I had driven to its final cul-de-sac in Leo Dicto's epitaph – the first of my duds. Dicto, that witness muted and abandoned to the flames.

'Correction. Eliot's last draft *but one*.' He handed me a business card, printed on it an address in London's East End, no name. 'You wouldn't want Laurel to reach a similar end. You two have grown quite fond.'

'Leave Laurel out of it. She is taken care of. The earl made provision, before he died.'

That caused the gentle ripple of a smile, and a brief, inquisitive cock of the head. 'Very good, Mr Joel. You will await further instructions.' He motioned to his two baboons in the background. I was led upstairs into the house, by a different stair we'd descended by, and was met on a polished parquet floor by Conrad Drake, a cute-looking blond boy of twenty-five or so, in a white jacket and black bowtie, and thrilled, apparently, to meet me.

'Mr Joel, I am so….'

'Do call me Humf.'

'Get on with it, Drake!'

Drake re-straightened himself into that servile role my gushing written reference had helped him to, the moment these two gangsters – men in thickly striped suits – retreated to the shadows, pained suspicion written in their faces. I gauged the surroundings – wood panelling and portraiture, windows long in the vertical, a candle chandelier – the formal anteroom of Barnadine's great hall, with a row of hooks for coats, a big bin for umbrellas, a walnut table with a pewter dish for calling cards, and a little silver Christmas tree. Conrad regretted I had missed much of the play, whose performance for the party faithful was well underway – he couldn't allow me to enter the hall until the next break. That came with the close of Act Two, when in a brief dimming of lights a single black-shirted sceneshifter entered the round and studiously positioned a screen. Drake showed me to a seat in the outer circle, and pushed into my hand a one-leafed, one-fold programme, with a cast list and political tractate written by Emerald-Hamm. I used my fob light. Two lamented absentees were Michaela Anchovy (the original, and inimitable Madame Z, perhaps honeymooning blissfully), and Melvyn Fish, whose return to the laboratory I found it hard to imagine. Their replacements were Judith du Pisanie, petite, dark like her predecessor, with a twanging, twangling timbre, and Dick Vermooten, a stolid, stocky rural type, with slow, deliberate locomotion on and off the stage.

11

Act Three, Scene One. A Madame Z I couldn't warm to at all has entered the King's Musician's chamber, these two the first motion in a drawn-out, detailed conclusion, the end and centre of Eliot's aristocratic summing-up of English history. I doubt if Hamm shares my solution, or my filter through the play's preceding acts, or agrees what their equations are or add up to. The boy next to me, seated on my left, has rolled his programme into a tube, and fidgets. The King's Musician and Madame Z are bound by the rules of collusion, and have in common the sleights of those whose business is practical illusion. On their agenda is Simon Star, a man whose ineptitude is double-edged. Laughable as that may be, his presence culturally represents an important problem of our age. It is the King's Musician in his eminence who is challenged by this new rival, now that Chads shows so much enthusiasm for him.

> ZEMLINSKY The merchant Palmers has petitioned the King, and has all but sold him that cube of flesh – that square-headed boy of his. A little entertainer, trussed up contractually.
> KING'S MUSICIAN The King's so easily fobbed off. I can't think why. Nowadays he'll buy the meanest jingle – bim without the bam – provided it leaves his mind untouched.
> ZEMLINSKY Sour!

Unfathomable too is the King's relationship with the EU, which has deteriorated to the extent that war is inevitable. The pair come no closer to a genuine insight into this (fair reflection of the current British view?) when Palmers arrives, knocking at the King's Musician's door. Before the latter lets him in, Madame Zemlinsky hides herself – in Pisanie's interpretation, a charmless strut across stage to a position behind that screen above, where she is static, wooden – no gesture at all. Palmers isn't slow in coming to the point. He has in his baggage a bundle of Star's newly written songs, merchandise he is willing to sell to the King's Musician. Aloud, he reads a letter addressed to Star, which outlines his plan to remove his protégé from court and place him in the sales department of Mr Pincher's shop. The King's Musician, in Star's absence, is thus given the opportunity to plagiarise as much material as he's willing to pay for – a sure route back into the King's favour. Palmers has 'other' business that night (his assignation with Mack the Metric Martyr), but agrees to meet the King's Musician at dawn, when they'll complete their transaction. In taking the letter to Star, the King's Musician willingly acts as go-between, on the understanding he makes the delivery while Palmers is away. Palmers leaves. Madame Zemlinsky reappears, in accent and in life a shrewish du Pisanie, and I mean by this her acting skills are limited. She has heard everything. Together she and the King's Musician reformulate Palmers's letter, with a planned outcome better suited to the bargain *they* have struck – among which is the theft of Palmers's purses. Their other ruse will ensure that Star is drafted into military service when his country calls, where mishap is sure to befall him on the field of battle. I don't know how familiar Eliot was with the Pardoner's tale.

III.2. A tube it was, but now it's palmed to a flatness on his knee. I appreciate fully why that boy with his ever-malleable programme notes is so distracted, and I anticipate bewildered looks when Toby's backbench address reverberates through the house, after the show. The girl to his left is dressed in a short scarlet skirt and black lace tights – I don't think these two youngsters are together. He ought to pay attention. The scene is set for the English as a nation of shopkeepers, with the wretched Pincher in his sheet-music shop. After a few routine tasks he sits in his chair and starts to doze. Enter Palmers (Andrew Venezuela), who begins to look around. In due course Pincher wakes from his slumbers, and soon he and his former employee are reminiscing on the past. Such a glow their hearts are warmed with. Not so happy is the present, when it now emerges that

Pincher's business partner, a Mr Pluckem – 'Pincher and Pluckem: Everythin Musickal' – is plagued with ill health and is therefore not able to help in the running of the shop.

> PALMERS Ah, it's a pity for the old days, Mr Pincher, when your own happy Palmers was young and fit and on top of things. Now don't you think you let me go a bit too soon? Why, if you got someone in, think of the time you'd have for Mr Pluckem! That's the thing about the old days. They're gone....
>
> PINCHER Ah do believe you're rart, Palmers. Ah do, really Ah do....

Palmers thinks he can offer a solution. He knows a young lad – able and willing and knowledgeable musically – who will soon be looking for work. At first reluctant, Pincher warms to the proposal. Before he leaves, Palmers offers to send the boy in to be vetted, in the next couple of days.

> PALMERS Goodbye, Mr Pincher. Give my regards to old Pluckem! [*Exit Palmers*]
>
> PINCHER Mr Pluckem! Mr Pluckem! Ah've got some very good news! [*Exit Pincher. Re-enter Palmers, careful not to be seen. He steals a manuscript and roars with laughter. Exit Palmers*]

Taylor Ess, in a circumvention of protocol, and unaccompanied by Conrad Drake, has strolled in casually by another door, and with legs apart, and arms folded, is standing in a gangway on the far side of the arena, where he alternates a repeated frown for me

with the longer spells he devotes to looking at the play. The play
has reached III.3, for which du Pisanie has doubled as crew,
positioning a bench outside the Rose and Crown. Madame Z is
purportedly reading the King's Musician's future.

> ZEMLINSKY Sit. Let me tell you what's to be. That steel
> ribbon the royal cartographer calls the Channel washes
> the feet of your destiny. I see success in all undertakings.
> KING'S MUSICIAN How?
> ZEMLINSKY There's quite a lot that comes my way when the
> King has his cards read. But hush! The street's no place
> for unguarded talk. Come on! Play my little game! A
> consultation.

In that guise the two discuss their plot for the theft of Palmers's
purses and other goods, a project that necessitates a pair of hired
thugs. Two drunks threaten to interrupt their conversation, but
after a bit of cajoling these they manage to brush aside. Z is
tempted to overstretch her hand, and offers the hint that should
she persuade Star (played by the plodding Dick Vermooten) to
return to courtly life – if of course he survives the war – the
King's Musician won't have solved his problems.

> ZEMLINSKY This is my prediction. It'll be your job soon to
> sing our English armies over foreign soil.
> KING'S MUSICIAN Any fool can see that.
> ZEMLINSKY Ah, but what else? What happens when our
> English yeomanry has finally saluted Chads's victory?
> When Chads's glory is hymned over the torn fields of
> France?

KING'S MUSICIAN Well, what?

ZEMLINSKY Should that boy at last think for himself, and remain in the service of the King, the last thing the royal musician will want is a renewal of old rivalries.

KING'S MUSICIAN The boy *can't* think for himself.

ZEMLINSKY I can do his thinking for him.

Du Pisanie's is not a voice to soothe, especially where Z shows how magnanimous a fortune-teller can be, insisting she will settle on a disproportionate share of the booty rather than carry out her threat. To her astonishment, the King's Musician agrees.

III.4. Dawn, the forest road. Palmers has made his first liaison with Mack the Martyr and is now waiting for the King's Musician, where he expects to exchange Star's manuscripts for a sample of the King's treasures. Instead of that, Palmers is overcome by two Assailants, an event witnessed by the King's Vassal, and gazed on detachedly by Taylor Ess – who shifts his weight from foot to foot – a scene predicted knowingly by me.

PALMERS Argh! [*Exeunt Assailants, dragging a floored Palmers*]

III.5. The girl in the scarlet skirt uncrosses, re-crosses her legs, provocatively. On the line 'What's it, boy?' – uttered by the Chancellor – Taylor Ess un-glues himself from his sentry position and glides out, with a thud of the door, through the hall's main egress. In that other hallway, in the King's fanta-sised estate, the Vassal has discovered what *he* thinks is a corpse, and casting back to III.4 fears he is witness to murder. The hullabaloo he raises sees the King, the Chancellor, the

Defence Secretary, the King's Musician and others rushing to the scene. There is an initial investigation, but all that's found is Palmers's coat, with its many secret compartments emptied of its purses, though still intact is its owner's original letter to Star, concealed in a pocket. The letter is read out.

'My dear boy, the worst thing has happened. It has ruined my plans. The King has got it into his head to march on France. Talk is all of the war effort. To help support it, he's certain to cancel his courtly entertainments, and just as you were making so much progress. Myself I'm of that age, and with my old wounds, when I've got to watch the crossfire. A man of my management flair can't get involved in that. I've got to take care, and sadly have gone into hiding – for hopefully these Europe-wide conflicts will one day blow over, and we can all settle down to civilised life. Please don't worry about me. I shall be fine. The good news for you is this. I bumped into an old friend, by chance, who is looking for someone like you – musical mind, natural talent. I said you'd pay him a visit, at his shop, where there's plenty of work. Here's the address…' et cetera.

Does the King, with all that Saxe-Coburg breeding, succeed in disguising his outrage? His other major shock is that an English army is even now marching for the Channel. Then, when Palmers's mobile phone, hidden in another of his coat pockets, starts to ring, the King's response is a call for his suit and tie. So attired, he intends to head off and parley with the martyrs marching on France.

By now his Chancellor is not his favourite minister. To add

to Sir Ossie's woes, his plan to use Madame Z as a source of misinformation, streamed to the tabloid press, is seen from the morning headlines not to have worked. Instead of an article fuelling anti-EU wrath among the common people, there's a vignette gently poking fun at the King's dependence on his Astrologer Royal.

It is left to the King's Musician to answer Palmers's phone, where he discusses a further arms deal with Mack the Metric Martyr. The King's Musician is also charged to deliver Palmers's coat to Simon Star. With what relish he takes his opportunity to exchange his reworked letter for the original.

> KING'S MUSICIAN [*Calm, having put phone to ear, and making his way slowly offstage*] A Mr Mack, you say…. And you are? Mm. I see. [*Shakes phone*] Representing a Captain Spavento. I think I know that name. Well now. And what would Captain Spavento want exactly? What's that? To broker another arms deal…. Well, you'll have to tell me more about this…. What sort of arms deal? [*Exit King's Musician, still in conversation*]

III.6. The forest. Palmers, who sees himself as a man more sinned against than sinning, is bound by rope and smothered in a sack. As he tries to struggle free, he swears he'll get even. The will to revenge is a powerful impetus, but the boy beside me has re-rolled his programme into a paper phallus and has both hands tightly gripping its girth. Freudians, no analysis required….

> PALMERS Rage-on-rage!

ॐ

III.7. A sunny glade in the forest. Madame Z and the King's Musician have taken possession of Palmers's purses. Zemlinsky has divided them into two equal piles, one for her, one for him. The King's Musician allows himself moments of distraction, plucking his lute. Z sees that as her moment to empty the contents of one of his purses into her pocket. She refills the purse with a handful of pebbles and puts it back in the King's Musician's pile. What value is placed on the manuscripts is now discussed, and they agree – as compensation – one purse shall be transferred from the King's Musician's pile to Madame Z's. The purse Zemlinsky transfers is the one full of pebbles. This done, the King's Musician more or less insinuates that if she doesn't now remove herself, and find a new habitat far away from him, he'll see to it personally that she too is dragooned into Mack the Metric Martyr's private war with France. He transfers not the purses set aside for him, but those for Zemlinsky into a sack, before he departs – that is to say, the pile where one of the purses contains only pebbles.

KING'S MUSICIAN [*Walks away with Zemlinsky's purses*]
Take my advice – make that long journey north…. Understand?

According to Eliot's maths, this left them evens.

III.8. On every professional stage that I have so far assessed this scene, smoke, light and laser effects. Here, maroon and violet beams from Barnadine's makeshift gantry. Enter Fool, Juggler, dressed for war. Enter Lady, dressed as medic. Enter Star, with flak jacket, helmet, sub-machine gun, folded letter visible in pocket, fife, drum. Enter Chancellor, Secretary for Foreign Affairs.

> CHANCELLOR The youth of England's on fire, whose silks lie in the wardrobe.
> FOREIGN AFFAIRS Armourers thrive.
> CHANCELLOR Thoughts of honour reign solely in every man's breast.
> FOREIGN AFFAIRS Pastures are sold, horses bought.
> CHANCELLOR See the sheen of all Christian kings, winged heels, English Mercuries. Expectation's in the air. [*Inspects ragbag representatives of army*] You stand like greyhounds in the slips, straining on the start. The game's afoot. Follow your spirit. Upon this charge, cry 'God for the King, for England, and Saint George!'

So to much conflict, carried out politely offstage, and a political period the perspiring boy to my left, and the Muse of his lust to his left, must think through for themselves imaginatively.

III.9. Pincher's shop, where a lean-looking Palmers, dressed as a salesman, and having lost everything, has come looking for a job. He is now a republican, and sees in the concept of Europeanisation something fundamentally commercial. Pincher's shop represents his first opportunity to claw his way back into the business world, where he envisages the role of magnate for himself, as a kind of medieval king at the head of a feudal concern or capitalist corporation. Unexpectedly, Star enters the shop, instructed by the Chancellor to buy sheet music suitable for a military band to march to. Palmers, though heavily disguised, almost betrays his true identity, yet manages to dupe Star yet again, and even has him mulling over becoming his employee.

> STAR [*Attempts salute*] For the glory of England!
> PALMERS [*Piling on more scores, till Star is over-burdened*] All that sabre-rattling! Really it's had its day. The future of music's in sales, and a nice job I could do you.
> STAR Sales?
> PALMERS My word yes, the length and breadth of the country. I need someone good – good, mind – to play my new tune, in my thousand and one new stores.
> STAR Stores?
> PALMERS Here – and all over Europe. It's all in my business plan. Interested?
> STAR [*Thinks*] Could be, I suppose....

So the cycle of striving and worldly ambition begins again – and here inescapably is Eliot's second circle of political and social power.

Curtain.

12

Or not quite curtain. The cast re-emerged in sunny pools of light, led by Palmers Ltd, entrepreneur, the beaming Andrew Venezuela, who took good-naturedly into his heart the stagy boos and hisses our young, sophisticated audience tacked to an extended round of applause. The floor cleared, bar the host, whose arm extended to the exit, with Dick Vermooten the last man out, in a kicking up of heels, elephantine as that seemed. Joking aside. A real, serious business, comedy, or so Hamm lectured and hectored, here at the heart of his solid, ancestral hectares. A new assault on those space-and-time-warped programme notes took place to my left, till an end came eventually with Toby telling us *class dismissed*. All present were invited into the pump room – the place festooned with gold and ruby tinsel – for a conversational bout fuelled by olives and cocktails. There, under the dark glossy portrait of his father, Toby Junior quizzed away at an uncomfortable-looking Laurel, that romance in my life I had long begun the process of erasing. 'You seem very distant,' is something she often says to me. What else do I note? Well, that girl in the scarlet skirt was a few inches taller than the boy she'd tortured and mesmerised, and dealt with his stuttering overtures with confident replies and an insouciant toss of her head. When one, two, three further suitors joined them, she left all to the vacuity of the closed circle they had formed, and went off in search of more intelligent conversation. Conrad Drake kept busy, his silver salver laden, first with fresh Martinis, then with empty glasses. He brushed my elbow, and offered me a drink. 'An orangeade,' I said. He'd have to return to the pantries for that. In the meantime that miniaturised white envelope I saw in his waistcoat pocket – that was for me.

I took it. Conrad went off to the pantries. When I opened it I found inside a replica of that business card pressed on me during interrogation – you remember, printed on it an address in London's East End, no name. On the reverse side, in a hand too elegant for Ess, was the written order to be at my office by nine, and I presumed the following morning. I crossed from my window-lit side of the room to Laurel, on the other, who was now in easy, relaxed mood with Letitia Columbine, Letitia stirring something deadly vodka-based with a plastic cocktail swirl.

I told her I'd urgent business meetings back at Finsbury Square, and I wouldn't be searching for Barnadine's secret passages this night. I wished her luck if she proposed staying, and if from her bedroom she was still planning on that adventure.

'I'll call you,' I said. She looked aghast.

I drove east to London, in a gathering pulse of m-way traffic, and a gradual fall in luminosity in the pearly starry sky arching round my windscreen, that horizon lost to a dirty orange glow over Reading, over Slough, then on into the depths of Hounslow. At home I was certain my wine rack was a bottle overstocked, of a château I rarely sampled, though I drank a solitary glass nevertheless. I got to my office at nine the following morning, as instructed, and there found in the boardroom a breakfast meeting underway – strategy, or product placement, or something – an exchange in full cry with my partners, here in the remnants of coffee and cornflakes, plates silver with grease after the sausage baps someone (a secretary) had been sent out for.

'Humf, you're late! We're about done.'

'Oh. Sorry. Send me the minutes.' In several weeks I hadn't checked my email.

My all-important phone call came at precisely twelve minutes past nine. Pert in my ear, it wasn't the voice of Taylor Ess – instead a strained, effeminate falsetto. I was left no room for manoeuvre, and was given three days to retrieve – wherever it was – the genuine final cut of that encoded *New King Palmers*, according to d'Oc's last wording.

'And if I don't?'

'We've already said. The girl gets it.' I had my directions. At that street address in the East End I was to wait for a blind man, who would lead me to my liaison. I put down the phone.

I picked it up again and dialled my travel agent. Within hours I had bought two one-way airline tickets – one for Auckland, New Zealand, the other was JFK. Then I hired a holiday cottage in the Yo Valley, just a few miles from Hoe, and told Laurel 'meet me there'.

'Humf, this is all so sudden.'

'It's the white one with the trellis porch and thatch roof. You know it.'

'Chocolate box.'

I drove down at furious motorway speeds, and got there late in the afternoon, ahead of Laurel. She arrived in plain ecstasy under a cascade of romantic moonlight, with news she could hardly wait to tell.

'Calm down. Come inside.'

She peeled off her coat and tossed it over the back of a sofa. 'The most wonderful thing has happened!' She produced a printed email, concrete evidence that a Charles P Eldonflower Junior, a Broadway impresario, was poised to lift her from the obscurity of the English provincial stage and appoint her as artistic director of the fledgling musical *Les Fleurs du mal*, a prospective career step delicious in the panic it wrought. 'I can't believe it. What on earth should I do?'

'You should go,' I said, and handed her her ticket, British Airways.

'Humf, I don't under—'

'There's no time. I've some biz to see to. Then we'll find a restaurant, celebrate….'

I drove up to the viewing point above the River Yo, a gravel patch in a screening of naked trees, where for company there was an abandoned motorbike and a campervan, the latter cloaked in darkness, its curtains drawn. I left the car and ambled cautiously down the grassy slopes, under a sooty sky and a swirl of violet cloud. An icy fragment of moon flirted briefly in the cold still water as I reached the riverbank, where I turned to face the fields and orchards of Hoe. I climbed in a ripple of damp grass, to the ruins of that old stone cottage where as a boy I had hidden my cigarettes, a niche in a weed-strewn gable, with its rusty sheet of corrugated iron. From my little crevice I retrieved, in its polythene sachet, the disc with d'Oc's last testament, which without duress I pocketed. The bike had gone when I returned to the car, but still the van slumbered, though now I noted a dog bowl had been put out at the rear. I got in my car quietly and drove back to Yo, where Laurel had changed clothes – blue jeans for a drop-waisted dress – and at the mirror upstairs had retouched her make-up. We strolled into Fore Street, Yo an Elizabethan market town, which had at its centre this one hilly thoroughfare, at its foot a hotel, from there a long wind to the summit past charity and outfitters' shops, and rough in its décor a tiny vegetarian restaurant where I cheered her and toasted absently, and we promised to keep in touch. A few days later we drove in our separate cars back into the anonymity of our metropolis, where I had got my date with the blind man, somewhere in a hellish industrial wasteland across in the East End. I stepped out of my car into a muddy pool.

'This way,' he said, having appeared from nowhere. With the confidence of someone it was hard to believe was unsighted he led me through a labyrinth of warehouse space and ruined machinery, and brought me to Roy Plateau, the monster behind all this. I was bundled into a rear office by two of Taylor

Ess's men, where the blinds were down and a harsh yellow globe shone in my face. I blinked, strained, adjusted – could make out the presence, the bullish silhouette, Plateau at his work. There was a scrape (it set my teeth on edge). A shadowy hand rummaged in a drawer, there was a pause while papers were sifted, then a document was tossed down on the desk into the periphery of light. In that falsetto I recognised from the phone, Plateau made clear just how much, and for how long, I had been under surveillance.

'The disc,' he said.

'Yes, I have it here.' I reached into my pocket, and could not eliminate hatred in my tone when I congratulated him on his MBE.

'Don't try it, Joel. We all of us know your petty resentments.'

'I don't think you do.'

'You and that guardian earl.'

'You know nothing about me.'

The dark presence of Roy Plateau, honoured and celebrated screen hack, brought his fist down heavily on the desk, but the voice was calm.

'You lose, Joel. The disc.'

I handed it over. He opened that document before me, and thrust a pen at me, and forced me to read—

I, Humfrey Joel, sole surviving issue of Earl Eliot d'Oc, do solemnly swear that I have rendered back to Crown or State said Earl Eliot d'Oc's true and final testament. I, Humfrey Joel, do solemnly swear....

'Sign!'

Peter Cowlam

I took up the ballpoint – the light was in my eyes – the presence calmly insisted – and I hesitated…hesitated…

…hesitated….

Encore

Conrad Drake, who for some reason assumed that Laurel was my wife, arranged for his interview during our last brief visit to Yo – just days before my descent into Roy Plateau's sordid little lair. I had first met him at Barnadine, of course, when he wasn't quite the youth I'd expected. Courageously in my view he had thrown himself into a degree course at Dartington as a mature student. Mature was twenty-five. He was slim, wiry-haired, tired-looking, and quietly spoken (though decisive in everything he said). He arrived at that thatched cottage in Yo on a dull-blue mountain bike, and had as luggage a hand-held recorder and a notepad and pen. I was later to put him right about Laurel, who as a young, single woman, was a Broadway producer, here to discuss a collaborative project with Channel 4, as both Broadway and Channel 4 had interests in Eliot's play. We passed an hour or so in the shade of the vines bestrewing the conservatory, and after that he left, promising to send me a transcript of our conversation. That document – highly doctored by him (my ums and ers excised) – arrived at the office just a few days before my departure for New Zealand. It wasn't until I'd reached the South Island – for a well-earned break, and cruising up the Milford Sound – that I paid it much attention.

It reads as follows—

Mr Joel's full postal address is The Mews House, The Mount, Yo Valley, AX9 5HJ, and aside from the pun is striking as a country retreat, set against ploughed red soil to the rear, whose fields are squared off by hawthorn and elderberry, and commanding at its north-western face a full panoramic view of Hoe, with its slate roofs and snaking River Yo. I have spent one sunny, wintry afternoon here with Humfrey Joel himself, in his beautifully furnished glasshouse, filled with herbal scents – one tiny slant into paradise – where I slaked my thirst on a glass of lemon tea (which my host had prepared). He was, as you'd appreciate, a very busy man. I doubt very much that I'd have got over his threshold had his stunningly beautiful wife, Daphne – or Laurel, as he insists I call her – been at home with him at that time. Fortunately for me she had left for London, and was on her way to New York.

'Mr Joel,' I asked, 'I wanted to talk for a short while about this extraordinary play, *New King Palmers*. I hope it doesn't bother you that I am running this pocket-size recorder.'

He replied: 'Not at all. All reporters must gather their data accurately.'

Our brief interview commenced—

DRAKE Much has been written in both the popular and academic press as to the nature of authorship generally, and identity per se in the particular case of *New King Palmers*.

JOEL Well, that is only a question among those bodies you mention. Earl d'Oc, though he does invade my waking imagination, was real enough to me, and from a very early age. I was a boy of only six or seven when he became my mentor of sorts. He remained my closest friend, right up to his recent death.

DRAKE There are those who dispute that he ever existed.

JOEL There are.

DRAKE Some would point to the central tenets of theatre itself as an explanation of that.

JOEL The 'central tenets of theatre' – theatre in general – form no part of any discipline that I have had to master. As you may know, my business is IT.

DRAKE I can't claim to be more than a novice myself, having come to tertiary education late (and even then without *absolute* conviction). What does however seem obvious is the one overarching reason why we have the theatre at all. Certain things that need to be said can be uttered on stage when they can't in everyday life.

JOEL I don't imagine the earl would have argued with that.

DRAKE One might say that much the same principle applies in adopting another persona.

JOEL Well, yes, that is what actors do.

DRAKE You misunderstand. I mean adopting another persona as author.

JOEL Ah, I see what you're getting at.

DRAKE Some would even posit that you, Humfrey Joel, have harked back to our ancient *literati*, messengers whose authority was written into their priesthood, or the fact that the ordinary members of the societies they operated in broadly agreed their status of prophet, or rhapsode, or bard. Not having that natural authority yourself, the mask of an English earl appropriates it for you.

JOEL I'm aware of that argument. But doesn't any public occupation – whatever the social standing of its practitioner – involve seizing the authority to carry it through?

DRAKE You are quoted as saying that embedded some-where in this play is a message from the House of Wind-sor to the constitutional architects of the European Union.

JOEL A certain Matthew Sells, once I'd confided that to him, did tend to use that information sneeringly, as part of his public programme in tarnishing my name.

DRAKE But it does beg the question, why would an English earl, and a member of the Privy Council, not simply write a diplomatic memo, or pick up the phone?

JOEL I think the answer to that is all bound up in those questions of authority we have already skirted round. In the broadest grammatical sense, plays are written, per-haps not in, but *for* the present tense (stage directions certainly *do* appear in the present tense). This is what gives the theatre its immediacy, the sense of its characters as living flesh and blood, and the action they're involved in as happening here and now.

DRAKE But a memo or phone call would still have been easier.

JOEL Not if you look at our play for what it is, rather than what Eliot said it is.

DRAKE You mean written by him, or you – bard, prophet, rhapsode – and addressed to the English people?

JOEL Perhaps you can see the problems in so grandiose a claim.

DRAKE Yes, I suppose so. Mr Joel, in the arts academic environment I currently inhabit – or cycle to every day – much emphasis is placed on the word 'juxtaposition', to the point that it almost becomes an obsession. This has its roots I believe in what in the jargon is known as the 'defamiliarised' object. Perhaps the most famous example of this is Duchamp's urinal – a real urinal actually exhibited as an artwork in a gallery environment. The theory is, the spectator looks at such an object in a completely new way, because so to speak it's in the wrong place. A striking juxtaposition in *New King Palmers* is its medieval courtiers co-existing with contemporary career and newspaper people. Do you think the playwright had in mind something similar to Duchamp?

JOEL Not exactly. However, conservative though Eliot was, he was quickly bored by convention. He never visited the theatre, loathing that as so much sameness, and he doubted the credentials of the latest prize-winning hack. He put it all down to an age where the styles and techniques of art have reached a kind of stasis – a mere exercise in formulas known to work – whose natural concomitant is an audience no longer required to exert its own imagination. As far as he was concerned, these were the evils of consumerism, where art becomes an anodyne, without vitality, and without any real capacity to engage. I remember once he helped me with a writing project when I was a student. It was a reworking of the William Tell legend. 'Make sure you know it,' he said, 'but roam as far as you can from it.' I think I now know what he meant. His own prescription involved either a measured departure towards something new, or the rediscovery of things that lay in the distant past – or a combination of the two. Also he wished to draw attention to the political truth of what we would call our modern democracy, a thing intimately snared in the ancient traditions of monarchism. Guaranteed to exercise his faculties was how problematic that will be for the future peoples of Europe, who will rightly ask what the constitution is exactly.

DRAKE A point lost on your first reviewer, Malcolm Blerby.

JOEL Mr Blerby is doubtless a conscientious, if in all respects a mediocre newspaperman.

DRAKE Mr Joel, when writing this up, I shall try not to be so ham-fisted.

JOEL I don't bear a grudge against Blerby or anyone. And no one should think that the earl himself was guilty of snobbery, as I most certainly am. He went out of his way with Simon Star in demonstrating that.

DRAKE I'm surprised to hear you say this.

JOEL Star is the product of an English education, a boy dumped on the world by a system caring nothing for his personal life or development – an arrangement fating him for the merciless clutches of commerce. Star of course is a musical dwarf, but that does not mean the earl had no respect for him. After all, anyone anywhere has the potential to be a King Chads, given a slightly different accident of birth.

DRAKE I'm glad you mentioned King Chads. How much of the House of Windsor, with all its recent troubles, went into the making of the court scenes – particularly in respect of Princess Moon?

JOEL I have never shared the earl's insights into that particular household. The answer to that question I am afraid my friend has taken to his grave.

DRAKE And the absence of any love scene – that's something many critics remark on.

JOEL That's because they're all conditioned by the strictures of Hollywood. And anyway, they've all overlooked that moment where Star is douched in fairy dust, in a dream of his Muse. But I am, Mr Drake, feeling really quite tired. Perhaps this is a good time to wind your interview up, trusting you have the information you need.

DRAKE I have, Mr Joel, encroached on your time and hospitality, and have more than enough to be going on with. Please give my regards to your astonishing wife.

JOEL Laurel will be glad you called. Let me just take that glass.

DRAKE Mr Joel, thank you for your time.

It was at this precise culmination that I renewed my pursuit of Melody, or Debonie, and Leader Books, and to that end shuffled discs and manuscripts into my document case and packed my bag for a working holiday in Remuera, where Deidre owned a cabriolet, a yacht, a four-wheel drive, and extensive shoreline property. Soon my mind was high up in the clouds, framed in one last lazy thought for all you little Englanders – you of the press and television, you of a fagged out arts (all propped up by the public purse), and especially you of a clapped-out party politics. Then my thoughts were turning once again to where I wanted Debonie to begin the process of editing my book—

'There was one among many ancient family myths that the Maison d'Oc deemed worth its salt…'

And finally…perhaps by now it is not beyond Eliot's electric canary, that sweet boy with his hobnail Muse, to pen the ten or so notes on his stave appropriate to the very last curtain, that little jingle going on over and over, remorselessly in my mind—

> Yo, Hoe, Hao
> And a bottle of rheum.

A Note on Sources

First published in 1996, Alan Bartlett's *The Deceivers* was due for re-launch under a new title five years after that, when the author came to me for editing. Alan, whom I met only once, was an industrialist and academic, with at least half a dozen other books to his credit. *The Deceivers* I worked on extensively over the spring and summer of 2001. At the suggestion of Jane Tatam, who had introduced me to him, his 'new' book emerged under the title *Hidden Agenda – a World History of Deceit and Deceivers* – a story-behind-the-story exposé. About one quarter of it is apportioned to a history and analysis of the Privy Council, and the rest to important historical figures, among them the Emperor Franz Joseph, of the Austro-Hungarian Empire, and Rudolf Hess, of the Third Reich. While clearly I am indebted to Alan for the promptings his own book gave me, all of that is eclipsed by his sudden and tragic death, just at that moment when his re-launched *Deceivers* was coming to fruition. So far as I know, it remains unpublished, but sits here among my files awaiting a kinder fate.

As intriguing in its own way was John Pollard's *The Paradise Co-ordinates*, whose opening draft first fell across my editorial desk in early 2000, and found publication in the spring of 2002. This was the story of the nineteenth-century priest, Bérenger Saunière, who reportedly unearthed an enormous cache of treasure in a disused salt mine under his tiny church in Rennes-le-Château, in the southwest of France. According to *The Paradise Co-ordinates* it was a discovery that interested both the Vatican and the Habsburgs, and over a century later enabled me to connect the fictitious Maison d'Oc with the Austro-Hungarian Empire and with the lucrative European salt market.

—Peter Cowlam, Totnes, 2016

More About the Press

CentreHouse Press is an independent publisher, specialising in memoirs, travel books, plays, literary fiction, children's books and non-fiction. The press also publishes ebooks. We have published, in either paper or electronic form, the following writers: Garry O'Connor, Peter Cowlam, Tony Phillips, Andrew Elsby, Jon Elsby, Eliza Granville, and Sam Richards. The press has also featured the work of artists Anne Boulting and Julie Oxenforth, and has worked with artists Thierry Naiglin, Dawn Hunter and M Elena M Rosillo.

For the latest news, visit our website, centrehousepress.com, or catch up with opinion and reviews at our blog, or find us on social media—

chpblog.centrehousepress.com
facebook.com/centrehousepress
@centrehouse

Peter Cowlam
Who's Afraid of the Booker Prize?

Winner of the 2015 Quagga Prize for Literary Fiction. For Alistair Wye, assistant to 'top' novelist Marshall Zob, Zob makes just two mistakes. First, he plans a commemorative book celebrating the life and work of his dead mentor, John Andrew Glaze, whose theory of 'literary time' is of dubious philosophical pedigree. Second, Zob turns the whole literary world on its head through the size of advance he instructs his agent to negotiate for his latest, and most mediocre novel to date.

Secretly Wye keeps a diary of Zob's professional and private life. Comic, resolute, Wye stalks through its every page, scattering his pearls with an imperious hand, while an unsuspecting Zob ensures perfect conditions for the chronicler of his downfall.

Set in the relatively safe remove of London's beau monde in the early 1990s, *Who's Afraid of the Booker Prize?* unremittingly debunks the phenomenon of literary celebrity. The plot revolves round a researcher working through an archive of computer discs, emails and faxes, and his own diary entries recording his reactions to life in proximity of bookish heavyweight Marshall Zob. It's a roaring satire, with a serious message, and remarkably funny, in the best English comedic tradition.

'Altogether, a wicked glance at the farce of prizes and the hype that precedes them.' **David James**

'…this gem of a book…. Superbly written, witty, intelligent…' **Danny, an Amazon reviewer**

'Deliciously wicked and extraordinarily funny, *Who's Afraid of the Booker Prize?* is satirical eloquence at its best….' **Book Viral**

Peter Cowlam
Across the Rebel Network

Anno centres a federated Europe in an uncertain, and not-too-distant digital future, when politics, the media and mass communications have fused into one amorphous whole. He works for the Bureau of Data Protection (BDP), a federal government department responsible for monitoring the full range of material, in all media, posted into cyberspace. The BDP is forced to do this when rebel states are seceding, small satellites once of the federation but now at a remove from it, economically and socially. A handful of organised outsiders threatens to undermine the central state through a concerted propaganda war, using the federation's own digital infrastructure. It is this climate of mutual suspicion that to Anno makes inevitable decades of digital guerrilla warfare. While his department takes steps to prevent this, he doesn't reckon on the intervention of his old college sparring partner, Craig Diamond, who is now a powerful media mogul. The two engage in combat conducted through cyberspace, in a rare concoction of literary sci-fi.

'*Across the Rebel Network* is a worthy successor to Peter Cowlam's *Who's Afraid of the Booker Prize?* The two novels together compose a single narrative: a dazzlingly inventive, bitingly satirical, and savagely funny critique of postmodern culture and society. They are an *Apes of God* for our time.' **Jon Elsby**

'Peppered throughout with references to Nabokov's *Bend Sinister*, *Across the Rebel Network* shares something of the purpose and aesthetic of that predecessor. It's a good night now, but not for mothing.' **Jack d'Argus**

Garry O'Connor
Debussy Was My Grandfather

Included in this volume are two plays by Garry O'Connor, *Debussy Was My Grandfather* and *The Madness of Vivien Leigh*. A theme common to both is the emotional and psychological turmoil underneath the veil of public careers, with an uncompromising look at the undercurrents: the dysfunction of domestic/family life, in all its anguish and floridity. There's a nicely judged balance between art in its moments of transcendence, and the reality underpinning it, with a flawed humanity put to its service. It's a theme O'Connor has explored in a substantial body of work as novelist, biographer and playwright.

'With real insight O'Connor gets plausibly close to what made Olivier and wife tick as artists...a penetrating, utterly objective mind at work. *Irish Times*

'Compulsive...the pair who were Charles and Di, Torville and Dean, Tragedy and Comedy, Scylla and Charybdis all rolled into one.' *Vogue*

'The mythology of one of the century's most celebrated marriages...a brilliantly perceptive portrait.' *The Observer*

Andrew Elsby
The Burghers of Ceylon

The Burghers of Ceylon traces the origins and history of the mixed-race populations of imperial Ceylon.

It explains how, and why, those populations emerged, how they developed, how they were distinguished – and how they distinguished themselves – from the Europeans and from the native populations. It explores the components of burgher identity. The author also provides answers to the following questions. How reliable is the evidence of the Dutch Burgher Union's genealogies? How prevalent is racial misrepresentation, and what were the motives behind it? How were the mixed-race populations treated by the European colonial powers? What happened to those mixed-race populations when colonial rule ended in 1948?

The author's interest in the burghers of Ceylon came about after his mother's death, when he discovered she was from a Dutch burgher family in Ceylon. Her mother was half English and half native, and her father, Raoul Frank, was a Dutch burgher descended from a long line of German, French, Dutch, Belgian and British European male ancestors, with native or mixed-race female ancestors from the Dutch and British periods in Ceylon.

Jon Elsby
Light in the Darkness

Christian apologetics is an important area of intellectual endeavour and achievement, standing at the boundaries between theology, philosophy and literature. Yet it has been largely neglected by historians of literature and ideas.

In these essays, the author attempts to establish apologetics as a subject deserving of respect in its own right. He analyses the apologetic arguments and strategies of four of the greatest Christian apologists of the twentieth century – Hilaire Belloc, G. K. Chesterton, Dorothy L. Sayers, and C. S. Lewis. He shows how different lines of argument support each other and converge on the same conclusion: that what Chesterton called 'orthodoxy' and Lewis 'mere Christianity' represents the fundamental truth about the relations between human beings, the universe, and God.

Jon Elsby
Wrestling With the Angel

Who am I? Am I an autonomous being, able to define myself by my own free choices, or a created being with a given human nature, living in a world which, in significant respects, does not depend on me? Are these two views necessarily opposed?

Wrestling With the Angel is one man's attempt to answer those questions. Raised as a Protestant, the author lost his faith in his teenage years, and then gradually regained it – but in an unexpected form. This is the story of a spiritual and intellectual journey from Protestantism to atheism, and beyond: a journey which finally, and much to the author's surprise, reached its terminus in the Catholic Church.

'*Wresting With the Angel* has the form of an intellectual autobiography, along the lines of Newman's *Apologia pro Vita Sua* but, like that older work, has much wider implications than that of a merely personal story. Elsby's style is engaging and the meaning of his prose – unlike much modern theology – clear.' **Stephen Lovatt**

Jon Elsby
Reassessing the Chesterbelloc

Hilaire Belloc and G. K. Chesterton were two of the biggest names on the Georgian literary scene. They were what today would be called 'public intellectuals'. Each wrote nearly a hundred books in a variety of genres and on a huge range of subjects. But they are now almost entirely unread.

The author argues that it is time to reassess their achievement. He maintains that, while their work is uneven and some of it is frankly ephemeral, their best work deserves to be rediscovered and read without bias. They will then be seen as writers who offered a robust critique of modernity, and thereby have provided us with resources with which to question and challenge the facile ideas, ingrained prejudices, and lazy assumptions of the ambient culture.

Sam Richards
The Engaged Musician

In *The Engaged Musician* is a passionate call to musicians, of whatever genre or discipline, to rescue themselves, and us, from the commercial tyrannies and dictates currently forming our musical life, and relocate it very determinedly in a meaningful social and aesthetic exchange. The book focuses on various themes typical of social, political and cultural engagement, without insisting on sectional interests.

Since his student years in London, Sam Richards – writer, musician, folklorist – has been equally devoted to experimental music and vernacular music, including the folksong revival. His sound archive of song, music and oral history recorded in the Westcountry is now housed by the British Library. Experimental music and improvisation are his core practices, focusing on music for large groups and using invented notations. He has previously written about musical democracy and the music of John Cage.

'…vital reading for anyone trying to understand the role of music and the arts in today's globalised world.' 'Anyone at all concerned with understanding the arts and their transformation in these problematic times should read it.' **Kipugandit, an Amazon reviewer**

www.ingramcontent.com/pod-product-compliance
Lightning Source LLC
Chambersburg PA
CBHW070724280626
47159CB00023B/2586